HE WOULD SETTLE THE MATTER
WITH A KISS

Bradenstoke looked down at Alice and felt aggravated in the extreme. Had he no heart, no soul? What did she know of him? Very little, indeed!

He stalked away from her, intent upon leaving the ballroom, but he happened to glance at her one last time and saw that the light from the mounting day was pouring through the layers of white muslin of her gown. He could see her figure outlined clearly and his interest in her sharpened once more. By all evidence, she would be as beautiful unclothed as she was draped in muslin.

He felt a sudden and quite profound desire to cross the room, slide his arm around the soft curve of her waist, drag her into his arms, and violate her lips as he had last night. He knew how soft and yielding she could be, and he wondered just what she would do if he attempted to kiss her now.

The same devilment that had prompted him to take his brother's identity last night possessed him again. His feet began to move swiftly in her direction; a moment more and his arm was indeed holding her fast about the waist.

"What are you doing, my lord?" she cried.

He did not try to argue with her, but caught the back of her head with his free hand and slanted his lips across hers with the same gentle kiss he had offered her last night.

He drew back, and she stared at him, apparently stunned.

"Oh," she murmured, searching his eyes . . .

BOOK YOUR PLACE ON OUR WEBSITE AND MAKE THE READING CONNECTION!

We've created a customized website just for our very special readers, where you can get the inside scoop on everything that's going on with Zebra, Pinnacle and Kensington books.

When you come online, you'll have the exciting opportunity to:

- View covers of upcoming books
- Read sample chapters
- Learn about our future publishing schedule (listed by publication month *and author*)
- Find out when your favorite authors will be visiting a city near you
- Search for and order backlist books from our online catalog
- Check out author bios and background information
- Send e-mail to your favorite authors
- Meet the Kensington staff online
- Join us in weekly chats with authors, readers and other guests
- Get writing guidelines
- AND MUCH MORE!

**Visit our website at
http://www.kensingtonbooks.com**

A ROGUE'S DECEPTION

Valerie King

ZEBRA BOOKS
Kensington Publishing Corp.

http://www.kensingtonbooks.com

ZEBRA BOOKS are published by

Kensington Publishing Corp.
850 Third Avenue
New York, NY 10022

All Kensington titles, imprints, and distributed lines are available at special quantity discounts for bulk purchases for sales promotion, premiums, fund-raising, educational or institutional use.

Special book excerpts or customized printings can also be created to fit specific needs. For details, write or phone the office of the Kensington Special Sales Manager: Kensington Publishing Corp., 850 Third Avenue, New York, NY 10022. Attn. Special Sales Department. Phone: 1-800-221-2647.

Zebra and the Z logo Reg. U.S. Pat. & TM Off.

First Printing: June 2002
10 9 8 7 6 5 4 3 2 1

Printed in the United States of America

One

London, 1817

The Earl of Bradenstoke cast his hardened gaze over the masked revellers just completing an elegant waltz at the Vauxhall Pleasure Gardens. The view was familiar: several inexperienced maidens arrived recently from the country and wishing for a little adventure, at least a dozen libertines scattered about in search of ignorant prey, and one young lady catching his notice who was forever glancing about as though everything she saw held an infinite fascination.

He was intrigued by her, for he could see at once she was not in the usual style. When she chose at that moment to unmask, he drew in a sharp breath for she was inutterably beautiful, a Diamond of the First Water, an Incomparable by even the strictest standards!

Her face was exquisite in every proportion and rendered even more lovely by her expression which was entirely alive with the pleasure of her surroundings. Her hair was a mass of flame red curls, decorously piled atop her head and draped with large pearls. Her gown, of a blue brocade embroidered in gold and adorned at the nape with a fantastic collar composed in part of peacock feathers, led him to believe she was costumed as a quite magnificent Queen Elizabeth. But it was her large blue eyes, sparkling like gems and dazzling even at such a distance, that truly captured his attention as she laughingly avoided the sweep of ostrich feathers from the hat of the older woman seated beside her. In her countenance was a curious sense of command reflected in the way she held her head and shoulders erect. He had never before seen such elegance and charm combined.

What wonderful good fortune to have found such a creature at Vauxhall of all places!

"She is the one," he whispered to his bosom bow, the honorable Mr. Geoffrey Quintin. "I will steal a kiss from her before the night is through."

An adventure was what he sought tonight to relieve the continual strain of his life. As a working member of the Lords, and the guardian of the Earldom of Bradenstoke, his responsibilities were extensive. He avoided as many of the usual London parties as he could, for he was not in search of a wife, but when Mr. Quintin, otherwise known as Quinney to his friends, had suggested an outing to the masquerade at Vauxhall, he found he could not resist. A little flirtation was precisely what he desired at the moment.

Mr. Quintin plucked the smallest speck of lint from his green velvet sleeve. "A Bird of Paradise I trust?" he queried, lifting his quizzing glass in the direction of his friend's gaze.

"Hardly," he stated. "But she will do just as well. Presently, she is situated in the box just opposite, costumed in a patterned blue gown as what I can only assume must be Elizabeth Regina, for the pearls in her red hair are dangling almost to her forehead. She is surrounded by three females, an older plumpish matron, and two young ladies in costume. The latter are presently being solicited for the country dance. Do you see them? I mean at once to find someone who can perform an introduction for I vow I must dance with that extraordinary creature."

Mr. Quintin glanced from one visage to the next. "Good God," he murmured, "I am acquainted with her, with the entire family as it happens."

Braden was stunned. "How the devil is it possible for you to have known of the existence of such a complete Nonpareil and yet to have said nothing to me?"

"For the simple reason that I met her only this afternoon

at Hyde. However, you will not be content with her, not by half."

Braden turned toward his friend. "Have you gone mad? How could I not be completely enamored of so much beauty in one face."

Mr. Quintin shook his head. "Because it belongs to Miss Alice Cherville recently of Wiltshire and now residing in Upper Brook Street."

Braden stared at his friend for a long, terrible moment. If Quinney had taken to joking with him then he was trying the patience of a very long friendship more severely than he could possibly comprehend. "I hope to God you are not teasing me in some thoughtless manner," he said darkly, an odd thumping having taken possession of his chest.

Mr. Quintin met his friend's gaze in a forthright manner. "Do not come the crab with me, old fellow," he responded crisply. "Though, I hope you know me better than to think I would torment you about anything concerned with Miss Cherville. I am so well acquainted with your sentiments that I would not for the world do so. That lady opposite us, Elizabeth if you will, is indeed Alice Cherville, who at this moment I am become convinced is your Nemesis, for how else can you explain your immediate interest in a lady who, by the nature of her correspondence, you have despised for the past decade?"

Braden slid his gaze back to Miss Cherville, who had indeed been a thorn in his side for the past ten years, from the time of the death of both her parents, when she and her five siblings had been orphaned. She had insisted that his own deceased father had made a promise to Mr. Cherville of a guardianship for which there had been no proof and therefore no legal basis. His father, having perished just two months prior to Mr. Cherville, had left nothing in his documents to indicate his intentions.

"So," he stated thoughtfully, "we are finally to meet. How is it you were introduced to her?"

"I was directing Lady Wroughton as to the proper use of rouge only this morning and she told me she had met a most unusual and charming family—her choice of expression, not mine. Later that day, at Hyde Park, she introduced me to Miss Cherville, along with her aunt, Mrs. Urchfont, and two of her three sisters. It would seem Lady Wroughton has been long acquainted with Mrs. Urchfont, who is even now seated beside Miss Cherville and sporting one, two, three, no— Good God!—five ostrich feathers. She and Lady Wroughton attended the same academy when they were young." He paused before adding, "I suppose now you will find some other quarry for your evening's amusement."

"On the contrary," Braden murmured, a quite ignoble scheme forming in his mind.

"Indeed?" Mr. Quintin, quite used to his friend's cynical view of life and of women, turned to stare at Braden. "What possible interest could you have in her, for, if I am not mistaken, you have referred to this lady as the worst Mushroom you have ever encountered?"

"You are not mistaken."

"And yet you still intend to, er, flirt with this maiden?"

Braden nodded.

Quinney shook his head and sighed anew. "I suppose you intend to take up your brother's identity again though I must say, one day you shall come to grief, see if you don't, particularly since Will is due to make land within the next fortnight or so!"

"A prophet this evening," he retorted, smiling. "You should have worn different garb. A robe perhaps, something of a more ecclesiastical nature than a doublet and tights."

"Do stubble it," Quinney returned, chuckling.

Braden smiled. "You must understand. My brother would not give a fig to any use I might make of his name while he is away and as for his arrival, when it comes to the sea, a fortnight can mean a disparity of weeks sometimes months. Besides, I strongly suspect a kiss stolen from Miss Cherville would be worth any risk attached to it. She ought to be punished a little for all the misery she has caused me."

"Yes," Quinney responded facetiously, "you have suffered terribly at her hands. All those minutes spent commanding your secretary to read her letters for you." He then lifted his quizzing glass and stared for a full minute upon the lovely features of Alice Cherville. "I will wager you ten pounds your efforts at getting that kiss will come to nought this evening. I found Miss Cherville to be an intelligent, rational creature, not given to any degree of sensibility. She will more likely bite your head off than offer a kiss to either you or a mere William Pinfrith."

"Not if her sympathies have been aroused by how wretchedly Mr. Pinfrith has suffered at the hands of Bradenstoke. Given her current dislike of me I believe she will be supremely receptive to 'William's' sad tale."

"You make my blood run cold!" Mr. Quintin exclaimed, turning once more to stare at his friend. "However did we manage to become friends?"

"That is simple—you are not a grasping female."

"So you mean to punish Miss Cherville for the sins of womankind?"

"No," he responded quietly. "For her own sins. Even you must admit she has gone beyond the pale. What manner of lady deserving of honor and respect would have written so many letters as she has, each imploring an office I have steadfastly refused these ten years and more?"

Quinney shook his head. "Her conduct, I would agree, seems rather bizarre. Perhaps she had a letter from your father, some proof of his intentions, which she lost?"

"There was no letter, no contract, nothing stated in his will, even she admitted as much. I have never been under the smallest obligation to her about which my solicitor informed her more than once. She has behaved the fool in fairly begging for my support when it would have been obvious from the first, even to a sapskull, that I had no intention of acquiescing."

Quinney sighed unexpectedly. "I believe Miss Cherville to be something of a mystery, for though I have always thought it strange her letters continued all these years, when I met her, I was agreeably struck with her."

"Indeed?"

"It is my sense of her, the way she conducted herself at Hyde, no flirtation, no dissimulation, an appraising eye, yet a careful reserve. At the same time there was something quite appealing in her expression, particularly her smile."

Braden laughed outright. "By God, you've tumbled in love with her!"

"No," Quinney responded scathingly.

"Have you never been in love?" he asked, curious of a sudden.

Quinney shook his head. "I haven't the faintest notion," he responded honestly. "Which is to say I do not believe I have."

"I wonder just what sort of lady would tempt your heart."

"Well not that one," he murmured, gesturing surreptitiously at a damsel nearby. "Her ankles are nearly as thick as tree stumps."

"Never mind that," Braden said, laughing as he pushed his friend further down the perimeter of the dance floor. The evening was very fine and the night sky full of stars. A cooling wind tugged at the edges of his domino. "Answer my question."

Quinney grimaced. "I cannot say precisely," he responded, stopping to once more observe the dancers. "Someone not quite in the usual style, I suppose, but if I could command one quality I would wish for a certain ability to set aside the confining rules of society at will. Caro Lamb had just such a gift for the outrageous."

"Yet, even Byron grew tired of her antics after a time."

"I suppose you are right," he murmured, after which he gasped. "Do but look at the Cherville box, Braden. Your Nemesis has just told that old roué, Gilles, to go the devil! I do not believe I have ever seen him bow so many times while making a retreat."

"She has at least shown a little good sense in setting him on his heels."

Quinney lifted his quizzing glass and peered at Gilles. "Someone should tell the old fop that even a tomato would not wear so much rouge."

Braden chuckled after which Quinney turned toward him,

his expression serious. "Do you think you will ever read Miss Cherville's letters?"

"I do not see why I would. Trickett has, of course, and occasionally would insist that I read one of them. However, I thought them rather ridiculous in nature, family antics, that sort of thing."

"The very thing your secretary would enjoy."

"Precisely so. What I have never understood is that not only is the brother well-shod, but Miss Cherville herself is an heiress, so why do you suppose she has hounded me these many years and more about the guardianship?"

Quinney, whose gaze was fixed on the dancing slippers of a nearby and quite comely shepherdess, shrugged. "I haven't the faintest notion. Perhaps what she desired of a guardian could not be purchased. Connections, that sort of thing."

Braden was not so satisfied with this answer. The guardianship of the Cherville children had been a sore point with him over the years. Generally, he ignored Miss Cherville's attempts to get him to reconsider his opinion and whenever his secretary, John Trickett, informed him of the arrival of another encroaching missive, he made it clear he was uninterested in knowing whether Nicholas had learned to ride or Miss Jane had completed her first embroidery sampler or Miss Frederica had written a fine poem or Miss Louisa had a new beau or that Master Hugh had been sent down from Cambridge for bringing a tame bear into his rooms just for a lark.

In truth, any reminder of the Chervilles tended to sharpen his temper. The guardianship had been one of the failures of his ascendancy to the Earldom of Bradenstoke, to which, had circumstance permitted, he might otherwise have generously agreed.

However, when his father passed away such a short time before Miss Cherville lost both her parents in a coaching accident, he had inherited an estate on the absolute brink of disaster. So deeply in debt had his father become in his love of gaming, that only by battling for two years had he salvaged even a portion of the estate. The turmoil of those early efforts to save his inheritance had absolutely forbidden his attention being drawn away by something that seemed so frivolous as a guardianship.

"What I should like to know," he stated hotly, "is why the deuce her brother is not in London? Master Hugh has attained his majority and has graduated from Cambridge, or so Trickett has informed me. Why is he not around to do the pretty with his sisters? If he were more responsible, I daresay Miss Cherville's letters would have ceased years ago."

"Good God."

"What? Are you disagreeing with me?"

"No, no. Sir Benedict Locksbury has just arrived and is addressing Miss Cherville. He is actually kissing her fingers and she appears to be welcoming his attentions. What do you suppose that means? She cannot know what he is!"

"Perhaps she does and does not care," Braden returned cynically.

"Someone should warn her of his reputation."

"Again, that would be Master Hugh's responsibility."

"He is obviously not here."

"My point exactly. If Mr. Cherville does not give a fig for the well-being of his sisters then why should anyone else? It is merely a reflection of a very bad education."

"Or the lack of a proper guardian," Quinney said, taunting him mercilessly.

Braden scowled. "Oh, go to the devil!" he snapped. "You know very well we should not even be speaking of the Chervilles."

"No, we should not for it always puts you sadly out of temper. However, I feel I ought to acknowledge Lady Wroughton's friend so you will forgive me if, after the dance I mean to have with this exquisite damsel who has lost her sheep, that I pay my respects to Miss Cherville."

"You do not need to ask for my permission," he said. "Besides, the fireworks will be commencing soon and I think that will be the moment I require to invoke the presence of 'poor Mr. Pinfrith.' "

"You make me shudder," Quinney said, laughing as he headed in the direction of the beguiling shepherdess.

Braden withdrew into the shadows to watch the female who had bedeviled him for so long. He had but one intent, to plot just how he was to steal a kiss from her.

Two

Alice Cherville lifted her fan to hide her smiles. Sir Benedict Locksbury's expression was wholly stoic, save for a faint twitching of his lips, as he gazed upon the monumental arrangement of bows, feathers, and artificial flowers which adorned her aunt's powdered locks.

Mrs. Urchfont, aware of his interest, preened before him, turning her head from side to side. "Oh, my dear Sir Benedict, do you not fancy my bonnet? Three of the feathers are new, five in all! I daresay you have never seen such beauty before. I wore this confection when I was first come out, which was a few years ago, let me tell you. Fashions then were so much more elegant than today's straight, rather uninteresting Grecian lines."

Sir Benedict swept his gaze over her hat. "I must admit, ma'am, I have never seen the like."

"Of course you have not," Mrs. Urchfont said, his facetiousness lost on her. "But then you are a most elegant gentleman and have such taste as must set you apart from some of these ridiculous fellows who call themselves dandies. Why, I was used to think Mr. Brummell looked like a skunk, arrayed as he always was in his blacks and whites. There is not a soul in England more genteel than our Sir Benedict! Why do you squint, Alice?"

"Your feathers, Aunt, have a tendency to brush over my face each time you turn your head."

Mrs. Urchfont clucked her tongue. "But you must not

squint, my dear, not if you are to get a husband for there is nothing worse than a squint. Why very soon the entire *beau monde* will be calling you platter-faced or something equally as horrid and then where shall you be—a spinster to your grave! Oh dear, the very thought of it makes me as blue-deviled as the Regent without his corset. My, my what a lovely masquerade! I do so enjoy looking at all the costumes." She twisted her head about to again view the dancers and once more caught Alice full in the face with one particular feather that hung quite low from her hat.

Alice sighed and drew her chair away from her aunt not for the first time that evening. It seemed that no matter how far she removed herself, however, the feathers found her.

Mrs. Urchfont, an impoverished widow of many years, was a rotund, shatter-brained creature who seemed perpetually unaware of her surroundings or the proximity of any object near her. She had already knocked over two glasses of champagne and her sisters had made a wager among themselves that before the night was through, a third would share a similar fate.

When the country dance ended, Louisa and Jane returned to the box, Jane as a lovely and quite clever green and white water lily and Louisa sporting a simple black domino since she had no interest in costumes generally. Each greeted Sir Benedict with warm smiles, for he had been a friend to the Cherville family for nigh on five years, having taken a house near Tilsford Hall, where he lived from Michaelmas through Easter. His own property in Northumberland was snowbound during January and February so that he wintered in the south until the snows melted along the Scottish border.

Alice glanced about the various boxes and the dancers now taking their places for the waltz. "I, too, love a masquerade," she said, addressing Sir Benedict. "One can be whatever one wishes at such a fete."

Sir Benedict sipped his champagne and settled his glass on the table. "I believe the same to be true of life."

"Not so," Alice disagreed readily. "Everyone is known to the world by their conduct if not by their words."

"Indeed?" he queried. "I must take exception. I believe we all wear a mask of sorts, though I must admit yours is a shimmering of tulle over one of the sweetest natures I have ever known."

Alice could not help but laugh. "What stuff!" she cried. "Though I must say your compliments are by far the prettiest I have ever heard. Only tell me, what is the mask you wear?"

He gave a low, rumbling chuckle. "A mask of goodness," he proclaimed with an arched brow lifted in a menacing fashion. "I am the very soul of what is dark and unworthy. I am the creature who haunts the dreams of young maidens, chasing them into the black of night until they awaken shivering."

Alice laughed anew, but Sir Benedict's playfulness was quite lost on Mrs. Urchfont, who laid a hand across her ample bosom. "Sir Benedict!" she cried. "How you do go on! I vow you have given me the worst fright!"

"Do not pay the smallest heed to him!" Alice cried, seeing at once that her aunt was indeed distressed by his remarks. "He only means to tease me and for that I should rap his knuckles and I would had I a strong-enough stick at hand."

"Now *I* am quaking with fear," Sir Benedict cried, his dark eyes dancing.

Louisa, seated on the opposite side of Mrs. Urchfont, squeezed her arm. "Dear aunt, who could ever be afraid of our dear Sir Benedict?"

"Indeed!" Jane agreed heartily. "When he has been Alice's strong right arm for so long a time!"

"I suppose I am being ridiculous," Mrs. Urchfont said, smiling sheepishly at the baronet. "After all, what would we have done without our good friend these many years and more?"

"You have spoken truly," Alice said. She glanced at Sir Benedict and found herself grateful yet again for his presence in her life. He had been a bulwark for the past several years and even tonight while he sat with them, she would not have to worry quite so much about being accosted by wholly unacceptable gentlemen like Mr. Gilles, who had been in his cups when he approached their table but a few minutes past.

No, the baronet had but to lift a brow and any such gentleman would scurry away. He was tall, strongly built, and though a little past forty, these attributes combined with black hair silvered at the temples and eyes of a shade no less dark than coal, presented a rather formidable appearance.

He had proven his devotion to her family a dozen times, not less so on one critical occasion when he had rescued Hugh after her brother's racing whiskey had collided with a wagon whose team had been hurtling down the same, narrow lane completely out of control. Hugh's left leg had been broken in two places, including a piercing of the skin, and he had suffered a severe blow to the head. Without Sir Benedict's swift assistance, along with the vicar, who chanced by at nearly the same moment, it was believed by all he would have been lamed for life or worse, he could easily have perished because of the severity of his wounds. The other driver had simply abandoned him to the mercy of the elements and had never been seen again.

Alice, therefore, had numerous reasons to be devoted to her dear friend. She had a great deal in common with Sir Benedict, a love of country life, a general interest in society, and a particular passion for the art of fencing, which she had taken up many years past. Both she and Sir Benedict had studied with a master by the name of Mr. Boscombe, who resided nearby in the village of Tilsford.

Three months prior, the baronet had paid her the highest compliment of offering for her hand in marriage. Although she had refused him for she did not love him as a woman should love her husband, still she had been touched by the depths of his love for her. She had even been tempted a little to accept of his kind proposals since as a husband he would have been a welcome shield against the unhappier aspects of the world.

The fact that she had actually considered wedding a man she did not love was perhaps the prime force that had driven her to London. Her parents' marriage had been a love-match, something she coveted for herself as well as for her brothers and sisters. Though she and her siblings enjoyed a wide society in Wiltshire, not one of them had been pricked by Cupid's gold-tipped arrow. She felt it most necessary that her sisters in particular enjoy the benefits of meeting any number of eligible young gentlemen in what was referred to as the Marriage Mart. Their portions were small, thus eliminating a great number of hopeful suitors from the prospect of matrimony. She wanted each of them to be able to marry exclusively for love.

Thus far, however, her own Season had not been successful in the manner she had hoped it would be. Although she had received three offers of marriage, all from gazetted fortune hunters since she was herself an heiress, her heart had not been in the least tempted by the gentlemen she had met over the course of the past four weeks. Here was a service Sir Benedict had performed for her—he frightened off any gentleman who courted her with an eye to her inheritance.

Unlike her sisters, she was in possession of a very fine fortune in excess of fifty thousand pounds and for that reason could have the man of her choosing. The only difficulty seemed to be that of the hundreds of gentlemen she had met, still her heart remained entirely untouched! She had even begun to wonder if she was not defective in some manner that she was so particular in her tastes. What sort of man would do for her?

Regardless, she was enjoying her first London Season prodigiously. Everything seemed so magical to her as she glanced about her and not just the Vauxhall Pleasure Gardens, but the Metropolis itself.

From the moment her coach had arrived at the outskirts of London she had felt as though forces she could not explain had been leading her a merry dance. She awoke each morning full of expectation and excitement and she could not recall a single event during the prior month of April that she had not fully enjoyed, whether it was a masquerade such as tonight in the cold swirling air of the gardens, or a play at Drury Lane, or receiving morning callers at their Tuesday and Thursday afternoon "at homes" in Upper Brook Street. She had numerous acquaintants now, enjoyed the spirited debates among

members of the House of Lords or Commons who frequented
the various evening entertainments, and particularly delighted
in shopping in New Bond Street for the latest fashions, for
specialty foodstuffs, or for articles that might improve the
appearance of her drawing room. She was in every particular
exceedingly well suited to the London Season.

Her sisters' experiences on the other hand differed from
hers in tone and interest. Louisa's court, in which she took
great pride, was growing steadily; Jane still longed for the
country; and Frederica from first setting foot in a ballroom
had become consumed with a ridiculous puppy by the name
of Mr. Dodds.

"And where is our charming Freddie this evening?" Sir
Benedict asked.

All the ladies groaned as one.

"Am I to understand she is with Mr. Dodds?" When a
general laughter ensued, he inquired, "I do not see Hugh
here this evening. Is it possible he has still not yet found his
way to London?"

Alice shook her head. "Unfortunately, no."

"I trust you are not worried on his account," he said.

"Not in the least," Alice assured him. "I am merely an-
noyed that he should keep us in suspense for an entire month
now."

"I shall be happy to speak to him once he does arrive,"
he offered. "All of you should be enjoying his protection,
particularly in such a place as this."

"Poor Hugh!" Mrs. Urchfont cried suddenly. "I am persuaded he has fallen into a ditch and broken his neck. Young
men are forever doing so, you know."

"Aunt!" Louisa protested. "How can you say such a terrible thing?"

"Yes, Aunt," Jane added. "I am certain he is perfectly
well, for you know what a Nonesuch he is."

Mrs. Urchfont screwed up her face. "Do not any of you
girls remember the time he fell from the apple tree and was
three months mending?"

The ladies all exchanged meaningful glances. Hugh was

a bruising rider, a skilled hunter, had remarkable physical acumen, and never so much as tripped even when the ice was heavy on the countryside. However, the fall from the tree when he was a lad had forever fixed in Mrs. Urchfont's mind that he was prone to misfortune.

Sir Benedict intervened. "Whether he has tumbled into a ditch or is merely being selfish, which I think a far more likely possibility given his general temperament, I know for certain Hugh would not want any of you to be either worried for his safety or to fail to enjoy the evening's amusements on his account."

"You are so right," Alice agreed at once. "I believe that is Hugh's finest quality, his desire for our happiness in everything."

"Just so," he said, rising to his feet in his dignified manner.

"You are not leaving us so soon, are you?" Louisa asked.

"Alas, though I would far prefer to remain here among friends, I was persuaded by an acquaintance to join him at Boodle's this evening, an invitation I could not refuse without giving offense. I hope you understand. I fear I stopped only to ascertain you were all situated happily."

Jane addressed him sweetly. "How kind of you to see to our comfort, Sir Benedict. You are a true friend."

"I am glad to be accounted as such." With that, he made his bows and quit their box.

A few minutes later, when the most recent set ended, Mrs. Urchfont whipped her head about, the feathers again striking Alice in the face as her attention became riveted on some object beyond Jane's shoulder. "Oh, my dears!" she exclaimed. "It is Mr. Quintin! Oh dear, oh dear! He has seen me and has smiled. He is even now lifting his hand to me. I believe he means to come to us. Just think of it! Should he deign to notice us tonight, we shall be made! He is a particular friend of Bradenstoke's, you know, and the pair of them travel in the *First Circles!*"

Alice turned slightly to view the man she had met earlier at Hyde Park and who had struck her as uncommonly intelligent. He was a dandy, but not in the usual order of such men. He lacked affectations of any kind and his dress was elegant and precise. This evening he wore a false moustachio and she saw at once that he was costumed as The Bard. How, she wondered, could a man of intelligence actually befriend a man of Lord Bradenstoke's stamp?

Thoughts of Bradenstoke forced Alice to recall with some pleasure all the letters she had sent to him over the past several weeks since having taken up residence in Upper Brook Street. When he had refused to meet with her upon her arrival in London, she had sent a shower of letters his direction merely to aggravate him for his unconscionable attitude toward her family. And yet, however much she had delighted in her quiet form of revenge, she was still on occasion saddened by his disinterest in the guardianship for which she had believed him from the first entirely responsible.

For the past ten years she had endeavored to encourage him to take an interest in her family by writing frequently about each of her siblings, their antics, their unique temperaments, and hundreds of anecdotes recounting the usual changes as each passed from childhood to adulthood. Still, Bradenstoke's heart had remained unmoved.

Even when she had expressed her deepest concerns, that both Hugh and Nicholas have a fatherly example in their lives, still he had not responded.

For some reason which she could not explain, hope had never died within her that one day Bradenstoke would take up the duties his father had promised so many years ago. Regardless, she had come to believe in recent months that her persistence in writing and posting her letters had emanated from a source quite apart from the guardianship. It would seem there had been something healing in the mere act of putting to paper the activities of her family which had not only kept her mind clear but had strengthened her ability to manage a household of growing children when she had been at the outset only a young lady of fifteen.

"Alice," Mrs. Urchfont said, turning toward her, "did I tell you that I saw Bradenstoke this morning? We have been much occupied today otherwise I cannot account for having forgotten so momentous an occasion. He was walking down Bond Street, and had just emerged from Berry Brothers, when I nearly rammed into him for the wind was blowing and my bonnet had come untied. My head was bent, pressing as I was against the wind, and the next moment he was begging my pardon.

"I looked up and nearly fainted for, my dears"—here she looked at all three of her nieces in turn and rolled her eyes in a meaningful fashion—"I had quite forgot that he is by far the handsomest man in all of the Kingdom. He has large brown eyes which fairly pierce the soul, his cheekbones are well defined in the manner of the Indians in the Colonies, his hair is the rich color of the coffee bean, and he is quite tall. There is always something about a tall man, especially one with shoulders so very broad. I vow my heart, even at my age, fluttered in my bosom." She fanned herself rather heartily and said, "Oh, my! It seems to have grown quite heated in our box. Are you heated Alice, Jane, Louisa?"

"No, ma'am," the ladies returned as one, all repressing their smiles yet again.

Alice sipped her champagne. "No matter how handsome a man might be, Aunt, of what use is he to any lady if his character is so very bad as we know Bradenstoke's to be? He is not a man of honor, nor is there the smallest speck of kindness in his bones. A lady would be a fool to tumble in love with such a creature."

"Of course she would," Mrs. Urchfont agreed readily. She leaned forward, squinting very hard into the crowds. "I see that Mr. Quintin is kept from us yet again. He has been stopped at least a dozen times by every toady here. Ah, well, I suppose he will eventually come to us. Speaking of Bradenstoke has put me in mind of something else I learned while actually in Berry's this morning."

"You are full of news," Alice cried.

"You will never credit it, but do you know this fellow Trickett who has recently formed part of your court, Louisa?"

"Yes, I like him very much," Louisa remarked.

"I as well," Alice said, addressing her sister. "In fact, of all of your numerous beaus, I would say he is my favorite. He is quite intelligent, always in excellent humor, and most considerate."

"He is not so handsome as some," Jane added, "but he has a gentle air about him that is most pleasing."

Mrs. Urchfont began to laugh. "Indeed! Indeed! But you will never guess who he is!" And in her merriment at knowing something her nieces did not, her hands began to flail. Alice lifted a brow and exchanged glances with Jane and Louisa. She bit her lip. She began to smile as though she could see the accident coming. Mrs. Urchfont waved an excited hand once more and promptly knocked over her third glass of champagne. "Oh dear, I am become as clumsy as poor Hugo."

All three ladies burst into peals of laughter.

"You need not be so very amused," she complained, at the same time calling for a waiter to sop up the pool of champagne.

Alice begged pardon, then continued. "Only tell me what you have learned of Louisa's beau."

At that, Mrs. Urchfont forgot their laughter and puffed up her chest. "Only that he is Bradenstoke's secretary!" she cried, triumphantly.

Alice stared at her aunt. "You astonish me!" she cried.

"I thought I might." She waggled her head and the feathers first struck Alice on her right then Louisa on her left.

"How is this possible!" Jane cried. "And we did not know! Louisa, were you aware of his connection to Bradenstoke?"

Louisa shook her head. "I have only danced with him on three occasions. He is a most elegant partner and polite to a fault but I have not had an opportunity to speak with him privately to any great extent." Her nose wrinkled in something Alice knew to be a measure of disgust. "I had no notion he was someone's secretary."

"Not just a secretary to *anyone,* though," Mrs. Urchfont cried. "To the Earl of Bradenstoke! Besides, I know even more about him than this!"

Once more, she became puffed up with the exalted position of knowing a bit of gossip before her nieces and would not speak.

"Do tell us!" Jane cried. "Before I succumb to a fit of apoplexy."

Mrs. Urchfont giggled with delight. "Well, if you must know, it would seem that though he is of a large family, he will one day inherit a rather tidy fortune from an uncle who favors him. However, Lady Wroughton told me Mr. Trickett has taken up the post as the earl's secretary so that he would not be a burden to his family. Apparently he did not wish, though I do not comprehend why, to live upon the expectation."

"I think his decision wholly admirable," Jane said.

Alice noted that throughout this conversation about Mr. Trickett Louisa's gaze had wandered through the crowds of revellers gathered about the dance floor. She knew her sister was hoping that Lord Tamerbeck would arrive to go down the waltz with her as he had told her he would. The hour was advanced, however, and still his lordship had not yet arrived.

Alice had no confidence in the viscount, who was clearly Louisa's favorite, and felt certain her sister was doomed to disappointment. As much as any lady might hope to be addressed as "her ladyship," she was convinced that Lord Tamerbeck was in no way suited to be any woman's husband, much less Louisa's. He was inconstant and entirely self-absorbed. His absence at the masquerade, when he had all but promised Louisa he would attend, was what she had come to expect of him. Still, she could see that her sister remained hopeful.

With a new set forming, both Jane and Louisa were solicited for another country dance. Louisa fairly bounced in her steps, for she was enjoying every aspect of the Season as much as Alice. However, Jane was polite in her smiles, a sight which rather wrenched her heart.

Mrs. Urchfont fanned herself and clucked her tongue. "Poor Jane," she murmured. "She is not in the least content in London."

"How well I know it," Alice said, sighing. "The smoke-filled air does not agree with her and she speaks of her gardens, chickens, and pets so as to leave no one in doubt of her longing to be back in Wiltshire."

Mrs. Urchfont, while little more than a peagoose, was of a loving disposition. "She will be happier tomorrow," she said. "For she is taking Nicky and Lady Wroughton's grandson to Kensington Gardens."

Alice's spirits brightened. "I had nearly forgot," she admitted. "Yes, Jane will enjoy the gardens."

Mrs. Urchfont grew agitated quite suddenly. "Oh, my dear!" she exclaimed beneath her breath. "Here is Mr. Quintin, at last." To the gentleman approaching the box, she called out, "How do you go on, Mr. Quintin? Is this not a delightful lark? I must say you appear to great advantage as Mr. William Shakespeare himself."

"Thank you, Mrs. Urchfont," he said, bowing in a simple, elegant fashion.

Alice watched him in some admiration for though he was a Pink of the Ton there was something in Mr. Quintin's quiet, almost gentle mode of expression as well as the frequent twinkle in his eye that drew her to him.

"Will you not sit with us while the young ladies have their dance?" Mrs. Urchfont urged.

"I should be delighted."

"Is Bradenstoke not in attendance this evening?" she asked as Mr. Quintin seated himself.

Alice watched him carefully and saw the smallest twitch of his lips and wondered what it could mean. "I fear not," he responded.

"We have been most anxious to make his acquaintance," Alice said, continuing to scrutinize his every feature.

Mr. Quintin turned sharp gray eyes toward her. "He can be quite elusive."

"So it would seem," she countered. "We had hoped to gain his sponsorship while we were in London since our respective fathers were great friends. Alas, circumstances quite beyond my control or comprehension have prevented our meeting."

"There is always a chance he will arrive unexpectedly at some event or other."

Alice felt an odd prickling at the back of her neck upon hearing these words and experienced the strangest inclination to look behind her.

"Do you not dance this evening?" Mrs. Urchfont queried.

Mr. Quintin smiled politely. "Only if Miss Cherville will be so kind as to oblige me for the next set, which I believe to be the quadrille." Again his gaze shifted back to her and she had the sense that there was the faintest challenge in his words as though questioning whether a set of rustic folk from the wilds of Wiltshire would actually know how to perform the intricacies of that particular dance.

"I should be honored, Mr. Quintin," Alice responded with a smile and a slight lift of her chin, "since I am told that you are a notable dancer." She held his gaze in a meaningful manner.

He chuckled warmly in response and she felt she understood him and believed at the same time that she had, at least for the moment, gained his respect. While the present *contre danse* progressed, the conversation ranged across a broad spectrum of subjects which appealed greatly to Alice, from the unhappy effects of the enclosures upon rural laborers, the loss of many fine woodlands to the lure of commerce, the unhappy lot of crippled soldiers returned from the Napoleonic Wars, the latest Paris fashions about which Mr. Quintin was particularly knowledgeable, and the manner in which the waltz continued to evolve, becoming more and more shocking to the high sticklers.

Time passed swiftly and before long, Alice found herself engaged in dancing the quadrille with Mr. Quintin and three other couples. The patterns were intricate and the dance lively. Alice felt she could not have been happier than at this moment.

When the set ended, Mr. Quintin flooded Mrs. Urchfont with joy by offering to escort the ladies to view the fireworks, which would be exploding over the nearby Thames shortly.

Three

"Miss Cherville?"

Alice, whose gaze had been pinned to the dark night sky as the first of the firework shells burst over the Thames, turned to find one of Vauxhall's serving maids at her side. "Yes?" she queried, startled at finding herself thus addressed.

"There be a Mr. Pinfrith," she said, leaning closer to Alice in order to keep her revelations confidential, "what has certain information for you concerning his brother, Lord Bradenstoke. His *half brother*. Will ye speak with him?"

"Mr. Pinfrith?" she queried, thinking she could not have heard correctly. Another shell burst overhead and the sky exploded in a dazzle of light.

"Aye, miss."

Alice knew Bradenstoke's half brother was to arrive sometime in May but there had been no indication from any quarter that his ship had actually reached the London docks. "But are you certain it was a Mr. Pinfrith?"

When another shell burst, the maid glanced indifferently toward the sky. "Aye, miss. That is wat 'e told me. Will ye follow after?"

Alice glanced at her sisters and aunt, as well as at Mr. Quintin, each of whom was engrossed in the succession of brilliant flashes. An excitement and trembling she had felt earlier upon entering the gardens began building in her heart. There was no question that she should refuse the request which, regardless of the gentleman's motives, was utterly clandestine in nature. A man of honor would introduce himself to her, in the presence of her aunt, and beg to speak privately with her or to call upon her in Upper Brook Street and request an audience in order to state his business. An invitation, during a fireworks display, was not entirely innocent in nature.

Alice turned to the serving maid. She meant to refuse, but her heart was not so easily dissuaded. "Word for me of Lord Bradenstoke?" she queried.

"Aye, miss. That is wat 'e said."

What harm could there be? Besides, perhaps he meant to discuss the guardianship with her.

She hesitated only a moment, then picked up her heavy brocade skirts. "Pray be quick," she murmured.

"Of course, miss," the maid responded.

She took her at her word and led her swiftly at a near run into the labyrinth of pathways. Before long, Alice knew she would have some difficulty finding a route back to the Thames. Only the presence of the continued fireworks showed her the direction of the river.

A few seconds more, however, planted her at the entrance to a dark path at the end of which a gentleman was seated on a stone bench, wearing a domino and mask, his identity completely disguised. The shrubberies had overgrown the usual low hedge and the darkness of the shadows prevented her from ascertaining anything about the man. As the maid disappeared, she began a slow progress down the path, her nerves prickling in anticipation.

"Mr. Pinfrith?" she called out.

"Here, Miss Cherville." The voice that returned to her was barely a whisper and set at an oddly high pitch. When the gentleman rose to his feet, she was a little startled to find that he was such a large man, quite tall and broad across the shoulders. She recalled Mrs. Urchfont's earlier description of Lord Bradenstoke. Well, the two men were brothers, after all.

For a moment she felt frightened and wondered if she was making a terrible mistake in having responded to his request as she had. She knew very little of Mr. Pinfrith, after all, only that he commanded the East Indies venture as one of the principal partners in the firm, Pinfrith, Stert, and Bradenstoke.

"You wished to speak with me?" she asked.

"Indeed, I do," he responded, his voice sounding hoarse. "You must forgive me. I have injured my throat from so much shouting into the wind. The last leg of our voyage was troubled with storms. Will you not sit with me for a few minutes? There is something I would say to you."

Alice felt the trembling in her heart increase. She was still several yards from him and did not feel she was at all wise in responding as she had to his request. "I should return to my aunt and my sisters. Why do you not call in Upper Brook Street tomorrow? We are having an at home at two o'clock."

"You honor me," he murmured, then slumped back onto the stone bench and dropped his head into his hands. A faint groan crossed the distance between them.

Alice was utterly confounded. "Mr. Pinfrith," she cried, taking several steps toward him, "whatever is the matter?" She could not imagine what was oversetting him, though she strongly suspected his brother might be at the heart of his distress.

"I was hoping you might be able to help me. You see . . ."

Alice thought she understood. "Has—has Bradenstoke used you ill?"

There was a long silence before his answer returned to her. "I fear he has."

She glanced back up the path, weighing just what she ought to do. The more prudent course would be to return to her aunt, which she knew very well she should do. However, she was fatigued of the moment with always being prudent, particularly since Cupid was still so disinterested in the state of her heart. Besides, what harm could there be in just speaking with Mr. Pinfrith? Clearly his wish that she attend him was with the view that she might be of service to him, though in what manner she could not imagine.

Drawing in a deep breath, she made her decision and com-

pleted the remainder of the distance to stand before him.
When he did not even lift his head to her, she felt the most
ridiculous impulse to lay her hand on his shoulder and to
offer what commiseration she could, for she believed she
knew precisely how he felt.

"It is very difficult," she began quietly, refraining from
touching him, "and quite sad when someone you hoped to
rely upon cannot find his way to be of assistance to those
to whom he is obligated by birth and honor. Do I much
mistake the matter in believing that such has been your experience with Lord Bradenstoke?"

"Precisely," he murmured, lifting his masked face to her.
"I hear in your voice a wonderful understanding and sympathy. Indeed, when I learned from Mr. Gilles that the beautiful *Elizabeth* was none other than Alice Cherville, I had
hoped to speak with you. I believe it was nothing less than
fate which drew me to Vauxhall on this my first day returned
from the East Indies, that I find you here and willing to
speak with me."

Alice felt a shiver go down her spine. "You are just arrived?" she asked, her pulse quickening. She could not credit
the fortuitous nature of their chance encounter.

"My ship docked this morning. Only Braden knows that
I am here. Will you not be seated?"

She hesitated but a moment, then settled herself beside
him. She realized that there were few things which could
have encouraged so bold an act on her part, but it so happened that her particular feelings of ill-use at the hands of
Bradenstoke was just such a reason. In Mr. Pinfrith she
sensed a kindred spirit, certainly in suffering.

Her thoughts shot suddenly down an odd path. She wondered, for instance, just what the man behind the mask
looked like and whether or not he had an agreeable countenance. Was he a man, for instance, with whom she could
tumble in love? Perhaps Cupid was not so indifferent as she
had believed.

But what was she thinking? What foolishness was this?
Mr. Pinfrith had obviously solicited her advice, perhaps even

her comfort, because of his sufferings. Surely any thoughts beyond a platonic offering of succor was ridiculous in the extreme.

Mr. Pinfrith turned toward her quite abruptly. "You must help me," he cried in his hoarse voice.

"How can I?" she returned. She did not know which shocked her more, his plea that she help him or that she was now facing him directly. "I have never even met your brother," she said. "His indifference to me, to my family, to the letters I have written him over the years must speak to his dislike of me. In what way, then, can I possibly be of use to you?"

"I was speaking with my brother only this morning. I found him reading your letters. Oh, yes, he has read them, all of them, more than once. He is not indifferent to you, not in the least. I believe he admires you excessively, in particular your determination to secure the guardianship in the face of his steadfast refusal to the contrary. I confess I never understood his reluctance to take up the guardianship. I know that I would never have refused you."

Entirely without ceremony, he took strong hold of her shoulders. "Will you help me?" There was something in the intensity with which he addressed her that made her hope he would go on holding her. It seemed odd that she would desire that something of a complete stranger, yet so she did. If only she could look into his eyes, then she would know the truth of who he was, but in the darkened shadows his eyes were but glints in the inconstant light of the fireworks.

"Whatever his opinions of me," she said, almost breathlessly, "I beg to know how I might be of use to you. Pray, tell me of your troubles."

He sighed. "I spoke with Braden only this morning," he explained. "We argued for at least an hour. You see, his father made a promise to our mother concerning a certain property in Hampshire. I told him that it was his duty to honor such a promise even if it had not been specified in our father's will."

Alice felt utterly mortified on behalf of the sensitive man

beside her. "My experience has been so similar," she cried. "I had always thought there was at least some justification to his denial of my claim but how could he refuse yours? I am astonished! I always knew Bradenstoke was a hard man, but I never thought him so bad as this. Your claim being much closer than mine, and yet rejected, must speak profoundly of that defect of character which the unfortunate man possesses. Only, tell me, what might I do for you? Anything within my power is yours for the asking."

The man still possessing her arms grew very still. "I ask that you go to him and speak with him."

"I would do so immediately but he has refused even to admit me into his house. I tell you, he will not receive me."

He shook his head and chuckled in a hopeless manner. "You are right," he whispered sadly. "Of course you are right. I do not know what I was thinking to have asked you to do the impossible. My brother is a hard man. He will never relent. I believe I have just now realized there is nothing you, nor anyone, can do."

"I am deeply saddened by his conduct toward you," she said, her heart wrung for him. "I only wish there was something I could do."

Another shell burst in the sky. He drew in his breath sharply. "The light from the fireworks has just crossed your face. What a beautiful queen you are. I saw you at a distance earlier but I must say, here, even in the shadows, you are so very lovely. I—" He broke off. "Forgive me. I should not be so bold."

Alice felt dizzy of a sudden. "You do not offend me," she offered. "If that is your concern." She could just see his smile in the darkness.

"Perhaps it is your sympathy, or the fireworks, or perhaps because I have always felt that in some inexplicable manner, you and I . . . that is, you are the kindest creature I have ever met, Miss Cherville. I would thank you . . ."

Before she knew what was happening, one of the hands still imprisoning her arm slid to her wrist and then in a swift movement slipped about her waist. He lifted her to her feet as though she had been a feather, dragging her tightly against him. A moment more, his lips were on hers in a kiss that was as gentle as his embrace was rough. She did not know which shocked her more, finding herself standing upright and locked unresisting in his firm embrace or feeling the first soft kiss become a second and a third until he was plying kisses all over her lips, her cheeks, and her lips once more.

Most certainly he had been away from England for a very long time!

In the midst of this tender assault she instructed herself repeatedly to stop such a wicked embrace, that she should desist from taking so much pleasure in his kisses, but another part of her would have none of it. She felt the deepest sympathy for the man holding her and not for the world would she reject him. In truth, she had never in her life felt anything so wonderful as being held in Mr. Pinfrith's arms.

"Miss Cherville," he whispered in his hoarse voice, "I never meant . . ." He seemed bereft of words as he drew back slightly, yet without releasing her, and stared at her through the slits in his mask.

"Of course you did not," she whispered. "Nor did I . . ." She then did the unthinkable and settled her own lips on his in a quite wanton manner.

Lord Bradenstoke received the unexpected kiss with a strong sensation that had nothing to do with the triumph he had initially felt at stealing a kiss from her. Instead, he was stunned by how she felt in his arms, how her lips tasted against his own, how he wished the moment would never end. These were things he had not expected to feel, not by half. He had meant to punish her and instead the pleasure she was giving him was like nothing he had ever experienced before.

Once more he drew her closely to him, surrounding her fully with his arms. He touched his tongue to her lips and miraculously her lips parted. He became lost in that moment as he searched the depths of her mouth and heard a faint cooing in her throat. Was he truly kissing Miss Alice

Cherville, the same female who had hounded him for a decade?

A sudden blinding passion took hold of him, driving every thought from his head. There was in this moment no past between them, only a banquet of present delights. He felt her arm tighten about his neck. When had she actually slid her arm just so and pressed herself against him? How sweetly she clung to him. He wanted to devour her and kissed her harder still. Her fingers sank into his hair, sliding beneath the strings of his mask. A wind swept over his back, sending a shiver snaking down his neck. A minute passed and then another. The peacock feathers of her collar drifted over his cheek. He should cease this madness yet he did not want the moment to end. Apparently the lady shared his sentiments, for she had taken to pulling on the strands of hair at the nape of his neck in a manner that kept his lips attached to hers and his tongue exploring the sweetness of her mouth.

Only as the last of the fireworks died away did Miss Cherville withdraw from him. "I must go," she whispered, unwrapping her arm slowly from about his neck. "What have I done?"

"You have kissed me," he whispered.

Her gaze drifted to his lips then back to his eyes. As ridiculous as it was, he did not want to let her go. He felt once he did that something precious, even innocent, would be passing from his life.

"St. James's," he said. "Meet me at St. James's Park on Wednesday at noon, where the milkmaids tender their milk."

Alice nodded and caressed his face. "Wednesday at noon," she said softly. "St. James's. And do not worry. We shall speak further of your difficulty."

For some unaccountable reason, the smile that attended her words, wrenched his heart. As she moved away, he caught her hand then released it in a gentle motion. When she had disappeared from the path, he remained in place, wondering why the earlier sensation of triumph he had experienced in kissing Alice Cherville had lasted only for a brief moment and why, in its stead, did he now experience an almost insatiable longing to see her again?

Another breeze stole over him, sending more shivers along his spine. Did he hear Cupid's laughter? He turned in a circle but nothing returned to him except the distant chatter of guests exclaiming over the fireworks.

Four

On the following morning, Alice lay on her feather pillows, her hands clasped across the thick layer of blue-flowered bed linens folded prettily over her stomach. She was smiling and felt warm to her toes even though the room was chilled, the once hot coals in the grate having grown cold in the night. In her five-and-twenty years she had never known such happiness as at this moment.

There had remained from the kiss she had shared with Mr. Pinfrith on the evening before a sensation unlike anything she had ever before experienced, as though her life had changed completely and would never again be the same. She could only wonder what Mr. Pinfrith's thoughts of her might be this morning.

She had rejoined her family after the fireworks, with Mr. Quintin by her side. He had found her emerging from the shrubbery and had informed her that Mrs. Urchfont was utterly distraught by her absence, believing she had been carried off by Gypsies. Alice had laughed but had permitted Mr. Quintin to tell a whisker or two about how she thought she had seen someone she knew and in pursuit had gotten lost in the pathways.

Of course this Banbury Tale had been strictly for the benefit of Mrs. Urchfont until her nerves grew calmer, but on the trip home she told them all the truth, that she had actually met Mr. Pinfrith. Though she felt most of what had been spoken between them was of a confidential nature, not to

mention the scandalous kiss, she revealed the nature of her
encounter, that Mr. Pinfrith desired her support in a matter
of some difficulty involving Lord Bradenstoke and, finally,
that she would be meeting him on Wednesday at St. James's
Park. She then asked if any of the ladies would be desirous
of accompanying her to the park and making the acquaintance of Mr. Pinfrith as well?

There had only been one response, a resounding "Yes!"
Even from Mrs. Urchfont.

Now, as she stared up at the canopy covering her bed, she
sighed with delight at the prospect of meeting the man she
had kissed so wonderfully. She then blushed at what he might
be thinking of a young lady who could be kissed so easily.
Her mind then took a rather large leap as she pondered the
possibility that love had found her at last.

This she dismissed as absurd. She had conversed with Mr.
Pinfrith for scarcely ten minutes and had kissed him for even
less time. It seemed wholly unlikely that love was what had
actually occurred between them, more like a sympathetic
communion and understanding based on a similar difficulty.
Was it, however, the beginnings of love? She simply did not
know and only time was capable of making such a determination.

Alice smiled and felt more content than she had in ages.
Even the chance that love was flitting about her door filled
her with gratitude. From the age of fifteen the events of her
life had been dictated by the governance of her house and
the education of not just herself but of her three sisters and
two brothers as well. To think she was actually contemplating
the mysteries of tumbling in love was beyond wonderful. In
truth, it was nothing short of miraculous.

She laughed aloud, her spirits soaring. To love and to be
loved. What more could any lady desire?

She remained in this blissful state for some few minutes
until her thoughts, as they were wont to do, drifted to the
day's requirements. Jane and Nicky would be going to
Kensington Gardens and at two o'clock the Cherville doors
were open to the *beau monde* at their twice-weekly at home.

In the evening, Lady Nettleford's ball. A good day, she thought, but a moment later a cloud crossed her soul. Where was Hugh?

She had not spoken her heart freely last night to Sir Benedict, for she was beginning to be worried about Hugh's extended absence. How could she fail to be? He was just one-and-twenty and more interested in kicking up a lark than in dancing attendance on his sisters. He had, however, promised most earnestly to be in London within the first fortnight of having quit Tilsford Hall.

She supposed his conduct was quite typical of young gentlemen his age and though he was showing steady improvement, she knew he had a long way to go before truly being a responsible young man.

She had even quarreled with him upon his leaving Tilsford an entire day in advance of his sisters and Nicky, for he had left several letters from their cousin's solicitor in Wales unread. She had insisted he take the letters with him so that he might read them while traveling, and to his credit he had finally promised to do so as well as to do better in minding his estate once they were returned to Wiltshire at the end of the Season.

On the whole, she was pleased with her brother's general conduct. He treated the estate servants with respect and kindness, he was adored by his sisters, and he fairly doted on Nicky, who would be eleven in less than a fortnight.

She could not help but smile at the thought of Nicky, her Nicky, for she had raised him as a mother would from the time he was a babe. He had never truly known their parents, only the love and affection of his siblings and the dotings of an aunt who even he had recently called a ridiculous ninny-hammer.

Dear Nicky and Hugh, Jane, Louisa, and Frederica. Alice sighed. She loved them all and was beyond satisfied that she had had the courage in the face of local disapproval of her scheme to bring her family to London. They were, with the exception of Jane, thriving in the Metropolis.

Thoughts of London returned her to her earlier reveries

of being caught up quite roughly in Mr. Pinfrith's embrace. She sighed anew. Of course once she met him she would have to declare to him that he must not trespass her lips in such a manner again, but for the present she would delight in her memories.

If only she could truly be of service to Mr. Pinfrith. He had honored her with his confidences yet she had felt completely powerless to be of the smallest use to him. Surely there was something she might accomplish on his behalf.

She began to feel restless. She sat up in bed, her brow pinched together as she pondered the nature of Bradenstoke's reprehensible conduct toward his own brother. Knowing that the earl would reject even his own brother's claim—half sibling or not!—only confirmed her opinion that the earl was a very bad man, indeed.

She twiddled her thumbs and pondered several quite excruciating means of torture which presented themselves to her eager mind. How much she would like to put Bradenstoke under the lash or perhaps set a pack of hounds after him or worse, place him among a set of hopeful young ladies and through a series of careful, thoughtful questions lead him to expose the true nature of his character to a completely horrified audience.

With these thoughts came the conviction that at the very least she should confront Bradenstoke about his misdeeds. Someone ought to perform the office. Why not Alice Cherville? With a surge of excitement, she rose from her bed and began her day. She would have sufficient time, following an excellent breakfast, to drive to Grosvenor Square and lay her reproving opinions before his lordship.

An hour later, with her hair dressed in a lovely knot of curls atop her head, Alice entered the morning room to the sounds of Nicky laughing almost hysterically. Jane and Louisa had taken to tickling him.

"Make them stop!" Nicky cried, catching sight of her.

Alice shook her head for she could not in good conscience

do any such thing. The merriment ceased only when Nicky was gasping for air between loud chortles and kicking his heels in the air.

Alice watched as her siblings resumed their places at the breakfast table. As she took a plate from the sideboard and spooned a portion of scrambled eggs onto her plate, to which she added a slice of fresh, warm bread, she could not help but smile, particularly at Louisa, for she thought her sophisticated sister was at her finest when she was at play with her family. She wondered what Lord Tamerbeck would think of her in this moment, with her features alive with the enjoyment of playfully tormenting her brother.

Ever since her arrival in London, Louisa had taken on an elegant air, though while enchanting in its way, did not allow society to see the charming, simple creature she truly was, in possession of a kind, generous heart, a quick wit, and a temperament open to experience and adventure. She was gowned in a simple white muslin, embroidered handsomely with small pink rosebuds. Her hair was a dark auburn, like Hugh's.

Jane, on the other hand, shared a coloring in common with both Nicky and Frederica. Each sported a head of blond, curly hair, and light blue eyes.

Sitting down to eat, Alice wished she could ask Louisa just what she thought of Tamerbeck's absence at Vauxhall last night. The subject, however, was a prickly one and unless Louisa opened a discussion she did not feel at liberty to speak of it. She withheld a sigh and adjusted the skirts of her own white muslin gown.

She had just taken a bite of eggs when Nicky asked, "Have you not heard yet from Hugh?"

Alice glanced at him and smiled. "I am sorry, dearest, I have not."

"I hope he comes to London soon. My birthday party is less than a fortnight away."

"I know, my darling, but he will be here, never fear. Hugh would not miss your birthday for the world. He spoke of it all winter long, how he intended to give you your first fencing lesson." Seeing a heavy frown descend on his brow, she gave the subject a soft turn. "But let me see, what are you doing today? Oh, that's right, Jane is taking you to Kensington Gardens, is she not?"

"Yes, and Peter is to come with us," he said, his expression brightening.

"I predict," she added, "that it will not even rain."

To that, Nicky smiled broadly. "It always rains."

"What, in England?" she cried. "Nonsense!"

At that moment, while everyone was enjoying a good laugh, the maid arrived bearing a beautiful bouquet of yellow roses.

"For Miss Louisa," she called out, a smile on her face. She settled the offering in the center of the table. "And two in the hall, but this were the loveliest."

Louisa withdrew a card tucked into the arrangement. "From Mr. Trickett," she said in a mild tone. "And the others?" She glanced at the serving maid, the expression in her dark blue eyes, so reminiscent of Hugh, wholly expectant.

"I cannot say, Miss Louisa. But I will fetch them for ye, if ye wish for it?"

"No, thank you. I shall tend to them myself." With that she left her seat and walked from the morning room.

Alice knew quite well what Louisa was hoping for—a bouquet from Lord Tamerbeck.

She pushed her eggs about her plate and took a bite or two. Jane sipped her coffee and stared rather sadly out the window to the small garden attached to the back of the town house. With thoughts of Louisa's hapless interest in Tamerbeck, Nicky's concern that he would not get his first fencing lesson on his birthday, and Jane's general dislike of London, Alice found herself longing for the strength of a man's presence in her life, someone she could turn to as a support for just such situations as this—an absent brother, a sister's longing for Wiltshire, and a potentially unhappy alliance looming just on the horizon.

She glanced at the doorway. Perhaps this would be a good

time to speak with Louisa, to see what her thoughts might be where the viscount was concerned.

She finished her eggs and toast and left the morning room. She found Louisa still in the entrance hall, her expression aglow as she held a simple bouquet of violets against her cheek and at the same time read what appeared to be a rather lengthy missive.

"Tamerbeck?" Alice asked, though she was certain she already knew the answer.

"Yes," Louisa returned mistily. "You must know by now that I have a *tendre* for him as I believe he does for me. He is so very handsome and witty and has written the sweetest poem in my honor."

"How very nice," she offered quietly.

Her lack of enthusiasm prompted Louisa to compress her lips. "I can see you do not approve," she said with a decided lift of her chin. "I can feel your disappointment in my choice but you do not even know him—"

"Nor do you," Alice returned, then wished she had left the words unsaid. Tears filled her sister's eyes and Alice quickly went to her. "I am sorry, dearest. How harsh I sound and I beg you will forgive me. It is true that none of us knows Lord Tamerbeck very well but I look forward in the next few days and weeks to becoming much better acquainted with him."

Louisa smiled hopefully. "You will like him, indeed you will. I promise you, he is the best of men. When we converse privately, he is everything I would want in a . . . in a friend."

Alice kissed her cheek. "I want only your happiness. You know that."

"I do. I only wish you saw Tamerbeck as I do."

"Perhaps one day I shall," she said quietly.

The raising of a masculine voice in the drawing room abovestairs averted her attention. "Who is that?" she asked. "One of the footmen?"

Louisa, who had already begun reading Tamerbeck's poem again, wrinkled up her nose. "Mr. Dodds is here."

"So early?"

"Yes, I know. It is such a nuisance but he and Freddie are practicing their vignette for Thursday next. He has written the piece in the manner of Byron's 'Corsair.' I think it ridiculous, for Freddie is to be portrayed as being held ransom by a Barbary Coast pirate. I believe he created the scene so that he could put our sister in yet another exotic costume and arrange her hair in yet another wild fashion, which of course will once more set the Tabbies to gossiping."

"Oh dear," Alice murmured. She thought it might be wise to at least see what mischief the hapless pair was inadvertently conjuring up so, after sending word for her carriage to be brought round from the mews, she mounted the stairs.

Upon arriving at the entrance to the drawing room, she found Freddie on her knees, in an extremely dramatic pose, apparently pleading for her life. Mr. Dodds, as beautiful as ever with his dark eyes blazing with passion as he held a large scimitar blade to her throat, continued to recite the verses.

Mr. Dodds was a hopeful poet in possession of a vast talent combined with a countenance that was all arrogance and pride. He was devilishly handsome with brooding brown eyes, petulant full lips, and a nose to defy the beauty of the Greek statues. He wore his hair in a riot of curls and had from the moment Freddie laid eyes upon his person won her heart and soul.

Most unfortuitously, Freddie had become beneath his guiding hand a personification of his notion of womankind. Her manner of dress was now wild and unruly, for she wore enormous turbans of violent shades of red, orange, purple, and blue, with her curly blond hair streaming from beneath nearly to her waist, and gowns to match. There had been more than one scathing comment from the high sticklers that she had the appearance of a Gypsy and nothing less.

At first, Alice had tried to reason with her, but Freddie had taken on the role of Mr. Dodds's muse and would not be shaken from what she professed was a holy purpose. Alice had therefore resigned herself to the truth that life itself must take Freddie, just seventeen, to task.

"You disturb us," Mr. Dodds called out.

Freddie, however, pushed the blade aside and rolled her eyes. "Do not be rude to Alice," she commanded.

"But do not you see?" he exclaimed. "The mood is entirely broken and I do not know when I shall achieve it again."

"In five minutes, for you have me to inspire you," Freddie countered with a smile that was so adorable even Alice's heart melted a trifle.

With that, Mr. Dodds smiled in return and chucked her chin. "You are right, of course. You do inspire me, Miss Frederica Cherville."

Alice watched her sister's cheeks turn a rosy hue and she could scarcely contain her own irritation that Mr. Dodds had succeeded so completely in gaining Freddie's slavish devotion.

Freddie crossed the room to greet her. Today she wore a turban of gold-and-green-striped silk and at least a dozen portions of her long blond hair were gathered into narrow braids. The rest was a frizz but all hung, as always, nearly to her waist.

Regardless of the impropriety of her costume, she was uncommonly striking in appearance, having a pronounced jaw, high cheekbones, and like Jane, beautiful light blue eyes. Had she not been a Lady of Quality, Alice rather suspected that she would have made an exemplary actress for the stage.

She had even asked her recently if she had ever wished for such an occupation but Freddie had spurned the notion immediately. "Of course not," she had cried in disgust. "I desire only to be of use to Mr. Dodds."

Alice had felt relieved, at least for the moment. Now, as she embraced Freddie she wondered what the end of her attachment to the unfortunate poet would be.

"Will you sit and listen to the whole of our vignette?" she asked. "There are a few difficult spots which require reworking but on the whole I believe you will enjoy it. Mr. Dodds has such a gift for the epic poem."

"I am afraid I cannot oblige you at the moment. I have an important call to make this morning which I am unable to set aside. I came up only to greet you both."

"Where are you going?" Freddie asked.

Alice chuckled. "To pay a long overdue morning call."

Freddie looked as though she would have liked to inquire further, but Mr. Dodds demanded her attention.

With that, she left the actors to their devices and descended the stairs to await the arrival of her carriage.

Five

"I came to settle our wager," Mr. Quintin said, taking up a seat opposite Braden and tossing a ten-pound bank note across the table.

"You have not even asked me whether I succeeded in my object last night," Braden said, holding a cup of coffee in hand and smiling broadly.

"I have no need to ask," he responded with a heavy sigh, "for I had occasion to witness the expression on Miss Cherville's face as she emerged from the pathways. If ever a lady had had her lips trespassed, she was that lady."

Braden could only laugh and feel exceedingly satisfied with himself. The breakfast parlor in which he and his most excellent friend were situated overlooked a well-kept garden at the back of his house in Grosvenor Square.

He crossed his legs, drawing the skirts of his burgundy brocade dressing gown over his knees. He wore embroidered Moroccan slippers in yellow, purple, and red hues and thought there were few finer things in existence than a good cup of coffee, conversing with an old friend, and of course winning a wager.

Braden watched as Quinney prepared his own cup of coffee, which he embellished with sugar, cream, and a stick of cinnamon. His thoughts drifted to his experience of the night before, in particular how delightful it had been to take Alice Cherville in his arms. In truth, the triumph he felt at winning his wager with Quinney was the barest fraction of the sentiments he presently experienced in recalling the kiss he had shared with her.

He still could not think of the manner in which she had suddenly kissed him in return without a renewed sense of awe. What he had never expected from Alice Cherville was that she would actually enter into a forbidden kiss with such enthusiasm, but so she had. Nor had she uttered even the smallest maidenly protest, which caused him briefly to wonder if she was not used to giving her kisses away.

Regardless, his only dissatisfaction with the evening's amusements was her opinion of him.

That defect of character!

How her words still rankled even if he had been deceiving her in order to provoke her. And yet he had to admit that while she could have waxed long on her ill opinion of him, instead, she had kept her attention fixed on poor Mr. Pinfrith's supposed dilemma. He would give her that much, that however vile the depths of her disdain for him, she had refrained last night from blasting "Mr. Pinfrith" with the entire extent of her animosity.

He realized he was in an odd predicament. He found himself desiring intensely to see Miss Cherville again, not as Mr. Pinfrith, but as himself. Why, he could not say, perhaps to see just how she would speak to him, whether she would give him a dressing-down for his supposed treatment of William or whether she would smile and simper and attempt to charm the guardianship from him.

He could not help but smile. At the very least, he would see her on Wednesday at St. James's Park, bearing a missive from "Mr. Pinfrith" who he had already decided must disappear from London for a time. Much could be communicated in letters of a provoking, punishing nature, certainly more skillfully than in a direct conversation.

He once more addressed his friend. "Did I tell you, Quinney, that Trickett has asked permission to see the Chervilles socially?"

Mr. Quintin lifted a curious brow. "John has an interest in Miss Cherville?"

"I have not the faintest notion."

"What did you tell him?"

"That he had no cause to even ask. His life is quite his own apart from his duties as my secretary."

"How intriguing," he mused, his expression thoughtful. "Although I would venture that any of the three sisters I have so far met might have captured his attention. They are all beauties. Miss Louisa has exquisite auburn hair, darker than even Miss Cherville's, but Miss Jane's is quite blond. There is another sister, Miss Frederica, whom I have not yet met, but I have been given to understand she has fallen under the influence of Mr. Dodds."

"Our most recent aspiring poet." He snorted. "He always chooses some absurd female to dominate. Why am I not surprised he has harnessed a Cherville?"

Quinney stirred the stick of cinnamon in his coffee. "You are far too harsh in your opinions," he said. "In truth, I was agreeably taken with all three of them last night, not less so by Miss Cherville in her conversation. I must admit I am looking forward to meeting Miss Frederica as well, regardless of Mr. Dodds's influence."

Braden sipped his coffee. "I daresay Miss Cherville was *aux anges* that *Mr. Quintin* had noticed her family."

"The aunt was," he responded dryly. "She could not stop chattering. As for Miss Cherville"—here he smiled—"she chose to challenge me, which I rather liked."

"Indeed?"

"Yes. She actually danced the quadrille with me."

"That is something," he said, grinning.

Mr. Quintin shook his head. "You have no notion how trying the dance can be with an inexpert partner. This, you would not know, however, being shy of company yourself."

"Not shy," he responded. "Indifferent, bored."

"Very bored."

"Yes."

He stirred the cinnamon stick again. "I read my *Times* this morning, but I did not see that your brother's ship has landed."

"I expect him perhaps late next week."

"How old is he now? Four-and-thirty?"

"Seven."

"Good God," he muttered. "We are all getting old, Robert."

Braden could only chuckle. "Speak for yourself."

"Do you think he intends to marry soon or will he remain a bachelor and die on some godforsaken island hunting for nutmeg in the East Indies with no one about to give him a proper burial?"

Braden chuckled. "He would like to take a wife but his preferences prevent him. He is never enamored of our London beauties since only a country wife will suit him. Yet all the ladies with whom he is acquainted in Hampshire are well married. Add to this his long absences and finding a wife becomes an impossibility, particularly since I know he should far prefer to marry for love."

"Like Miss Cherville."

"What?" Braden queried. He cannot have heard his friend correctly.

"When we were dancing I asked her if she hoped to make a brilliant match. She told me she had no interest in such nonsense and that only love would do for her."

"I find myself shocked."

"I can see that you do, but why?"

"Because I do not think such a philosophy in keeping with her general character. I vow she said as much for the strict purpose of appearing to advantage in your eyes."

"I did not know your opinion of her was so very bad."

"Why on earth would you think I believed her to be anything but an encroaching Mushroom, for I cannot explain her letters otherwise. No, my good man. Alice Cherville's ambition knows no bounds. Of this, I am certain."

"Have it as you will, I believed her."

"You are entitled to your opinion, but I promise you her actions will confirm the truth of her character."

In the distance the sound of a knocker reached the breakfast parlor. "I wonder who that might be at this hour. Although if you were not already seated opposite me, I should know in a trice."

A moment later, his butler, Stevens, entered the small chamber and promptly announced that Miss Cherville begged a word with him and was awaiting him in the entrance hall.

He was stunned. The enemy had actually dared to approach his gates? "Tell her I am not at home."

"I did, m'lord," Stevens stated somberly, "knowing that you were in a state of undress. However, the lady was quite adamant that she speak with you and said she intended to, in her words, set up a caterwaul if you did not receive her. Had she not been elegantly dressed besides speaking with an unexceptionable accent, I would have turned her away. As it was, I felt I should lay the matter before you."

Braden eyed his butler carefully. "She is also quite beautiful, or did you not notice?"

"As to that," Stevens responded, his lips twitching ever so slightly, "I could not say."

"The devil you could not," he retorted.

However much Braden might have delighted in Miss Cherville's beauty or her kisses, he was never in a mood to be threatened at his own door.

"Then let Trickett deal with her." His secretary had been privy to Miss Cherville's letters almost from the first and knew what his employer would wish in this situation.

"He is not yet arrived. If you will recall, m'lord, he spent the night escorting his sister and mother through a series of balls and soirees last night."

"Of course." He was about to tell Stevens that Miss Cherville could scream herself hoarse for the next several hours for all he cared, but another quite promising thought occurred to him.

"You may show our guest to the drawing room. Tell her I shall receive her directly."

"Directly, m'lord?" he queried, a shocked brow lifted ever so faintly.

"Yes, Stevens," he said, rising to tie his dressing gown more securely about his waist. "Directly."

Stevens turned on his heel, his expression rather stunned as he quit the morning room.

Braden glanced down at his friend. "Have you an objection?"

"Only that propriety dictates I must remain here. I vow I would give my entire fortune to hear the following exchange."

Braden could only laugh as he quit the room.

Alice seated herself on the edge of an elegant sofa, her nerves sorely afflicted. Her courage had not failed her once during the entire journey from Upper Brook Street to Grosvenor Square. However, the moment she actually entered the earl's quite magnificent home, her boldness flagged ominously.

The drawing room, decorated in so elegant a style as to take her breath away, reminded her that this was the home of an exalted Peer, a friend to the Regent and to Wellington, a member of the very pinnacle of the nobility. Her conduct in so storming the bastions of Bradenstoke's home was audacious, impertinent, in every respect absurd, and her knees had begun to quake. Whatever was she doing here?

She glanced about the chamber utterly awestruck. The walls were covered in a pale green silk damask, echoed in the draperies and in several of the chairs scattered about the tall, handsome room. The sofa upon which she was seated was in wide bands of silk stripes, a soft beige against a stark white all of which was contrasted to the furniture in black lacquer, lending the softest hints of the style known as *à la Chinoise*.

She had been in dozens of receiving rooms over the past month since her arrival in London, but what she saw here, in the home of a man she despised, was by far the loveliest she had yet witnessed. The display of several pieces of delicately carved jade, flowery porcelain, and a playful automaton, brought an unexpected warmth to the chamber.

She was stunned, even charmed, and could not seem to keep her mouth closed. Was this indeed the work of a man whom she felt to be coldhearted? It did not seem at all possible. She stretched her arm along the back of the sofa, that she might better see the automaton. She could not help but smile and wondered just what antics the country girl in the large hoop skirt would perform once set in motion.

Bradenstoke stood on the threshold of the drawing room, his slippered feet having kept his arrival a secret. He had meant to storm the chamber and to so overpower Miss Cherville that her only recourse would be to run from his house in terror. However, when he reached the threshold, he found her enrapt by the sight of the toy his mother had given him many years ago for his birthday.

He found himself unable to tear his gaze from the beauty before him. She wore a poke bonnet of pale yellow silk trimmed with white ruching. Her pelisse was of a matching hue, which set her dove white complexion to extreme advantage as well as her fiery locks, which just touched her face in feathery curls. He found he could not move, he could not think except to grasp at flashes of memory as he recalled kissing her last night. Once more he felt awash in the unexpected magic of the shared embrace.

There occurred within him a rupture of thought and for the longest moment as he waited, poised on the threshold, he desired nothing more than to kiss her again, to see if she might respond with the same degree of passion she had so clearly experienced with "Mr. Pinfrith" last night. His anger toward her was forgotten, he felt an urge to offer his guardianship at long last, to beg forgiveness, to plant himself in the shade of her countenance, to drink from her mind and to kiss her for an eternity. How was it possible the mere sight of her could evoke such completely bizarre impulses?

Layered over these thoughts was the overpowering sensation that he would be wise to return to his bedchamber and don a proper set of morning clothes.

She turned at that moment, however, her expression one of utter shock as her gaze raked his burgundy gown. A blush suffused her cheeks. There was in the immobility of the moment a flicker in her eye that dazzled him. He was not certain of its meaning as she met his gaze and stared into his eyes, but he felt certain disinterest was not what was reflected to him.

"Bradenstoke, I presume," she stated at last, the gentle beauty of her features dissolving into an expression of disgust. She rose to her feet in a slow, purposeful movement that set his every muscle on guard.

He chuckled sardonically to himself and the spell she had cast over him shattered like thin ice on a shallow pond. How easily he might have been misled as to the truth of her character merely because she was a beauty. What he saw presently in the harsh light of her blue eyes was the person he knew her to be.

"Yes, I am Bradenstoke," he said, his gaze riveted coolly to her face. "What the devil brings you here, Miss Cherville, although I can well imagine? Still grasping after my patronage, no doubt, which I will tell you again I have not the smallest intention of settling upon you or your siblings."

Alice felt all her rage against the man lounging so carelessly in the doorway. Could he have insulted her more profoundly than to receive her in a state of undress or to speak words that made her sound as though she had come a-begging? She did not think so and how very like the man she had come to despise to behave so very badly.

"Why did you not respond to my letters?" she asked, to the point. "I believe given the nature of our relationship the very least you owe me is an explanation."

"I do not have one that would satisfy you. I daresay nothing short of my blessing at every turn would make you feel I had properly discharged my father's debt to you. Therefore, I have no intention of attempting to justify myself to you in the least."

"What an ignorant man you are," she stated evenly.

"Were you a man . . ." he countered, his complexion darkening.

"I am skilled in the art of fencing. Do not let my sex deter you, my lord." She began unbuttoning her pelisse, sloughing it off her shoulders. "Although I daresay you would have to don at least a pair of breeches or would that be too great an effort for you?"

Alice was not certain where she had found the brazenness to throw down the gauntlet at the feet of the terrible man before her. He was tall, powerfully built, and certainly were he to take up her challenge she would soon find herself in the basket. She did not care. From the moment she had seen him in the doorway in just his robe, all her ire and courage had returned to her. She recalled Mr. Pinfrith's downcast state when she had first met him and knew such a profound outrage for both his and her own circumstances that she felt she could do battle with Zeus himself were he present at this moment.

Bradenstoke's jaw worked strongly. A muscle on his cheek twitched. He struggled to draw a deep breath. "By God, if I were not a gentleman," he cried, hoarse with suppressed anger.

She pressed a hand to her bosom and presented as sarcastic a countenance as she could manage. "Again, you hide behind your belief in your own chivalry." She met his gaze without flinching. "I find myself amazed. You are as much a hypocrite as you are a man of dishonor." She lifted her chin.

"Miss Cherville, your gauntlet is accepted. I shall return forthwith."

Six

Alice watched him go and only when he had disappeared into the hallway beyond did her knees begin to tremble anew. What madness was this, she wondered, that she had actually challenged Lord Bradenstoke to a fencing match? She knew the strongest desire to run from Grosvenor Square, to hasten to Upper Brook Street, to throw her siblings in a large coach, and to immediately escape back to Wiltshire. If only she had shown a little more restraint, but somehow Bradenstoke's complete indifference had sent her into the boughs.

The butler arrived, obviously out of countenance, for his complexion was quite high. "Miss Cherville," he said, "I am to show you to the ballroom and, I believe, to give you this."

He presented her with a long mahogany box, beautifully inlaid. He lifted the lid and within were a pair of exquisite fencing foils. "Yes," she whispered, moving forward.

He closed the lid and cradling it in his arms, murmured, "Follow me."

Alice gathered up her yellow pelisse and marched behind him, the sensation that she was a soldier at war not too far off the mark, only what the deuce was she doing fencing with Bradenstoke?

Bradenstoke arrived scarcely five minutes later, wearing only a shirt, buff breeches, stockings, and slippers, the latter of which he promptly removed once he noticed she was no longer sporting her half boots. Alice had hooked the bulk of her muslin skirts over the ribbon she wore tightly about the high waist of her gown. The effect was scandalous, for much of her finely knit stockings were exposed, but she did not care. Bradenstoke, to his credit, or perhaps because of the rage he felt at her insults, did not so much as glance in the direction of her ankles.

She had already taken up one of the swords. When he had tested his own foil with several swipes through the air, she addressed him. "*En Guard*, m'lord!" she cried.

She assumed the proper position, her left arm elevated for balance. He did the same and when she saw him hesitate, she thrust quickly. He parried, danced about on unusually light feet for a man of his size, eyeing her closely, then, with lightning flicks of his wrist, engaged battle.

Alice responded in kind and became lost in what was soon an utterly exhilarating experience. Bradenstoke was no longer the man who had refused to honor his father's word, but a skilled opponent in a sport centuries old.

Mr. Boscombe, who lived but two miles from her home in Wiltshire, had trained her well. One of her truest friends, he had suggested she take up the art of fencing as a means of helping her to bear both the terrible grief which had beset her upon the death of her dear mother and father as well as the weight of the terrific responsibility which had fallen solely on her shoulders at the same time. She had begun her lessons but a handful of weeks after the funeral. Never had she expected to make use of his vital, experienced instruction in such a manner as this.

She felt Bradenstoke testing her, much as Mr. Boscombe would do. She could hear her teacher's voice in her head: *You must watch every conceivable part of your opponent, for indications of intent, if you hope to win the day.* Bradenstoke became a blur of particulars, the bend of his wrist, the tilt of an ankle, the shifting of his eyes, the slide of his abdomen, the subtle lift of a shoulder.

He began pressing her harder and she responded as she had been taught, with an increased concentration so that she saw nothing but the man opposite her. She watched sweat splatter from his brow, she noted how his brown hair was soon sticking to his forehead, she heard his labored breaths, she saw that his shirt clung to his chest and that every time he lunged the muscles of his thighs stretched the knit of his breeches.

He caught her suddenly at crossed swords, so that he held her tightly, pinning her close to him with the force of his sword and wrist. She wondered what he hoped to gain as he glared at her.

She lifted her chin, turned her wrist, and slid the blade of her sword the length of his, moving away from him swiftly. Once more she engaged him, but this time she could feel that he was withholding nothing from her, a circumstance for which she found herself grateful. She smiled. He was a powerful man of considerable skill and whatever complaints he might have of her he was at this moment honoring her with his respect.

After a few minutes, however, she began to flag. His superior strength, if not skill, soon forced her back time and again. She was spent and knew it, yet she continued on for a few minutes more until he simply backed away from her and shook his head. That he was himself fairly panting did not escape her notice.

"Is this . . . all you have, Miss Cherville?" He eyed her in some hostility, even though he gasped for air as sweat dripped from his chin.

"I would at this moment . . . wish I were a man!" she cried in response, sorely disappointed she could not follow and challenge him further, but she was done. "Oh . . . how I would run you through!"

"I . . . have no doubt of it and . . . were you a man I should tender you the same compliment."

She said nothing further but walked toward the French doors which opened onto a narrow garden, at the same time letting down her skirts. She threw open one of the doors and drew the cool May air deeply into her lungs. Her throat was on fire and her heart beat so fast she felt if she took even one more step, the overtaxed organ would simply burst.

She glanced at Bradenstoke and saw that his sword was

on the floor and that he was bent over at the waist. His shirt was soaked. "You are not used to such exertion," she called to him, her tone scathing.

He did not look up. "No more than yourself."

"On the contrary," she retorted. "Mr. Boscombe and I sparred thrice weekly for at least two hours a day for the past eight years."

Bradenstoke chuckled. "Boscombe, eh? I should have known." He rose up from his bent posture and after picking up his sword struggled toward the French doors to stand beside her. "My God."

Alice's breath had returned to her but the earl was still laboring. He settled his sword in the box that Stevens had placed on the floor beside the doors. He rose and after opening the adjacent door, closed his eyes and began breathing deeply as well.

She watched him, her hand still grasping the silver chased hilt of her sword. How simple it would be to merely thrust once and end his life. At least then his betrayal of his own brother would be avenged.

"You make me nervous," he said, opening his eyes and watching her closely. "I could feel your venom even without looking at you."

"Am I supposed to be impressed?" she queried. She withdrew her kerchief from the pocket of her white muslin gown and mopped her brow, which she realized was nearly as wet as Bradenstoke's. Her hair was hanging all about her face, down her shoulders, and her back. She pulled at it and heard some of the pins drop to the floor. "Good heavens!" she murmured.

She heard Bradenstoke laugh. Glancing up at him, she found he was watching her and that his face was lit with amusement. Her heart, which had only in the last minute or so resumed its normal beat, suddenly thrummed to life all over again. There was something so youthful, even boyish in his expression, that she found herself caught. Just as her aunt had said, the Earl of Bradenstoke was indeed a notably handsome man.

She had never before seen him since he lived a life quite apart from the *beau monde* and only on select occasions, such as at Carlton House at the Prince's invitation, appeared in public. His white muslin shirt clung to his shoulders and back provocatively. His physique was something to admire, his broad shoulders tapering to a lean waist, his legs muscular. Had she not despised him so very much she rather thought she might have been attracted to the man.

He laughed once more, took her sword from her, and replaced it in the box as well.

Her thoughts had so startled her, that she averted her gaze to the floor and began collecting the few pins scattered about her feet.

"You do fence exceptionally well," he said. "Even formidably."

"Thank you," she said, frowning as she stood up, sliding the pins into her pocket.

"It is perhaps unfortunate you have been unable to forgive me for not, as you have said, honoring my father's agreement, otherwise we might even be friends."

"You and I could never be friends," she said.

"Because I refused to become your guardian?"

"That and your treatment of your own brother. Yes, well you may stare but as it happens I met him last night at Vauxhall and his own suffering at your hands is what brought me here today. I felt it important that someone address your conduct."

He seemed both startled and amused at the same time. "William has been indiscreet I see."

"I believe the confidences he shared with me were more necessary than indiscreet. He was greatly distressed and I was sorry for him."

"So you have come to plead his cause."

"I suppose I have," she said.

"I know that you think me a hard man," he said quietly, "but I do not act hastily or with an eye to doing injury when I make my decisions. The property that William and I frequently argue about has been in the Bradenstoke estate for many generations. I would be remiss in my duties were I to relinquish it to a Pinfrith. As for your own interests, I was sorry at the time that I could not offer the guardianship to your family and had my circumstances been other than what they were, I should have obliged you most happily. However, I will always maintain that I was never, at any point, under a legal obligation to become your guardian. Your letters, miss, should have ceased years ago. I consider your conduct the height of impertinence and audacity."

She straightened her shoulders. "Whatever you may think of me, I wrote because I believed it was a matter of honor and nothing less."

"Then we disagree sorely on this point."

"Regardless of your decision where the guardianship is concerned, what I do not understand is how you can possibly justify your conduct toward your brother."

He lowered his gaze and she could see that he was struggling with some strong emotion. After a time, he said, "I do not comprehend in the least why William felt it necessary to discuss his concerns with you. For myself, I choose not to give you an answer except to say that whatever difficulties lie between my brother and me remain there exclusively."

Alice searched his gaze. "But where is your compassion, Lord Bradenstoke? Have you no soul, no heart? How could you deny your own brother the wish of his stepfather? Every feeling is offended that you have done so. As for myself, what I wrote in my letters, if you were too obtuse to comprehend it, was that I desired if not a father for Hugh and for young Nicholas, then at least an elder brother who might offer them guidance from time to time."

"And whatever assistance I could give them and your sisters while you were here in London?" he suggested.

"Of course."

He shook his head as though disgusted anew. "I have known a score of young ladies like yourself. Always grasping for as much as your purse can hold."

Alice was shocked. "Is this indeed how you feel, what you believe?" she asked. She doubted she had ever known such a cold heart in her entire existence and she began to pity him.

"Then you shan't hear from me again. I had always supposed that if just once we met and discussed the matter, I would be able to persuade you, but now that I see the stubbornness in your face and hear it in your voice, I know it is hopeless. You may consider the matter finished, my lord."

He seemed stunned. "Had I known you would have left me in peace in such a simple manner, a few flurries of the sword, an exchange of insults, I would have called on you in Wiltshire ten years ago."

"Indeed, now that I have met you, I wish you had."

She turned away from him and let a gentle May breeze sweep over her face, cooling her a little more. She began to gather her locks into a knot atop her head, bringing her red curls into a semblance of order. The exertion of the match had given her skin a wonderful tingling sensation and so long as she was not pondering what she felt to be Bradenstoke's flaws, she found even at this moment she could be content. She closed her eyes and enjoyed the feel of the breeze against her damp gown creating a sharp cooling effect on her skin.

Bradenstoke looked down at her and felt aggravated in the extreme. Had he no heart, no soul? What did she know of him? Very little, indeed!

He stalked away from her, intent upon leaving the ballroom, but he happened to glance at her one last time and saw that the light from the mounting day was pouring through the layers of white muslin of her gown. He could see her figure outlined clearly and his interest in her sharpened once more. By all evidence she would be as beautiful unclothed as she was draped in muslin.

He felt a sudden and quite profound desire to cross the room, to slide his arm around the soft curve of her waist, drag her into his arms, and violate her lips as he had last night. He knew how soft and yielding she could be and he wondered just what she would do if he attempted to kiss her now.

The same devilment which had prompted him to take his brother's identity last night possessed him again. His feet began to move swiftly in her direction, a moment more and his arm was indeed holding her fast about the waist. She began to struggle immediately.

"What are you doing, my lord?" she cried, pushing with all her might against his shoulders. "Would you add this to your heinous conduct?"

He did not try to argue with her but caught the back of her head with his free hand and slanted his lips across hers with the same gentle kiss he had offered her last night.

He drew back, and she stared at him, apparently stunned.

"Oh," she murmured, searching his eyes.

He kissed her again, but this time she did not attempt to disengage his firm hold on her. He believed he understood why she was so astonished and took advantage of it, kissing her with no small degree of pleasure over and over.

He heard the faintest moan from her throat.

He drew back and looked at her.

"I do not understand," she murmured, clearly astonished.

"Though we cannot be friends, perhaps lovers?" he suggested, taunting her. He lessened his grip and she immediately pulled away from his embrace.

"What a beast you are!" she cried, taking another step away from him.

"You liked kissing me," he said. "Tell me you did not."

"I . . . I was merely startled because—" She broke off and a blush stole up her cheeks.

"You were merely startled because . . . ?" He was enjoying himself hugely.

She narrowed her eyes. "Because you kiss very much like your brother."

In a thousand years he would never have expected her to admit as much. She had surprised him again and he was rarely surprised by anything. "You have kissed William?" he queried innocently.

Her blush deepened. "I should not be speaking of such things to you."

He took hold of her arm. "Whom did you prefer?" he asked, his face close to hers once more.

She gasped. "Why your brother, of course!"

This was too much for Braden, he could keep his countenance no longer and roared his laughter.

The lady before him was obviously piqued by his amusement, which only made him laugh harder.

"Do you intend to share the joke with me, my lord?" she queried, her spine stiffening.

"I promise you," he said, between chuckles, "you would not find it amusing."

"I daresay I would not." She turned away from him and moved to a chair across the room, where she had left her belongings. She sat down and began putting on her half boots.

He crossed the room and held her pelisse for her while she slipped it on. "Thank you," she murmured. She was greatly subdued. When she placed her bonnet over the loose, jumbled knot of curls atop her head, she grew very serious. "I promised myself this morning that I would do what I could on your brother's behalf. If you must know, he confided in me because he believed you admired me. He thought I might have some unexpected influence with you."

"I cannot imagine in what way he thought I admired you." He watched her closely, wondering just what she meant to say next although he supposed she would attempt to browbeat him one last time, whatever her earlier protestations.

"Mr. Pinfrith said you admired my persistence in writing to you as I had, year after year. Whether or not this is true"— here she drew in a deep breath, straightened her shoulders, and plunged on—"I am asking you to reconsider your decision."

He was surprised—again. "Indeed? Well, as I have said before, this is a matter between brothers but I am certain he will be much gratified to hear of your efforts on his behalf. Only tell me, Miss Cherville, do you not mean one last time to force the guardianship from me or do you mean to continue doing so with a thousand future letters?"

Very slowly, she set about tying the ribbons of her bonnet beneath her chin. A frown settled over her brow and she now searched his eyes. "I must know something, my lord," she began. "Is it possible you have never read my letters?"

"Why do you ask?"

"It is just an impression I have been forming throughout our conversation."

"As it happens," he stated coldly, "I have not. Only a handful of them."

The lady before him grew as still as the surface of a pond on a windless day. Not once in his entire exchange with her had she looked so dejected as she did at this moment.

"You did not even read my letters," she murmured. "But your brother told me you had read all of them, more than once?"

"He was mistaken, Miss Cherville. He may have seen me peruse one or two of them and perhaps believed I had actually given them the attention he thought I had but not so. Indeed, I had no need to read them." He wondered why the devil this was distressing her so very much. "I was fully conversant with their contents, or at least their purpose. I had no reason to bother my head over them."

"But I told you so much about my family, my brothers, and sisters. I cannot credit you then know nothing of us."

There was a stricken look in her eyes that made him deuced uncomfortable, even more than anything she had said or done previously during the past hour since her arrival.

She turned away from him. "I suppose this is better in some way," she added. "I have nothing more to say to you."

Without so much as a backward glance, she quit the ballroom. He watched her go and for a long time stared at the empty doorway. In the distance, he heard her exchange a handful of words with Stevens, then there was just silence.

A confusion reigned in his mind for several minutes, as he reviewed all that had happened, from first seeing her in his drawing room and experiencing a rush of desire for her, to hearing her insults, to fencing with her, to arguing with her, and finally to kissing her. What seemed to remain, however, was the way she had looked upon learning he had never read her letters.

Now why the devil that would give him the smallest degree of trouble, he could not imagine, but so it did.

Seven

Several hours later, what Alice noticed first about the stream of visitors which had begun to arrive and pass through her drawing room was that the volume of guests had fairly trebled since last night.

"What did I tell you!" Mrs. Urchfont murmured excitedly into her ear. "Mr. Quintin's influence has prevailed!"

"Do you really think so, Aunt?" Alice asked, stunned. "Is his ability to persuade the *beau monde* so very profound?"

"Indeed, it is. The very fact that he sat in our box at Vauxhall and afterward danced with you has been the making of us. You will see very soon that we shall be receiving more invitations than a duck has feathers."

"Who is Mr. Quintin?" Freddie asked, drawing near. "I have heard him spoken of everywhere but I do not know if I have ever met him?" Alice glanced at her sister and shuddered faintly. Whatever would Mr. Quintin think of their dear Freddie, of her enormous purple-and-red turban and her blond her streaming in frizzed curls down her back.

Mrs. Urchfont swelled her chest. "Mr. Quintin travels only in the First Circles, my dear, and is quite the Pink of the Ton. A true Arbiter of Fashion."

"Oh, you mean like Mr. Dodds?"

Alice stared at her sister for a long moment as did her aunt.

Mrs. Urchfont shook her head and wrung her hands. "Not precisely, my dear. While Mr. Dodds is a very unique man it is Mr. Quintin who is our undisputed Leader of Fashion."

"I would not argue with you for the world, Aunt, but I believe you to be mistaken. Mr. Dodds now sets the example for others to follow."

All three ladies turned to look at the gentleman in question. Alice had never seen tails so long on a coat before, nor tassels dangling from the ends of each and fairly brushing the back of his white embroidered slippers.

"Wherever did his tailor find silk in that particular shade of green?" Mrs. Urchfont asked. "I am reminded of peas, you know the color they turn when they have been cooked forever."

Freddie smiled and released a sigh. "Is he not the handsomest creature ever designed by the gods?"

Alice and Mrs. Urchfont exchanged a glance and also released sighs, but not of the same quality as Freddie's.

"There can be few to match the beauty of his face," Alice agreed, although she could think of one man and was a little startled when the image of the earl dressed only in his burgundy brocade robe rose up to remind her anew of just how handsome he was. For some reason, since returning from Grosvenor Square, Lord Bradenstoke had never been very far from her thoughts even though she was fairly certain she would never see him again.

A new set of arrivals was announced and Mrs. Urchfont crossed the room quickly to greet her good friend Lady Wroughton. Next to cross the threshold was Mr. Trickett, who after exchanging pleasantries with several people, crossed to her.

"How do you go on, Miss Cherville?" he queried, bowing to her in his friendly manner.

"Very well, thank you."

"Your drawing room is fairly full to overflowing," he remarked with a smile.

Alice chuckled. "Mr. Quintin's influence, I believe. We chanced to meet him at Vauxhall last night."

"Did you also dance with him?" he asked.

"As it happens, I did."

Mr. Trickett smiled broadly. "Then of course you are made!"

Alice could only laugh for it seemed to her the most ridiculous thing in the world that a mere dance would have such an effect, but there was no denying that half the personages present had been but names on an invitation list before today.

She watched as Mr. Trickett let his gaze drift over the assembled guests. He was nearly as tall as Braden but of a leaner figure than the earl. He had a pleasing countenance, blue eyes which were precise and appraising, and light brown hair cut formally *à la Brutus*. She did not think he could be accounted a handsome man but there was something of command in his posture and elegance in his dress that bespoke the gentleman.

She watched his gaze become fixed on a particular object. His expression softened immediately and his chest rose in a silent sigh. She followed the line of his gaze and saw that it rested on Louisa, who was sitting at the end of a chaise longue with Lord Tamerbeck reclining on the carpeted floor at her feet and reading poetry to her. Her expression was entirely enrapt. Only a simpleton could fail to see that his lordship had engaged her fancy.

"Are you acquainted with Lord Tamerbeck?" Alice inquired.

"Only a trifle. We were at Oxford together but our interests were so dissimilar that we rarely conversed."

"I have been hoping to find someone who knows him well. When I have attempted to engage him in any manner of discussion, he will not be brought to the point. May I ask your impression of him generally?"

At that, Mr. Trickett turned to her and smiled faintly. "I believe him to be a gentleman of fashion, who travels in the best circles and does not want for feminine attention. Beyond this, I fear I have no true knowledge of the man."

"Your tact is to your credit, sir," Alice said, smiling. "However, you cannot wound me nor offend me by offering your opinion. My own, which is based on his conduct over the past three weeks with my sister, is that he is inconstant in his feelings and his conduct."

Mr. Trickett met her gaze forcefully. "Then let us hope," he returned quietly, "that the *tendre* which holds her bound to him will pass."

Alice nodded. "You have expressed my thoughts exactly. Mr. Trickett, do you mind my asking you something?"

"No, of course not."

She lowered her voice, "Only that I have wondered how it is you have tumbled in love with my sister without knowing her?"

He laughed. "Is it so very obvious?" he asked. When she nodded, he responded to her question. "But I do know Miss Louisa."

Alice was surprised. "She tells me that though you have danced with her but a handful of times, she has barely had occasion to converse with you."

"That much is true," he admitted. "However, I feel I should confess to you that as Bradenstoke's secretary, I was required to read all of your letters, Miss Cherville."

"All of them?" she asked, astonished.

He nodded. "In so doing, I came to know Miss Louisa. Indeed, your entire family. You cannot conceive how happy I am that you have come to London at last for I have so much I would say to you. Your management of five younger siblings, and that from the age of fifteen, was no small feat. You have my eternal respect and admiration."

"How very kind you are, Mr. Trickett," she said, her heart flowering with warmth. "And Louisa has your love, then?"

"Precisely so," he said.

Alice felt at the very least she should bring Mr. Trickett the object of his affection and called to her sister. Louisa came immediately and extended her hand to him in a friendly manner.

"How do you go on, Mr. Trickett?"

He shook her hand readily. "Very well, thank you, Miss Louisa."

"I was deeply gratified to receive your flowers. They are

quite lovely and rest in a prominent place in our morning room where the family gathers for breakfast."

"You do me a great honor."

Though he smiled warmly at her, Louisa's gaze strayed to Tamerbeck, who was still reclining on the floor as though waiting for her to return. She grew nervous and though Alice could see Mr. Trickett desired to converse with her, his gaze as well was drawn to the sight of the open volume of poetry which the viscount was holding in full view of their small group.

Alice was irritated by the sight of the book, knowing that it was held aloft as a sort of imperious command. She would have intervened and prevented Louisa from leaving, for in doing so she felt that her sister's conduct would border on the uncivil, but Mr. Trickett was before her.

"I begged only to know," he said in his dignified manner, "that you enjoyed my offering, Miss Louisa, but I can see that we have disturbed Lord Tamerbeck's reading. Please, return to him that he might continue."

The relief she obviously experienced lit her features in a glow. "You are very kind, Mr. Trickett and yes, he was greatly disappointed to have the sonnet interrupted—Byron, you know." With that, Louisa dipped a small curtsy and hurried back to take up her place before the viscount.

"You were wise," Alice murmured.

"The war will not be won in a single skirmish. I only hope I have not engaged my adversary at too late an hour."

"I am persuaded you have not," she assured him. "Louisa's head may be turned for the moment, but she possesses a great deal of sense and will one day see what he is."

Mr. Trickett turned to her. "Miss Cherville, there is another matter I have long wished to address with you. Would you permit me to speak openly about . . . the guardianship?"

Alice was startled both by his request and by the intensity with which he had addressed her. "Yes, I beg you will," she responded, drawing him aside a little. She had not the smallest notion what he meant to say to her.

"Over the years, I have desired times out of mind that Bradenstoke would relent and finally take on the guardianship. Though I may not entirely agree with his refusals, I do however comprehend them. You cannot know the terrible scope of the difficulties he faced at the very moment you presented your claim to him. Though I was not his secretary during those early years, I have since become fully acquainted with all the details of his situation at the time. He was under enormous pressures for years upon coming into his inheritance."

Alice frowned slightly, recalling that Bradenstoke had said that he would have assumed the guardianship had his circumstances been other than what they were.

"You obviously have a very kind heart," Alice said. "But I am persuaded that the sole reason Lord Bradenstoke has not acquiesced to the guardianship is because his heart is about the size of a shriveled walnut."

Mr. Trickett could not help but laugh but his expression soon grew quite animated. "You do him the worst injustice. I promise, you do! As his friend, these many years and more, I have known him to extend great kindnesses in a hundred different directions."

Alice was entirely taken aback. She could not in the least understand the depths of such loyalty as he obviously possessed. "And you are a true friend to say as much so I will ask you this—if his heart is indeed as large as you suggest, why would he deny his own brother a property promised to him by his own stepfather?"

"What?" he cried, obviously shocked. "I do not know to what you refer or from whence you have learned anything so—so abhorrent. I know nothing of what you speak and I believe I am conversant with all of Braden's affairs. Tell me, Miss Cherville, who has been slandering his good name in such a vile fashion?"

"Lord Bradenstoke confirmed this morning what his very own brother told me," Alice responded, lowering her voice further, for their conversation had grown quite intense.

"His brother?" Mr. Trickett cried. "Forgive me if I express my shock, but you cannot mean William?"

"The very one. William Pinfrith."

"Wh—when did you have occasion to speak with Will?"

"Last night, at Vauxhall."

Mr. Trickett stared at her for a long, long moment. "I had thought Mr. Pinfrith was not yet arrived in London, that he was not due for two or three more weeks."

"The tides must have been more favorable than usual," she responded, "for I spoke with him at Vauxhall last night and he told me of the property in Hampshire which Bradenstoke has withheld from him. His distress quite wrung my heart. So, you see, I have not only my own circumstances by which I have cast my judgment upon your employer but by reason of his conduct toward Mr. Pinfrith as well. How you have remained ignorant of this transgression I cannot imagine, though I can only suppose that Mr. Pinfrith did not wish to let it be known generally how badly his brother has used him."

Mr. Trickett grew suddenly quite conscious and no longer met her gaze. "There was a masquerade last night, was there not?"

"Yes, indeed," she responded.

He shook his head. "I wonder how it is that Will has not yet called at my lodgings," he mused.

At that moment an interesting hush fell on the guests and Alice's attention was drawn away from this most curious conversation with Mr. Trickett.

Mr. Quintin had arrived.

He was quickly beseiged by a bevy of hostesses, each exclaiming over him, and the guests returned to their former prattle.

"So Quinney has made his way here," Mr. Trickett murmured, a crooked smile on his lips. "I am grateful for your sake, Miss Cherville. You will want for no attention from the *beau monde* because of it."

At that moment, however, Mr. Dodds's voice rose above the gentle din. "A sonnet!" he cried.

"Oh dear," Alice murmured. "I do hope Mr. Dodds and Freddie's questionable appearance will not give him a disgust of our drawing room."

Mr. Trickett merely laughed. "Quinney, while fastidious, would never permit his interests to be set aside for such a reason as that."

Since Mr. Dodds had garnered the attention of everyone present, he brought Freddie forward and bade her sit on a footstool at his feet, which she did quite obligingly. She even appeared to great advantage, her expression alive as it was with her obvious devotion to the poet.

Mr. Dodds launched into a sonnet he himself had written which was indeed crafted quite beautifully and which brought more than one feminine sigh issuing from any number of young ladies present.

Alice's attention, however, was directed elsewhere. Her gaze had become fixed upon Mr. Quintin, who had raised his quizzing glass to Freddie's beautiful face. He seemed transfixed and his lips were slightly parted as he watched her. The smile which followed did not fade for some time, even after Mr. Dodds's performance had been applauded and Freddie lifted to her feet.

Well! This was an interesting turn of events!

Eight

"You must be so very excited!" Jane said, linking arms with Alice.

"I am," she murmured, her heart leaping in her breast. "I will confess something to you. Throughout the entirety of Lady Nettleford's ball last night I kept hoping Mr. Pinfrith might arrive and put me out of my suspense."

"What do you suppose he looks like?"

"I wish I had thought to ask him or at the very least to have him lower his mask."

"To think he kissed you," she whispered. "Oh, Alice, it is all so romantic. I only wish—"

"What?" Alice pressed her, for Jane's cheeks were suddenly flushed.

"I, too, wish that my heart would awaken as yours has. I seem to be the only one that love has not touched."

Alice gave her sister's arm a squeeze. "My dear, I have not seen a more woeful expression since Nicky told his last joke and no one laughed."

Jane could not help but smile. However, the amusement on her face disappeared as quickly as a swiftly moving cloud obliterated the sun from the beauty of St. James's Park below. "I have tried, Alice, truly I have, but I cannot be content in London. I miss my cats and my dogs, and though it may seem quite odd to you, I daresay Cook will not know how to encourage the hens or in just what manner they like their seed cast about."

"It is not the casting," Alice mused, "but your singing. I am convinced they enjoy your lovely voice above all things."

"They will be completely off their laying by now as well as the pigeons and when we finally return home at the beginning of summer we will have to purchase eggs from the vicar's wife who will gloat over her success for she has always been convinced hers were a superior breed." A heavy sigh followed this terrible prediction.

"All of this leads me to ask, my dear, where were you during the ball last night? When I was not dancing, which I admit was not very often—"

"And how could it be when you are so pretty and lively. I vow you have nearly as many admirers as Louisa."

"No one has that many beaus. At any rate, do not detract me from my purpose for you must by now have comprehended what I wished to ask you."

Jane pouted. "I was in the orangerie picking off all the dead leaves and then I went about watering every pot for they were drier than was at all wise. Lady Nettleford ought to tend to her trees better or they will not give the fruit of which I know her to be so desirous."

"That at least would explain the note her ladyship sent me this morning expressing her appreciation for the tidiness of her conservatory."

"She did not!" Jane cried.

Alice chuckled. "No, of course not, I was only teasing you, but, Jane—watering lemon and orange trees was not why I brought you to London."

"You brought me to find a husband but I have met no one who intrigues me in the least."

Alice shook her head and gave her arm a gentle nip with her fingers then released her. Seeing her brother running wildly with his hoop and stick, she called to him. "Have a care for the cows, Nicky, or you will frighten them!"

Jane caught her shawl before it fell to the grass and wrapped it more securely about her elbows. "Dear Nicky! If he were not here I vow I should return to Wiltshire on the very next Mail Coach, see if I wouldn't!"

"And I should let you go," Alice assured her. "But you do see how necessary you are to him?"

"Of course I do," she said. "Besides, how can I complain when we are walking in such a beautiful park."

St. James's Park was the oldest of the royal parks, consisting of some one hundred twenty acres. Rosamund's pond had long been filled in, but the canal was in good condition and since the middle of the last century the park had been cared for by excellent rangers, showing steady improvement.

"Do you think Mr. Pinfrith is that gentleman standing near the bridge?"

Alice directed her gaze beyond the stretch of water to the yellow bridge which had been erected in 1814 along with a seven storey Chinese pagoda for the purpose of celebrating the Battle of the Nile. The pagoda had been burnt to the ground during the fireworks display but the bridge yet remained.

Alice tried to imagine the tall stranger in a close domino and mask, but could not. "I cannot say," she murmured with a little shrug. "To own the truth, he could be anyone."

Nicky called to them, shouting and waving, happy to be able to run amuck in a park. Jane sighed. "I wish Hugh were here. He would enjoy such an outing as this."

"He certainly would."

Since they were nearing the row of cows, where Louisa was surrounded by at least five of her numerous beaus, Alice asked, "Will you be having a mug of milk?"

"I should like that," she said. Her contented expression however was short-lived as she caught sight of Freddie, who was also nearing the row of cows. "How can our sister leave Upper Brook Street wearing a gown of green, red, and yellow stripes! She appears more and more like a Gypsy!"

"Not a Gypsy," Alice replied. "More of a lady held ransom by Barbary Coast pirates."

"The vignette of course. She still thinks of herself as Mr. Dodds's muse."

"Yes, she does," Alice said, sighing heavily.

When Freddie drew near, Jane addressed her. "So tell me,

Freddie," she inquired, "is Mr. Dodds's foot broken or merely sprained from having danced with you last night?"

Freddie's cheeks grew quite pink. At Lady Nettleford's ball, Mr. Dodds had missed his steps, tripped over Freddie, fallen on his face, and arisen in some pain. "At least I danced," Freddie retorted sharply, "instead of standing about frowning and scowling and setting all the Tabbies to gossiping as you do."

A squabble in St. James's Park was not precisely what Alice desired Mr. Pinfrith to witness once he arrived. Before Jane could respond, she addressed Freddie. "I could not help but notice the set you went down with Mr. Quintin last night. I vow I have never seen anything so graceful and you seemed so well suited as partners. Was it as pleasant as it appeared?"

Louisa, having left her several beaus for a moment to converse with her sisters, agreed. "It was wondrous, Freddie, as though you had been dancing together for ages and I was not the only one to remark on it. Several of my beaus made mention of it."

Freddie smiled, quite softly, and for the barest moment, Alice saw the young lady she had known before the arrival of Mr. Dodds in Upper Brook Street. "I must confess," she said, smiling, "that I have never enjoyed a dance so much. Mr. Quintin is quite expert and the whole time I had the impression he could make any young lady appear to advantage beside him."

Louisa nodded vigorously. "You would do well to draw him into your court. He is beseiged by every hostess for if you do not know already he travels only in the First Circles."

Freddie lifted her chin. "Is that all you think of, Louisa, how someone many be of advantage to you?"

"Of course not!" Louisa cried, growing quite flustered.

Alice held back a sigh. It seemed to her that the exigencies of the Season were taking a toll on the goodwill in her home. "Enough," she murmured softly but with just such a tone and expression that caused all three of her sisters to turn to her.

As one, Jane, Louisa, and Freddie offered an apology first

to her and then to one another. Jane and Freddie moved to
the milkmaids, where they purchased their mugs of milk.
Alice would have asked Louisa if she had any notion why
Lord Tamerbeck had not attended Lady Nettleford's ball as
promised, but Louisa's attention had at that moment become
diverted by some sight which caused her eyes to grow very
wide.

"The handsomest man I have ever before witnessed!" she
exclaimed. "And Mr. Trickett is with him. I wonder who he
might be and why we have never seen him before."

A brief surge of hope shot through her that perhaps Mr.
Pinfrith had arrived in the company of Bradenstoke's secretary, but as she turned, all hope died.

"Oh dear," she murmured.

"You know him? I can only suppose by your expression
it is not Mr. Pinfrith?"

"No," she stated quietly. "That man is Bradenstoke."

"Our guardian?" she queried.

"Not our guardian. He never accepted the post."

"Of course he is not. I do not know why I called him
such. Do not fear for I shall support you now. You cannot
like meeting him so soon after having fenced with him yesterday."

Alice had told her siblings of her unhappy and rather bizarre encounter with Lord Bradenstoke, of the exchange of
insults, of the fencing match, and of having learned he had
never even bothered to read her letters over the years.

"Thank you, Louisa. And you are right. I do not like it
one whit."

She drew in a deep breath and at the same time felt Louisa
slip her arm about hers supportively. Was it only yesterday
she had had the audacity to force her way into the man's
house? How small the park suddenly seemed and how
strange her thoughts became, flitting as they did to the particular memory of seeing him just after their fencing match
had ended. His sword lay on the floor, his shirt was drenched
in sweat, and he had been bent over at the waist in an attempt
to regain his breath. She realized with a start that as angry

as she had been with him at the time, there had been the briefest moment when she had thought him magnificent.

"Bradenstoke carries himself like a general," Louisa whispered.

"Yes, you are right. He does. I wonder what he is doing here." Alice's heart began to thrum in a quite unusual manner. There was indeed a great deal of strength, even command, in his countenance and his stride was long and purposeful.

He wore a dark gray coat, a black waistcoat, and a snowy neckcloth arranged in intricate folds. Black pantaloons clung to muscular thighs and his black top boots gleamed in the scattered sunshine. The wind buffeted his beaver hat and with a stiff pop he settled it firmly on his head. He lifted his face to her and smiled, if crookedly.

Had she really fenced with him yesterday and all but told him to go to the devil? Had he really kissed her and that so roughly? And had there been that portentous moment when she had enjoyed his kiss? Oh dear, it was true, she had enjoyed the manner in which he had kissed her so completely out of hand! How dreadful!

She felt as though some sort of madness characterized her relationship with Bradenstoke, not less so in this situation when he was here, in the very place, at the very time, she was supposed to meet his half brother. Was it possible he knew of the assignation?

"Well met, Miss Cherville," he said, approaching her. "I have little doubt you are surprised to see me today. You know my secretary of course?"

"Yes, how do you do, Mr. Trickett?"

"Miss Cherville. Miss Louisa." Mr. Trickett bowed to them both in turn.

Alice, aware that none of her family had as yet met the man who should have been their guardian, made the first introduction. "Lord Bradenstoke," she began formally. "May I present my sister, Miss Louisa Cherville?"

Bradenstoke bowed to her. "I am pleased to make your acquaintance, Miss Louisa."

In response, Louisa offered him a perfunctory smile and a slight inclination of the head. Alice felt her sister's strong disapproval and could not help but smile, if but a trifle.

Jane and Freddie, having imbibed their mugs of the fresh milk, returned at that moment to Alice and were also introduced to Bradenstoke. Alice could not fail to notice how frosty her sisters were to the man who had rejected the guardianship all these years. In their countenances, as they formed a solid wall of disapprobation, Alice was put forcibly in mind of the decade she had spent trying to encourage his interest through her letters. Somehow, as she shifted her gaze back to the earl, she felt she would never be able to forgive him for his callous treatment of his father's promise to her family.

Lord Bradenstoke thought that he had never before seen such a beautiful collection of ladies in all his life and understood why Trickett was so intent on making his way as frequently as possible to Upper Brook Street. For the barest moment, he felt a tug as well, particularly as he shifted his gaze to the eldest daughter, his Nemesis, Alice.

She was gowned in spring loveliness in an underdress of pale green twilled cotton, an overdress of sheer white lawn embroidered with green and pale yellow flowers, a shawl of a finely woven merino wool of a darker green which she carried elegantly over her elbows. Her white bonnet was decorated jauntily with artificial flowers and her red hair graced her forehead in a series of delicate curls. She was more beautiful in the light of this early May day than even when gowned so exquisitely as she had been at Vauxhall.

His mind was shattered suddenly by images of fencing with her yesterday, of the wild, intent look in her eye as she matched blade for blade, of her skill and her passion, of her desire to meet him fully with every trick she had learned from her fencing master. There had been no holding back in Miss Cherville.

He felt on fire suddenly, a brilliant, blue-white longing sweeping hard over him. His gaze drifted to her lips, such sweet, kissable lips, and the longing intensified. He wished he were alone with her, as he had been at Vauxhall, that he might place his lips once more on hers. Only, why the devil was he feeling this way when his purpose in coming to St. James's Park was entirely juxtaposed?

The ladies excused themselves, Freddie to enjoy another mug of milk, Jane to chase after Nicholas, who was near the canal practicing his cartwheels, and Louisa, who Trickett drew off in the direction of her waiting beaus.

"Are you not astonished to see me?" he asked.

"Yes, of course I would be. I can only suppose your brother informed you of our meeting."

"He did. I am here on his behalf since he has left London for a time, business in Portsmouth, and cannot attend you as he wished."

"Portsmouth?" she cried. He watched her chin rise and her eyes flash with ill-concealed aggravation. "Did you know we were to meet before you sent him away?"

He felt triumphant, even powerful, that he could get her to rise to the fly so easily. "I did not send him away. The nature of his, of our shipping firm, performed that feat all by itself. As it happens, you wound me, Miss Cherville. I am not so bad a fellow as you think. In truth, I am here in an attempt to make up for the misery which his leaving has undoubtedly caused you." He drew a letter from the pocket of his coat, written by his hand, but signed with his brother's name. "This, I hope, will soften the inconvenience of having to wait for a day or two before again being in my brother's company."

He watched Miss Cherville stare at the letter and press a hand to her bosom. He could see the anticipation in the way her lips parted ever so slightly.

"Thank you," she murmured, sliding the letter into the pocket of her gown. Lifting her gaze to him, she continued. "You were very kind to have performed this office for both your brother and myself and I do beg your pardon."

His breath caught once more as he saw the sincerity in her eyes. He would not in a hundred years have expected an apology. She had succeeded in surprising him again, just as she had yesterday in picking up her sword and laying it so fiercely against his. He watched her expression grow very still. She tilted her head, her lips parted anew. He did not understand why these movements affected him as they did, but with each second that passed, he felt as though she were reaching into his soul.

After a time, she gave herself a shake. "For a moment," she said quietly, a faint smile forming on her lips as she adjusted her green shawl, "you seemed familiar to me, like an old friend. I cannot explain it."

Nor could he.

What he might have said next was lost in the sound of Nicholas crying out to be noticed. "Alice, see how many cartwheels I can do in a row?"

"Nicky, be careful of the canal." However, the wind picked up her words and carried them off in the opposite direction.

Alice began moving toward Jane, who was closer to him than any of the others. "How many has he done?" she called out.

"Fifteen," Jane replied.

"He is too close to the canal."

"I know. Nicky, you must stop!"

Braden heard a voice from behind. "How many, Alice?" Miss Frederica had a line of cream on her lip from the milk she was drinking.

"Eighteen, nineteen, twenty . . ."

Miss Cherville was laughing.

Braden followed after Alice. Louisa's voice also joined in. "Nicky, you are too close to the canal!"

Braden could see that if the lad continued on his course, he would soon be in the water. Alice began to run, as did all the sisters. Jane's voice grew shrill. "Nicky, stop! Stop!"

Nicky stopped at the water's edge at her command, but he was too dizzy to do anything but tumble in backward. He stood up laughing and crawled out of the water. His sisters were on him immediately, but instead of chiding him as Braden had expected they would, the lad was cosseted, laughed at, his chin chucked, and in the end he was wrapped up in Alice's elegant wool shawl with her praise for the number of cartwheels he had achieved.

As Braden approached, she looked up at him, her face beautifully alive with laughter and said, "I am sorry, my lord, but we must take our leave. Thank you for bringing the letter."

That was all. She had dismissed him as tidily as she had enveloped her brother in her shawl.

He stood back, with a disappointed Mr. Trickett drawing up beside him, and watched them go. He could not quite comprehend for the longest time the sense of desolation he experienced upon their departing.

"I feel as though the fair came to town," Mr. Trickett said quietly, "but left before I could attend."

Braden chuckled. Yes, that was how he felt. Precisely.

"Come, old fellow," he said to his secretary. "Shall we return to the work of creating new laws for England?"

"Dull stuff, what?" Trickett responded, laughing.

"Dull, indeed."

Nine

When Alice had Nicky safely in dry clothes, she excused herself to her office, where she sat at her desk and removed Mr. Pinfrith's letter from her reticule. She found that her fingers were trembling as she recalled yet again the kiss she had shared with him at Vauxhall. The disappointment she had felt upon seeing not Mr. Pinfrith, but Lord Bradenstoke at the park, eased from her mind, for she felt that in this missive her connection with the earl's brother was reestablished.

She broke the seal and smoothed out the folded page. The script was bold and lacking in the smallest ostentation. She found she approved. She could only imagine Bradenstoke's pen. He undoubtedly would scribble his words with great flourish. Mr. Pinfrith's was just what she preferred in a gentleman's script.

She began to read, very slowly, savoring each word.

My Dear Miss Cherville,
I was deeply saddened on Tuesday morning when I learned from Braden that I must away to Portsmouth and in doing so forsake our assignation at St. James's Park. But there was nothing for it. Duty summoned me and I had to go but not before securing my brother's willingness to attend you in my stead and to make certain you received my letter. Should you desire to correspond with me, you may send your letters to Grosvenor

Square. A courier leaves daily for Portsmouth. Do I hope too much that you will write to me?

How can I express to you my most profound gratitude for your kindnesses of Monday night. It is a rarity, indeed, when one finds another spirit so capable of sympathetic understanding as yourself. Before leaving for Portsmouth, I was emboldened to speak with my brother, as you suggested, about purchasing the property from him which has been at the heart of my interest for so long. Though he was visibly disturbed by my request and spoke as he always does of maintaining the integrity of the Bradenstoke estate, I sensed he was not entirely opposed to the notion. I was overjoyed for I know him well and believe in time that he will relent. I was in that moment aware of his love for me and that only a powerful sense of duty has prevented him from relinquishing the property.

I would add that when I spoke with you on Monday night, I was for that moment out of patience with my brother. I fear that I may have given you an unequal portrait of him as a monster, which I assure you he is not. As a partner in business with him, for instance, I have found him just and equitable in all things.

On an entirely different matter, but one which pertains to both you and I more nearly, would I be too forward or insensitive to your feelings in saying that I have never found such inordinate pleasure in my entire existence as when I held you in my arms?

Alice felt her cheeks grow warm upon reading these last words. Her heart felt awash with new and strange flutterings. Was it possible, could it be possible, she might tumble in love with William Pinfrith?

She could only smile as another thought struck her, that it would be such a perfect punishment for Bradenstoke to be required to greet her one day as his sister. She chuckled with delight then reproved herself for having such wicked thoughts when it was Mr. Pinfrith who was deserving of her attention.

His letter concluded. *There is more I would say to you, but not until we meet again, which I trust will be very soon. I should be leaving Portsmouth within the next three days. Yours, etcetera, William Pinfrith.*

With a heartfelt sigh, Alice refolded his letter, drew forward a sheet of fine vellum from her desk drawer, and composed a responding missive of her own.

When she had completed the letter and sealed it, she was just about to send for a footman to deliver it to Grosvenor Square when Freddie entered her office, her cheeks flaming.

"Alice!" she cried, her lower lip quivering slightly. "I beg you will tell Louisa to cease tormenting me."

Louisa was close on her heels and entered the chamber, trying to suppress her laughter. "I did not mean to be unkind," she said, a wicked light in her eye. "I only asked if she wished me to teach Mr. Dodds the steps to the quadrille."

"Louisa," Alice said, admonishing her with a scowl and a shake of her head.

"You see how horrid my sister is this afternoon!" Freddie retorted sharply.

"Louisa," Alice said, as Freddie came to stand next to her, "I beg you will cease at once."

"I only meant it as a kindness," Louisa said triumphantly, afterward turning on her heel and flouncing from the chamber.

"You must speak with Louisa," Freddie said, "and make it clear that her character is grievously flawed."

Alice looked up at her youngest sister. "I might be willing to do so if you would promise to forsake teasing her about Lord Tamerbeck's inconstancies."

"That is a different matter entirely but I knew how it would be. You always favored Louisa!" She sniffed loudly and Alice did not prevent her when she, too, stalked from the room. There was no use in attempting to resolve such squabbles, certainly not until Freddie actually gave up the ridiculous Mr. Dodds and Louisa forsook her inconstant beau. Until such time, she expected her sisters would be given to finding fault anywhere but in their own actions and choices.

For the present, she had a matter of much greater importance to attend to as she went in search of her footman.

That evening, Braden had just returned from dining at White's when he took up a seat before his own desk and found a letter directed to "The Honorable William Pinfrith." The smile which resulted was so broad that his face ached for the wicked pleasure he felt in receiving so quick a response from Miss Cherville.

He took up his seat and read her missive eagerly.

My dear Mr. Pinfrith,

I was utterly delighted to receive your kind letter which you will be happy to know your brother delivered to me as promised at St. James's Park this afternoon. He could easily have directed any one of his servants to perform the duty so I believe it is to your credit that he performed the office himself.

I read your compliments with no small degree of pleasure and can only say that it was your character, your humble manner in addressing me as you did at Vauxhall, which was the basis for any kindnesses I extended to you that night. What surprised me in your recent correspondence was how very gently you spoke of your brother when he has used you so very ill. I vow the notion that you must now offer to pay for what by right should belong to you already has deepened my belief in the unhappy defects of your brother's character. I do not believe that Bradenstoke can be "just and equitable" in all things for that would be an impossibility given his nature. But your insistence otherwise only leads me to the conviction that yours is the finer heart and mind.

Braden was stunned upon reading these words. The devil take it! He had meant for his letter to soften her opinions of him, not to increase her dislike of him, even if the whole situation of the property was a complete whisker. His first act upon ascending to the earldom was to bestow the property in question upon William. Miss Cherville, it would seem, was clearly more prejudiced against him than he could have believed possible and apparently sought every opportunity to think badly of him. His mind immediately began searching for ways he might begin overturning such dislike and wondered if perhaps he should call on the Chervilles tomorrow afternoon.

This he dismissed readily enough. He had no desire whatsoever to dance attendance upon her even if he thought her a great beauty and even if for a moment at St. James's Park he had been drawn to her so powerfully that he wondered if his world would ever right itself. He was not a man to be commanded by either his heart or his impulses, however, and certainly not where Alice Cherville was concerned.

He drew in a deep breath, scowled a little more, and read on.

I long for you to make the acquaintance of my family. My eldest brother, Hugh, is not yet arrived in London but I think you will be delighted to meet Nicky, not yet eleven, who is our particular darling. He accomplished one too many cartwheels today and fell into the canal at the park, but we got him home quickly so that he did not suffer even the smallest complaint from having become wet through. I cannot imagine what your brother thought of us, for we all descended upon Nicky like a flock of birds and fairly ignored his lordship. I do not think Bradenstoke would care for being ignored although this puts me in mind of a circumstance which occurred upon his arrival. My sisters welcomed him quite coolly as I suppose could not be helped for there is not a one of them who has not felt the lack of a proper guardian over the years. However, I shall say no more for I am convinced the subject must be as old to your ears as it certainly is to my heart.

When you are returned from Portsmouth, therefore,

*I do anticipate a great measure of joy in introducing
you to Jane, Louisa, Freddie, Nicholas and hopefully
Hugh, who we expect momentarily.*

Braden sat back in his chair. Had the Cherville ladies received him coolly? He had not noticed, which was perhaps to their credit. He did not think it fair, however, that they had judged him so harshly, but of course none of them could possibly know or comprehend what a horror it had been so many years ago to have inherited an estate in shambles, only to be told that in addition to dealing with the absolute terror of a score of creditors, he must take on the guardianship of a family of six children about whom he knew absolutely nothing.

But judged he had been and it rankled sorely. He almost tore the letter in shreds but something drew him to the last paragraph.

*As for the embrace we shared, which you mentioned
in your missive to me, I hope I do not shock you when
I say that I was quite pleased in learning of your sentiments. For myself, I found the experience to be extraordinary for there was, for a brief moment, an
unearthly quality to the exchange, one that I shall never
in the entire course of my life forget. Oh, how my cheeks
are burning even now for speaking of such things and
only a curious boldness on my part prevents me from
destroying this entire letter and beginning anew. Regardless of my discomfiture, I wish you to know that I
most earnestly look forward to your return in three
days' time and to the prospect of furthering our friendship.*

> *Most sincerely,*
> *Alice Cherville*

Braden now sat stunned as he read and reread her closing remarks. She had surprised him again. Never in a thousand years would he have expected her to give expression to her feelings on the subject of the kisses he had showered upon her. Forgotten in this moment was his sense of ill-use and in its stead was the truth that she had described very nearly his own response to the very same experience he had had on Monday evening. There had been an unearthly quality to the feel of her in his arms and he would not forget it in the course of his life either.

Whatever her opinions of his character might be, the words describing the kisses he had stolen from her were worth the whole of the missive. He therefore refrained from tearing the letter to bits, refolded it, and tucked it into the packet he kept for his personal correspondence, to which no one, not even Trickett, was privy.

Miss Cherville could not possibly expect an immediate response since a courier would require at least two days to ride to Portsmouth and return with word from "Mr. Pinfrith" so he would have several days to decide just how he wanted to respond to her letter. What he knew for certain was that he must find a way to begin the process of softening her heart toward "Bradenstoke," regardless of how many "defects of character" she believed him to have. He could hardly successfully punish a lady who held him at arm's length.

That evening, Alice was in attendance at Mrs. Ivy's musicale along with her sisters. Louisa was presently gliding her fingers over the keys of the pianoforte with her usual strength and vivacity and truly had no equal in her ability to perform the works of Bach, Haydn, or even Mozart. The entire audience listened awestruck, save for Lord Tamerbeck, who flirted outrageously with Miss Reed throughout the entire performance. Miss Reed was a tall, elegant young woman in possession of a large dowry. The pair of them were presently treating Louisa's sonata as but a piece of stage-dressing for their private amusements.

Standing in the very back of the room, Alice could barely control her irritation at Tamerbeck's supremely inconsiderate conduct. Had she been seated next to him, she vowed she would have given him a severe dressing-down for behaving without the smallest thought for Louisa's feelings. As it was, she could only fume on behalf of her sister, who, when she rose to her feet at the completion of the sonata, entirely lost her expression of exhilaration upon hearing Miss Reed trill her laughter loudly at something Tamerbeck had just said to her.

It was odd, Alice thought as she continued to applaud her sister's performance, how murderous one's thoughts could become over a flirtation in a music room.

Her attention, however, was swiftly drawn away by the happy sight of Mr. Quintin, who approached Freddie and promptly engaged her in conversation. This at least was promising, she thought, and for the barest moment found herself grateful that Mr. Dodds had injured his ankle last night at Lady Nettleford's ball. She doubted that had the handsome poet been in attendance, Freddie would have smiled so warmly at Mr. Quintin or laughed so heartily at some joke or other he had just told her. Promising, indeed.

Jane approached her. "Did you see Tamerbeck flirting shamelessly with Miss Reed?" she asked, whispering.

"Did anyone not see him doing so?" she responded. "Oh, Jane, you cannot imagine how many times I wished to drag him from the chamber with a strong hold on his ear."

Jane giggled. "I should like to have seen that!" she cried.

On the following morning, Alice found herself in the unhappy predicament of being seated alone in the drawing room with Sir Benedict kneeling at her feet.

"Oh, pray, my good friend, do not speak!" she cried.

"But I must. My heart requires it." He then launched into a renewed discussion of his feelings, which he confessed to be so powerful as to have brought him here today to once more declare his hopes of at long last making her his wife.

Alice listened in some agony, for she knew what her answer must be since she simply did not love him. At the end of his speech, therefore, she bade him rise from his humble position. When he took up a seat beside her, she spoke at length of her admiration for him and of her certain knowledge that she would always account him the very dearest of her friends, but alas her heart was still not inclined to matrimony.

He chuckled softly and kissed her fingers. "Then I have embarrassed you and for that I am sorry," he said, sighing heartily but smiling at the same time. "I promise I shall do better in controlling my ardor at least until the Season ends. For if, at that time, I find you are still not betrothed I mean to try again."

His manner was so teasing that she could only smile in return, thinking that there was no better example of graciousness in a man than Sir Benedict. He gave the subject a turn, asking after the musicale of last night. She told him of Tamerbeck's antics, to which he shook his head and rolled his eyes. "He was always a rascal," he said.

"However, you will be interested to know that Mr. Quintin paid particular attention to Freddie. I believe he may be forming a *tendre* for her."

"Indeed?" he queried, smiling anew. "This is most hopeful. He is not disgusted in the least by her costumes generally?"

"Apparently not. In fact, I think he admires her for not letting the criticisms of others deter her from dressing as she wishes to."

"Then let us hope," he whispered conspiratorially, "that at some point Freddie will become enamored of Mr. Quintin for I am persuaded she will then give up her turbans."

Alice could only laugh.

He rose to take his leave and she extended her hand to him. He took it in a gentle clasp. "Will the ladies of the house be attending Lady Dassett's ball tomorrow night?" he asked.

"Indeed, we will," she responded, also rising to her feet.

"Then I hope you will save at least a country dance for me."

"Of course." With that, he walked sedately from the room.

Alice remained in the drawing room, listening to the sound of his steps as he descended the stairs. She had been entirely taken aback by his renewed addresses, but not less so by the fact that for a moment she had almost been tempted to accept his hand in marriage. He would be an easy companion, he would make an agreeable husband, and she could for once have an arm to lean on whenever she required it.

Her senses had quickly righted themselves, however. There might be a convenience in marrying Sir Benedict, but she did not think she could ever embrace matrimony for such a reason.

On the following morning, Braden entered the small office apportioned to his secretary. "Where the deuce are my invitations for this evening? Where do you keep them, man? I have looked through every packet in my desk drawers and can find hide nor hair of them!"

Mr. Trickett, obviously startled by Braden's sudden demands, lifted a brow. "Your invitations? You mean, of a social nature?"

"Are there any other kind?" he inquired, repressing the aggravation he felt.

Trickett eyed him narrowly for a long moment, then sifted through his own documents, withdrawing a ribbon-bound stack from the whole, which he handed to the earl.

Braden, who never looked at his invitations, stared at the size of the bundle. "Good God! How many are there?"

"I should think at least a score."

"And just for tonight?"

"Yes."

"Good God. I had no notion. You mean even though I have refused for years to go about in society, the invitations still arrive."

"Hope never dies in the truly ambitious hostess."

Braden untied the ribbon and let the mass fall on Trickett's desk. He pushed them apart and began examining one after the other. He quickly became aware that the information he was seeking could not be found merely by looking at the invitations.

"Which of these," he cried at last, "will the Chervilles be

attending and do not pretend you haven't the faintest idea since I know perfectly well you have planted yourself in their drawing room every day this week."

Once more Trickett narrowed his eyes, even frowning slightly.

"You need not gape at me," he complained, scowling heavily upon his good friend. "I have asked you an honest question."

Trickett's mouth worked as he turned to the numerous invitations before him. He cleared his throat, he compressed his lips together, he cleared his throat again.

"You seem amused in some manner."

"Not by half," Trickett responded, his lips turning white from the pressure exerted upon them. "Ah, here we are." He passed an invitation over his shoulder, but kept his face averted.

Braden could see that his friend was having a great deal of difficulty in keeping his countenance, which only served to aggravate him further. "Lady Dassett's ball?" he inquired, glancing at the invitation.

"Yes. Berkeley Square." Trickett coughed and cleared his throat a little more.

"So you think my interest laughable?" he inquired. "Perhaps I have a reason for attending Lady Dassett's ball. She is an excellent friend to my mother."

"I am certain she is," Trickett said, turning to face him fully. However, when he met the earl's gaze, he began to chuckle and could not prevent a very broad grin from suffusing his face. A roll of laughter ensued and only between gasps was he able to say, "Caught . . . in your own . . . net, eh?"

"I might have expected a little more decorum from you, John!" Braden cried. He turned hard on his heel and stalked the short distance from the desk to the doorway, only to call back over his shoulder. "I shall be attending. Send the appropriate word to her ladyship."

"And a physician as well?" he asked sardonically, between chortles of glee. "For I vow Lady Dassett will fall into a fit of apoplexy with the surge of shock and delight she will undoubtedly experience upon your arrival."

"Oh, go to the devil, you worthless fellow," he cried. But as he quit the small chamber, hearing more of Trickett's amusement ring through the walls, he could not help but laugh at himself a little as well. How had it come about that he had actually deigned to attend a ball and strictly for the purpose of seeing Alice Cherville again?

Ten

Braden stood at the threshold of Lady Dassett's ballroom, his gaze fixed on the sight of Alice Cherville going down a country dance. She was radiant, there could be no two opinions on that score. Her light blue eyes shone with enjoyment, her complexion, probably due to the exercise of dancing, was in a glow, and she moved like an angel on feet so light and expert that he could only wonder that the entire assemblage did not pause to watch her. She wore a gown of the palest blue silk and tucked amongst her fiery red curls were a dozen small white flowers. Her jewelry was simple in nature, a gold necklace, dangling opal earbobs that swayed as she moved through her steps, and a small ivory-and-gold brooch pinned to the high waist of her gown.

He wished he had never kissed her now, for the only thought he had at present as he watched her was that he already knew what she felt like gathered up in his arms. A longing for a life greater than the very full one he was presently living descended on him so powerfully that he felt undone by it. He could not put a name to the sensation, nor did he understand it at all, except that when the tune ended, and Miss Cherville was suddenly surrounded by Miss Louisa, Miss Jane, and a rather wild-looking creature who, he finally recognized as being the youngest sister, Miss Frederica, his longing intensified. How was he to succeed in punishing her if the mere sight of her could disturb him so deeply?

He should not have come, he knew that now. He should return to Grosvenor Square, sit at his writing desk, take pen and paper in hand, and set about crushing her with a series of letters from a fictitious Mr. Pinfrith. Yet he was here and he could not seem to make himself leave.

In truth, he felt utterly and hopelessly confused by Miss Cherville. In the space of five days, she had somehow managed to snag his mind and invade his thoughts one out of every two. Her poor opinion of him had worked in his soul like a wound that refused to heal. She disturbed his sleep and he had awakened more than once, having dreamt about her. He did not understand what was happening. The only thing he knew was that he needed to converse with her, to see if he could alter her unhappy opinions of his character.

More importantly, he wondered if she had already given away her waltz.

He might have continued watching her, but he was soon engaged in conversation with Lord Wroughton's heir, who was hopeful of a political career. Before long, he was surrounded by a fairly large group of both friends of the young man as well as ladies of his acquaintance. Miss Cherville would have to wait.

Alice was chatting with her sisters when she noted that Mr. Quintin, who conversed nearby with Lady Nettleford, frequently stole glances at Freddie. She felt embarrassed for her sister, whose blond hair appeared to have been arranged by a florist, for three large red flowers were pinned in her hair while several long fern fronds dangled down the back. Even so, she had to admit that her coiffure was not so grand as it might have been otherwise and she strongly suspected that Mr. Dodds's influence was beginning to wane.

"Mr. Quintin is looking very fine tonight," Alice observed.

Freddie glanced in his direction but her expression remained impassive. "He is a very unusual man," she said.

"I like his unaffected manners," Louisa offered. "He has a directness which cannot help but please."

Jane smiled. "Lady Dassett is convinced her ball is a success merely because he is in attendance."

"Imagine one person having such power," Freddie mused.

At that moment, Mr. Quintin disengaged himself from Lady Nettleford and moved to join Alice and her sisters.

After an exchange of pleasantries, he cast his gaze swiftly about the ballroom. "I do not see Mr. Dodds," he said. "Is he not in attendance this evening?"

Freddie flipped open her fan gently and began wafting it over her features. "Not as yet, though I am still hopeful. I take it most kindly of you to have asked."

Mr. Quintin turned and smiled down into her face. Alice's breath caught, for if ever there was a gentleman in love it was the honorable Mr. Quintin. Louisa, who was standing next to her, gave her a gentle nudge with her elbow and a quickly exchanged glance confirmed that her sister was of a similar opinion.

"And how is Mr. Dodds's ankle?" he asked.

"Not very well, I fear. He was uncertain even this afternoon whether or not he would be attending the ball tonight."

Movement across the chamber, at the entrance to the ballroom, caught Alice's eyes. "Oh dear," she murmured. "I . . . I believe Mr. Dodds is just arrived."

The entire group, indeed, the entire ballroom turned almost as one to stare at the brooding poet. His foot was bandaged thickly in gold silk, his black locks had been feathered into a ridiculous bubble, a collection of fobs and seals dangled heavily from his waistcoat, and a silver chain draped from one habitually long tail of his bottle green velvet coat to the other.

Espying Freddie, he began limping forward in her direction on a large crutch decorated in several vibrant shades of silk.

Alice thought he looked ridiculous in the extreme.

A quick glance at Freddie told her that she, too, was embarrassed by his extravagant appearance, for a ruby blush washed over her cheeks. To her credit, however, she squared her shoulders. "If you will excuse me, Mr. Quintin, I believe Mr. Dodds will have need of my assistance."

"Of course."

Alice, though feeling for Freddie's intense mortification, had never been prouder of her sister than at this moment. That she would not even consider forsaking a man who deserved to be forsaken was infinitely to her credit. She glanced at Mr. Quintin and saw that his own expression was one of admiration as he watched Freddie begin what would undoubtedly be a very long trek across the ballroom floor.

"Mr. Quintin," she said quietly, "I fear Freddie's deep sense of loyalty will not permit her to do ought else but acknowledge Mr. Dodds. Would you be so kind as to support her in this moment?"

Mr. Quintin glanced sharply at her. "I only wonder I did not think of it myself," he responded promptly. With that, he smiled hugely and hurried to Freddie's side. The radiant, beaming expression she bestowed upon him caused Mr. Quintin to glance back at Alice and wink at her.

Louisa nudged Alice again. "He loves her!" she stated in some finality. "What a triumph for Freddie and the worst of it is she does not even realize what a conquest she has made."

"I think it the very best part," Alice said, slipping her arm about Louisa's and giving it a gentle squeeze.

"You are right," Louisa said, her voice softening. "I have been a great deal too harsh with her of late and for that I am sorry."

Lord Tamerbeck walked by with Miss Reed on his arm, fairly snubbing Louisa by ignoring her, or at least pretending to. It would seem Lord Tamerbeck enjoyed keeping his favorites entirely uncertain of what his regard for them truly was.

"I know you think very highly of him," Alice began, "but I become quite angry when I see that he treats you in what I can only describe as a despicable manner. How do you bear it?"

"He did something similar at the musicale on Wednesday

night," Louisa responded rather sadly. "He spoke with Miss
Reed throughout my whole performance. I promised myself
I would never forgive him for such conduct but then yesterday he took me to Hyde Park and introduced me to at least
a dozen of his acquaintances. Even this morning, he sent me
another bouquet, this time of the most fragrant gardenias.
Once more, he drew me under his spell, but now this." She
waved a hand toward the viscount, whose attention was all
for Miss Reed. "I simply do not understand him for in so
many other respects he is just what I would want in a—that
is, he is just what I admire in a gentleman."

"There is no accounting for his conduct," Alice said quietly. "Perhaps he is not as skilled in the art of dalliance as
he would like to think."

At that moment, Mr. Trickett joined them and, with timing
that seemed to Alice to be impeccable, asked Louisa to go
down the next set with him. She agreed readily and since a
lively Scottish reel was just forming, he led her immediately
onto the ballroom floor.

Alice smiled as she watched them go. How very promising, she thought and how fortunate that Mr. Trickett should
be so very close on the heels of Tamerbeck's defection.
Somehow she rather thought he might have calculated his
timely arrival and was sure of it when, just as Mr. Quintin
had done earlier, he looked over his shoulder and winked at
her.

She could only laugh and trust that Louisa would not be
backward in her assessment as to which of these two suitors
was the better man.

For herself, she was very content. She had gone down
nearly every set thus far and because of the delight she experienced merely from the nature of dancing, she found that
her feelings of the moment bordered on the sublime.

The sudden trilling of laughter at a point behind her drew
her attention from the dancers now engaged in the reel. She
glanced over her shoulder and discovered, as the cacophony
of feminine amusement repeated itself, that Lord Bradenstoke was but a few yards from her, surrounded by five, no

six, beautiful young ladies and an equal number of younger gentlemen who appeared to be hanging on his every word.

He happened to glance at her in that moment and actually smiled!

Alice was so stunned that she dropped her fan and even more amazed when Bradenstoke excused himself from his admirers for the strict purpose of crossing to her in order to retrieve the feathered object.

"Th—thank you," she murmured, completely astonished, her gaze fixed on his face as he rose up before her.

"You are most welcome," he responded, looking down at her, his smile broadening.

She unfurled the fan and wafted the loose collection of white feathers over features. She felt oddly warm. "I thought you never attended such fetes," she said.

"On occasion. Lady Dassett is a particular friend of my mother's."

"Oh, I see. And is your mother in attendance as well?"

"I have not seen her as yet," he responded.

Alice could not stop staring at him. He seemed but a phantom and she could not credit he was actually standing before her.

"Are you well, Miss Cherville? You seem to be distressed."

"I am merely so surprised to see you that I cannot shake the feeling I have tumbled into a dream."

"A dream," he mused. "What an intriguing notion."

She could hardly ignore the hostile stares directed toward her from the bevy of hopeful ladies still waiting for the earl to resume his place among them. "Should you not be returning to your friends?"

He glanced at the nearby group. "They are even now deciding on partners for the next several sets. I do not think I shall be greatly missed."

Alice disagreed strongly for at least three of the ladies continued to eye her with considerable venom, but she kept her peace.

As she looked up at him, she was reminded once more of

her aunt's fluttery pronouncements of how very handsome he was. She could hardly disagree and thought he appeared to great advantage in the formal dress of the ballroom. He wore an elegant black coat and waistcoat, both of very fine fabric, along with knee breeches to match and slippers suited to a ballroom. His white neckcloth was tied to perfection in an elegant form she recognized as *trone d'amour* and his clothes generally seemed molded to his excellent figure. For some reason a very strange sensation, something like butterflies rioting, assaulted her stomach.

When an awkward silence settled between them, she searched her mind for some subject or other to bring forward. "You are looking quite handsome this evening," she ventured. "Black suits you." Oh, what a ridiculous thing to say, even if it was true. She felt herself blushing.

"Thank you," he said, smiling. "Though I must say I never expected to hear such praise fall from your lips. However, I shall return the compliment. I happened to see you dancing earlier and was much struck by your abilities. Your movements have an elegance unmatched."

She was stunned—again. Did he truly mean what he said? "Thank you," she responded, searching his eyes. "I enjoy dancing very much."

Why on earth could she think of nothing more gracious or even more interesting to say to him? What was worse, she could not seem to tear her gaze away from him. There was a shape or perhaps an expression to his large, brown eyes that seemed to have but one purpose, to command the object of his view.

"Miss Cherville," he murmured, "you are staring at me." His lips twitched and he touched his collar. "Are my shirt points wilting, perchance?"

"Of course not," she responded, with a faint chuckle. "The trouble is you ought not to be so very handsome. I cannot keep from looking at you, though I must say you might avert your own gaze just to be polite and then I could be at ease again. For instance, why do you not watch Mr. Trickett and Louisa, whom I know to be dancing?"

"Because I had much rather look at you," he said, lowering his voice, his smile widening a trifle.

Alice felt the challenge of it and smiled as well then lifted a brow. He seemed to understand she had thrown down the gauntlet.

After a full minute, when he refused to look away and she was still meeting his gaze just as forcefully, he laughed outright. "You realize we will create a terrible scandal if we continue this absurd behavior. Therefore, I will ask you, would you care for a glass of champagne?"

"Yes, my lord," she responded.

When he offered his arm, she took it and at the same time looked away from him.

"I knew I should win our little battle," he stated, directing her around the perimeter of the floor.

She gasped. "You did not win!" she cried.

"Yes, I did. You looked away first!"

"You are a very rude man," she countered, lifting her chin.

"And you are an extraordinarily beautiful woman. Only tell me, Miss Cherville, will you give me the pleasure of a waltz this evening?"

"Does the elusive Earl of Bradenstoke waltz as well?"

"Not so well as I fence, but sufficiently to twirl you about the ballroom floor without ruining your slippers."

Alice could only laugh. "Then I suppose I must accept although I promise you if you dare trod on my slippers as a half dozen gentlemen have done this evening, I shall never let you forget it. So be warned!"

"I vow I am quaking with fear."

"I can see that you are," she said, laughing once more.

He guided her carefully around a rather boisterous group of young gentlemen. "And to think I was afraid you would bite my head off if I dared address you this evening."

"I suppose I should have," she countered.

"I fully expected you to do so since you were not precisely charmed with me on either Tuesday or Wednesday. We have been enemies for such a long time that you cannot know the courage I had to summon in order to ask you to go down a set with me."

"You are being very absurd this evening for though I have known you but a handful of days, I would say you are the sort of man who has never been frightened of anything in his life."

"There you are out. When I crossed swords with you on Tuesday, particularly during the first few minutes of our match, I vow I felt as though my life would soon come to an end."

"You were never in any real danger for I never wanted you dead. Maimed, perhaps!"

He chuckled. "You did fence well enough, however, to strike fear in my heart and I was forced to be more careful. But I do not think that a bad thing."

As they passed from the ballroom, she noticed that Mr. Quintin had remained beside Freddie, while she in turn conversed with Mr. Dodds. "I admire your friend, Mr. Quintin, very much," she said, "and I do not refer solely to his excellence of manners, wit, and fashion."

"Indeed?"

"Though I have been in his company only on a few occasions, I believe him to be in possession of a very good heart."

At that, Braden chuckled. "I could not agree more. He took me under his wing at a time when I was not such good company, I fear. Ah, here is a servant bearing champagne." He retrieved two glasses for them.

She thanked him for the champagne as she took a glass from him, wondering all the while that he would confide in her. "Are you better company now?" she inquired. She did not know what to make of him or of his presence at the ball or even of his apparent desire to dance with her.

"I like to think so though you ought to ask my friends for their opinions. I daresay they would not hesitate to give you an honest answer."

"Perhaps I shall do just that," she stated archly.

"I have no doubt you will," he responded, sipping his

champagne. "Only tell me, why have you so stubbornly pursued my guardianship?"

She nearly choked on her champagne. "You are very brave to have asked me as much when the last time we spoke of it, I challenged you to a fencing match."

"So you did," he said. The smile on his face was so unexpected that it fairly took her breath away. Suddenly, Alice felt in the worst danger but of what she did not know.

She glanced about her. They had reached the blue salon, which was nothing short of a sad crush of fellow guests. "I cannot possibly answer your question in such a crowd," she murmured.

He nodded and gently took her elbow. "If we go to the music room which is just down the hall, then we may converse with greater ease, for I doubt there will be many guests within. Would that suit you?"

She nodded, once more taking his arm but holding her glass of champagne in her free hand.

As the chatter of the crowd diminished in quick stages, he soon led her into the music room, which was a tall, elegant chamber in which a handful of guests were scattered about, conversing quietly. The chamber overlooked a small garden and one or two couples were out-of-doors cooling themselves after having danced.

He settled her on a settee near a tall harp. "So you wish to know why I pressed for the guardianship despite your disinterest?" she queried, smiling at him.

"Yes," he responded quietly.

Alice sipped her champagne again and looked away from him. "In truth," she began, "I have asked myself the same question at least a hundred times over the years. I am not certain I have an adequate answer or to quote you, 'I do not have one that would satisfy you.' "

"At least tell me what comes to mind when you ponder the question."

"Well, I always think of Nicholas, I suppose. He was but a year old when my parents died. I desired more than anything that he might have every possible advantage since he had been robbed of even his mother's love at such a tender age."

"Primarily for young Nicholas's sake, then?" he queried.

"Yes, I think so. And yet, I desired the support of a guardian for all my siblings, not just Nicky. I was also thinking of myself. You must remember, I was but fifteen at the time and the only adult who supported me in those early years was Mrs. Urchfont."

"I understand," he said. "You must have missed your parents a great deal over the years."

"You can have no notion."

"There is something I have been wondering about of late. Was your father well acquainted with mine?"

"Do you not know?" she asked, once more surprised.

"You must forgive me if I do not. My father and I did not have the gentlest of relations."

"I see," she said. "So you know very little of their friendship?" If this was true, then she thought she understood something of his unwillingness to take up the guardianship.

"Nothing really. If we are to speak of disinterest . . ."

Since he did not seem inclined to elaborate, she continued. "And your mother? Was she equally uninvolved in your life or your interests and pursuits?"

"Mama is a different sort altogether, an admirable woman. I have often wondered why the deuce she ever married my father."

At that, Alice chuckled. "Having met the former Earl of Bradenstoke on any number of occasions, for he was used to come to Wiltshire and stay at Tilsford Hall, I believe I know of at least one reason."

"Indeed?"

She smiled at her various memories of the fourth earl. "He could walk into a room and light every candle with the mere force of his presence. I see the same quality in you. I was much younger, of course, when I knew him, but he would take hold of my chin quite gently but firmly and give it a little shake, 'Is this my little Alice?' he would ask. 'How you have grown. You will break a dozen hearts before long.'

I could not help but beam under such praise even though I was but a child. I was used to sit and talk with him for a quarter of an hour at a time which is a great deal for an adult to be conversing with one so young. But it was not so much anything he might have said to me that I valued as it was the laughing light in his eye."

Braden stared at Alice, wondering who this creature was beside him. The only memories he had of his father were glaringly critical, painfully abrupt, and always riddled with a sense that he had yet again disappointed him. When his solicitor, ten years ago, had explained to him the depth of the fourth earl's indebtedness, he had come to a place of scathing contempt for the man who had so belittled him over the years. He had come to see that whatever his own youthful indiscretions had been at the time, and there had been sufficient to earn him the epithet *a rogue amongst rogues,* his father's animadversions had been rather like the pot calling the kettle black.

However, time had softened his view of his parent, particularly in light of his evolving understanding of the ever-present difficulties of life. Hearing Alice speak so charmingly of his parent served to add a new perspective of the previous Earl of Bradenstoke. "I must say, I am grateful to hear you speak of my father in such kind terms."

He realized she was nothing like the lady he had imagined. For some reason, he had supposed she would be despotic and harsh in nature, having had the governance of her family for so long. Instead, she seemed to be all that was kind and generous in both manner and opinion, except where he was concerned, of course. Oddly enough, in this moment, he wished he had never pretended to be William Pinfrith.

"I think we should return to the ballroom," he said. "I daresay the waltz will commence very soon."

She rose and once more took his arm.

"There is something I must confess to you," he said. "I did not come to the ball tonight because of my mother's friendship with Lady Dassett. I came to see you." He did not mistake the startled expression in her eyes.

"You cannot possibly be serious," she said, frowning slightly, "when we dislike one another so very much."

A servant bearing a tray drew close and Braden paused to quickly relieve her of her empty glass of champagne. After placing his own glass on the tray as well, he continued guiding her down the hall, which was thronged with more guests moving toward the ballroom. "I do not dislike you," he said. "Well, perhaps a little since you called me, now what was it? Ah, yes, *ignorant, unchivalrous, hypocritical, and dishonorable.* All in one breath, if I remember correctly."

"Oh dear," she murmured. "Did I truly say such dreadful things to you?"

"Yes," he responded succinctly.

She surprised him by chuckling. "I imagine those were words you had never heard addressed to you before."

When he glanced at her he saw that her expression was teasing, a circumstance which pleased him very much. He could only laugh. "I did not like that you thought so meanly of me. I suppose I have come here in hopes of redeeming something of your opinion of me."

He led her into the swell of guests entering the ballroom. An answering swell met them as the former participants in a recent country dance which followed the reel departed the long chamber.

Once onto the floor, he guided her to a position at the far end of the ballroom. He bowed to her and she curtsied slightly in return, a formal beginning to the dance they would next share.

The orchestra struck the first note and soon, he was whirling her about the floor. She did not speak and he could see that she was minding her steps as she became accustomed to his manner of going down the dance. She was delightful to hold in his arms and as light on her feet as he had supposed she would be after having watched her during the earlier country dance.

After they had made a complete revolution of the chamber, she queried, "Is it possible you have come here for the purpose of punishing me?"

Since this was so near to his original purpose, he nearly missed his steps. "You offend me," he responded with a laugh.

"I thought as much," she countered, but there did not seem to be the smallest degree of pique in her expression.

"You have found me out," he confessed. "I did attend Lady Dassett's ball in order to discover some means of punishing you for having been so cruel to me not just on Tuesday but for abandoning me on Wednesday, and that so near the cows at St. James's Park. Only, once I arrived this evening, I could not conceive of just how to go about achieving my object. How does one go about punishing another creature in a ballroom?" he asked.

She met his gaze fully. "You could release me in one of the turns of this waltz and fling me into another set of partners, complaining all the while that I have the grace of a cow."

He burst out laughing. "I suppose I could, but that would be rather vulgar. Were my purpose to punish you, I would hope for something with greater dignity."

"A dignified punishment. Now there is a notion to be considered. Let me see. The waltz could end, you could stare at me coldly as though I had offended you and then you could stalk away. The entire room would wonder what *Miss Cherville* could possibly have said to have so wounded the sensibilities of the elusive Earl of Bradenstoke. I daresay my social reputation would be ruined and I would be invited nowhere."

He nodded. "Not a bad notion and rather dignified in nature. However, I think it a bit lacking in finesse. Have you any more ideas, perhaps something with a decided flair?"

She smiled as though the idea charmed her. He guided her up and back, around and around, the music swelling in a marked three-quarter rhythm the length of the long chamber. She floated with him, her feet but a whisper against the wood floor. As she pondered what her next suggestion would be, he took the moment merely to look at her, at the gentle cream of her complexion, at the vivacity in her eyes and expression, at the beautiful arch of her auburn brows, the delicate cheekbones and oval face. The balance of her features was perfection itself. What was it about her beauty that moved his heart as it did, for he vowed he could look at her for hours and still not grow fatigued?

At last, apparently having solved the dilemma of a third, more interesting punishment, she looked at him and smiled wickedly. "You could pretend to tumble in love with me, lead me a merry chase, and then jilt me just short of the altar."

"A most promising notion," he responded, smiling in kind. "And had you not suggested it, I might have taken it up myself."

Alice did not know what to make of so much teasing banter or what his purpose might be in dancing with her. She even felt that his professed purpose in attending the ball was suspect. She wondered if it was possible, however unlikely, that he might be experiencing some interest in her? She could not help but smile, for that seemed utterly ridiculous. How could Lord Bradenstoke ever think of her as anything more than a thorn in his side?

For some reason she would never comprehend, she was suddenly put forcibly in mind of the moment she had seen him for the first time, in his drawing room, when he had arrived on the threshold, wearing only his robe. A decided warmth flooded her and she nearly missed her steps.

Thoughts scurried about the edge of her awareness, snippets of notions far too passionate to be brought to full knowledge. She could only continue to stare at Bradenstoke and wish for the barest and most unreasonable moment that at some point in the very near future he would kiss her again.

His gaze, which had been keeping an eye on the general movement of all the dancers presently on the floor, shifted quite suddenly to her. Had he somehow read her mind and divined the nature of her thoughts? She suffered a shock as though a hot wind had just struck her face. Was he even now reading her mind, for a dark, inexplicable expression gradually overtook his features?

Lord Bradenstoke felt himself flying apart from within. He had saved the waltz for her with the intention of continuing his assault on her opinion of him. He meant to be charming, to dance well with her, to engage her in a manner that would not allow for her to continue thinking so poorly of him. But this! He had not expected to be undone by her, by the sudden desire he could read in the flushed expressions of her face.

His original intentions began spinning away from him, revealing a core of truth about why he had really come to Lady Dassett's ball—he had wanted to gather her up in his arms, to hold her again, to kiss her if he could. By God instead of the ballroom, he should have led her to some deserted corner where neither guests nor servants were wont to trespass. He might then have had the prize he was truly seeking.

"Lord Bradenstoke," she called to him, piercing the depths of his reverie with her musical voice, "are you feeling well?"

"Yes," he responded, giving himself a mental shake. He glanced about the dance floor, regaining his bearings once more and forcing the waltz to become a little more vigorous. "Of course I am."

"You seemed overset. I trust you were not thinking about my letters."

"No, not in the least," he assured her though he could hardly tell her the exact nature of his thoughts.

"I am glad of it," she said. "Only, I beg you will not move so swiftly, 'else we are likely to collide with Louisa and her partner."

"You are right," he stated, easing into a more gentle rhythm.

"Come," she coaxed, "something must have disturbed you."

"You, Miss Cherville. You disturb me. Why the deuce have you intruded into my world? You are changing everything. By God, I wish we were anywhere but in this deuced ballroom."

Alice gasped faintly, her heart swelling with a delightful ache. She could not mistake the meaning of his words and was reminded that but a minute earlier she had been wishful of the very same thing.

The waltz drew to a close at that moment. He regarded her for a long moment then slowly led her from the floor. He shook his head as though in some disbelief. "I do not know why I have said such absurd things to you," he whispered, leaning close. "I beg you will forget they have been spoken."

Alice, holding his arm, tilted her head to look at him. She smiled suddenly. "Do you know, I think the waltz always makes me a little dizzy, even reckless. Perhaps you tend to suffer in the same way, which might explain why you do not go about in company much. Might I suggest we forget what has been said, and what has *not* been said, laying the blame upon the waltz, which many have called a paltry excuse for hugging."

He seemed rather astounded. "And in this moment," he observed, "you would be gracious. Thank you, Miss Cherville."

She parted from him when Mr. Trickett, to whom she had promised the quadrille, claimed her for the next dance. As she took up her place on the ballroom floor once more, she glanced in the earl's direction and saw him watching her. He smiled faintly and nodded. She did the same, but the moment the music started he was forgotten in the intricacies of the *beau monde's* most difficult dance.

Eleven

On Saturday morning, Alice looked up from the menus she was reviewing, unable to comprehend what had put her aunt in such a state.

"You should have married Sir Benedict years ago!" Mrs. Urchfont cried. "Then we would not be in this muddle."

Alice spread her hands wide in some confusion. "What muddle?"

"Hugh, of course!" she cried. "Where is he? I . . . I have a tick beneath my right eye which always tells me that something dreadful has happened. There! Do you see it?"

She leaned forward, but Alice could detect nothing untoward as she scrutinized her aunt's face. "I am sorry, but I do not."

Mrs. Urchfont wrung her hands. "Something has happened to Hugh! Something terrible, I tell you."

Alice leaned back in her chair, her impatience mounting. "Aunt," she began again in a coaxing manner. "We have discussed this matter at least a dozen—"

"Oh, do not speak so condescendingly to me! I detest it above all things. I tell you, there has been an accident or something but had you married Sir Benedict years ago he would never have permitted your brother to have traveled apart from his family. He should have forbade it entirely!"

"I would never marry a man in hopes he might be able to keep my brother in check. This entire conversation is ridiculous." Alice returned her attention to the numerous papers and ledger books on her desk. "If . . . if you are so concerned over the matter, why do you not place an advertisement in *The Times*."

When Mrs. Urchfont remained silent, Alice turned toward her. Her expression was one of utter disbelief. Alice realized she had been unforgiveably cross with her and would have apologized, but her aunt turned swiftly on her heel and quit Alice's office, all the while muttering, *"The Times. The Times."*

The chagrin Alice felt was beyond description. She would not for the world intentionally wound her aunt but so she had. Yet at the same time she was irritated that there rarely seemed to be a moment's peace in her home. All she had wanted to do upon arising on what was an unusually sunny Saturday morning was to review the menus that Cook had placed on her desk, work on the household accounts for an hour or two, and if possible enjoy a cup of tea on the small terrace at the back of the house before beginning the day's round of social engagements.

So far, Freddie had complained that Louisa had hidden several of her large red silk flowers, Jane had expressed her frustration that there were so few birds in London compared to the country, and Nicky had come in from a walk with his best breeches torn at both knees.

"But it was a famous lark, Alice," he cried, his blue eyes shining with joy. "For Peter has just got a hobbyhorse and I rode it all the way from the top of the street to our front door, but then somehow I lost control and fell. I am not hurt, if that is why you are so out of patience with me!"

When the noon hour arrived, Alice sat down to nuncheon with her family and immediately apologized to her aunt. "I do beg your pardon for coming the crab this morning."

"Whatever do you mean, dearest?" she queried. "You spoke your mind. I was not in the least offended. On the contrary, you have given me hope." She then dipped her spoon into a bowl of steaming beef soup.

Alice regarded her aunt closely, wondering what she meant by "hope," but since she seemed content, she chose

instead to address another matter and asked Freddie if she
had yet found her flowers.

"No," Freddie responded sharply, glaring at Louisa.

"You should not wear them anyway," Louisa responded
with a sniff, a certain sign she had indeed taken them.

Alice glanced from sister to sister and decided they could
settle this particular conflict for themselves.

Later that afternoon, Alice took the family to the British
Museum, where she was rather taken aback to find herself
approached by at least a score of personages asking after her
acquaintance with Lord Bradenstoke and inquiring particularly whether or not he was indeed her family's guardian.
She was not certain where such a rumor had begun but was
quick to deny that though their respective fathers had been
excellent friends, and that she indeed accounted Lord
Bradenstoke a most excellent friend, the relationship had not
extended to a formal guardianship. Time and again she was
congratulated on her success in London and even given a
few hints that the gabblemongers were speaking of little else
than Miss Cherville's triumph in finally tempting Lord
Bradenstoke into society.

Alice was bewildered by such gossip but could find no
words to counter what she felt to be an impossibility. How
could she ever tempt or persuade the earl to do anything?

At the same time, these well-wishers, both the ladies as
well as the gentlemen, took the opportunity while addressing
her to extol his lordship's virtues. *Such a fine man, so witty
and handsome, one of the most intelligent gentlemen I have
ever known, works for reform day and night in the Lords,
bruising rider,* and even *I would trust him with my life!*

She had been stunned by the stream of compliments, not
less so than by Lord Wroughton, who whispered in her ear,
*Marry him, my dear. You could not do better in a thousand
years.* With a wink, he drew his wife and Mrs. Urchfont
away to look at a display of Etruscan antiquities.

Alice had been left to ponder the meaning of so many

compliments where Bradenstoke was concerned. Though she discounted several of them since they came from confirmed toadeaters, there remained a large portion which were utterly sincere. It would seem that Lord Bradenstoke, for all her dislike of him in his refusal to honor his father's promise, was admired and respected by many, a circumstance which quite strangely caused her heart to flutter.

On Sunday morning, Alice stared at a most startling event—Bradenstoke had come to church!

"I wonder why he is here," Mrs. Urchfont whispered to her, prayer book in hand.

"I cannot say but I think it a good thing that he would attend his mother."

Mrs. Urchfont sighed. "He is so incredibly handsome. I vow I could look at him for hours. I only wish I were ten . . . no twenty . . . no thirty years younger! Oh, do but look, he is smiling at you and nodding and directing his mother's attention toward you! Goodness gracious"—she dropped her voice to a whisper—"is it possible he has a *tendre* for you?"

This made Alice chuckle. "Of course not! I can think of few things more absurd."

"You are right of course though I vow I cannot account for such a marked attention to you."

"Nor can I," Alice returned, her heart fluttering anew.

Fortunately, the service commenced and she was able to forget for at least one minute out of every two that Bradenstoke was actually sitting across the aisle from her.

Ever since she had danced with him at Lady Dassett's ball, her thoughts had begun to take increasingly odd starts and turns where he was concerned. One moment she would be irritated by his surly attitude where the guardianship was concerned, another moment she would remember quite wickedly that he had kissed her while dressed only in the thinnest of shirts, knee breeches, and stockings, and in another she would wonder how soon she might waltz with him again.

More than once, while the good reverend was admonish-

ing his flock, Alice found she had to force herself to attend
to his fine, polished words.

After services, thinking she would but offer Lord Bradenstoke a polite nod as she passed by, Alice was utterly astonished when he brought his mother across the aisle to meet
her family. She knew such a marked attention would give
rise to any manner of gossip, not least of which would be a
confirmation that he was indeed her family's guardian, a circumstance she knew very well he would not like.

Upon meeting his mother, Alice decided the countess was
an instant favorite with her. She was neither proud, as she
might have expected her to be, and certainly not in the least
disagreeable. Her manners were friendly and open and she
spoke with Mrs. Urchfont and every Cherville sibling as
though they were friends long parted but now returned.

While Lady Bradenstoke was thus engaged, Alice found
herself addressed by the earl. "I have heard that you account
me *a most excellent friend,"* he said, startling her.

Alice wrinkled her nose as she looked up at him. "You
have heard reports from my visit to the British Museum yesterday."

"Indeed, I have."

"I know it must seem as though I was trespassing on what
is between us the merest acquaintance, but I said as much
because of an unfortunate rumor that was repeated to me
time and again. I was asked, no, I was told several times that
you were my family's guardian. It seemed imperative to me
that I deny such a relationship immediately and in doing so
said that though you were *a most excellent friend* you were
not our legal guardian. I was attempting to be polite, and to
honor your feelings on the subject. I hope you are not offended."

"Of course not," he returned with a smile.

"Indeed?"

"Why do you seem so shocked?"

She lowered her voice. "Because I know very well you
despise me, that you think me little more than a . . . a grasp-

ing sort of person, who has pursued you all these years merely for the advantages you could give me."

His mouth had fallen slightly agape.

"There you see," she said with a smile. "I have not been too far off the mark, have I?"

"I suppose not," he returned quietly, his eyes searching hers intently.

"I do not know how these rumors have begun, my lord, but even Lady Dassett intimated you were our guardian. I hope you do not think I have initiated such gabblemongering."

"I would never think that," he responded promptly. "I am only distressed that you are concerned I would believe it of you."

"What?" she queried, startled.

He laughed outright. "Perhaps I have questioned your motivations in writing all the letters you did but from my brief acquaintance with you, I have detected nothing in you of, as Quinney once put it, artifice or dissimulation. Indeed, what I have found is a lady who does not hesitate to speak her thoughts, though who frequently does so in a manner as painful as it is direct."

It was her turn to laugh for his expression had grown quite confounded. She might have boldly asked him to what he was referring specifically, but by that time her ladyship was ready to be escorted to her coach and the moment had passed.

The remainder of the day was spent quietly. The evening became an enjoyable family party in which Mr. Quintin was in attendance. The subject arose about horsemanship and driving skill. Mr. Quintin announced that he had an anecdote that would surprise them all.

Once his audience was captured, he began. "We had been out driving, trying out a new team of matched grays. I had whipped them up to a spanking pace, when suddenly I lost the reins. The horses took this as their cue to gallop away. I thought we were done for.

"However, Braden, without a moment's hesitation, leaped

onto the back of the horse nearest him, as neatly as you please, gathered up the reins, and brought the equipage to a standstill at the very brink of a deep ditch. My entire existence passed before my eyes. It was three days before I stopped trembling."

"Did he do so really?" Nicky had asked, his eyes glowing with admiration.

"Indeed, he is also a bruising rider," Mr. Quintin responded with a gentle smile. "A complete Nonesuch, rather like your brother I believe, or so Miss Frederica has told me. Is not Mr. Hugh Cherville handy with the ribbons and more comfortable on the back of his horse than in a chair?"

"Precisely so!" Nicky exclaimed emphatically.

During the remainder of the evening, in particular while Mr. Trickett turned the music for Louisa, who in turn played a beautiful Haydn sonata for the family, Alice pondered all that she had learned of Bradenstoke from his numerous friends. So many anecdotes and compliments had the most peculiar affect of shifting about her harsh opinions of the earl. It would appear he was not entirely the hard man she had believed him to be.

On Monday morning, Alice awoke to a scratching at her door. She sat up in bed, sleep curling abruptly away from her brain as a din from the street below suddenly reached her ears.

"Come," she called out, yawning. She could not imagine who or what could be setting up such a caterwaul on her street.

Her maid, a tray in hand, entered the chamber quite cheerfully. At the same moment, a shouting arose from below along with the rumble of more carriage wheels. "Betsy, whatever is going forward outside? With so much noise I would think a hunt was in progress."

"It is, Miss Cherville."

"Whatever do you mean?" she asked, laughing, for the notion of a hunt in London seemed quite ridiculous.

"The gentlemen are hunting you!" she cried, smiling broadly. She settled the bed tray over Alice's lap and handed a copy of *The Times* to her, which had been opened to a page of advertisements and a star drawn near one in particular which Alice read aloud.

> *A young lady of quality and fortune desires a husband. Applicants may apply in Upper Brook Street at the residence of Miss Alice Cherville. Only gentlemen of breeding need apply. All fortune hunters will be turned away at the door.*

Alice would have laughed, for it was the silliest thing she had ever read, yet her horror was too great! In terms of social standing such a breach of etiquette could only be considered a complete disaster.

"Take the tray away, Betsy, and pray help me to dress quickly. Are my sisters about? Has Mrs. Urchfont left her bed?" Her poor aunt, upon reading anything so wretched, would surely fall into a decline faster than the cat could lick her ear. She could not imagine who would have done this terrible thing to her!

"Aye, miss," she responded, removing the tray. "Miss Jane took Nicky to Hyde Park for an early ride, and both Miss Louisa and Miss Frederica are presently dressing for the day. Mrs. Urchfont, however, arose early, and is interviewing the gentlemen even now and that with great enthusiasm."

"My aunt is conducting the interviews?" she asked, dumbfounded.

The truth of the situation dawned on her in a sudden painful burst of understanding. "Oh, no," she cried, groaning at the same time. "She did not . . . that is, oh, Betsy, tell me my aunt did not . . . ?"

"I believe she did, miss."

With that, Alice leaped from her bed and dressed in lightninglike bursts.

* * *

Braden spewed coffee over his newspaper at the precise moment he read the advertisement in *The Times*.

"Good God!" he cried, lifting his horrified gaze to his secretary, who had fallen into a fit of laughter.

"You knew of this?" he exclaimed.

Mr. Trickett stood opposite him and between chortles and gasps for breath nodded his head. "I was . . . waiting for the moment . . . you discovered it. You have coffee . . . still dripping from your chin." He bent over at the waist and laughed until he cried.

Braden was not so amused. He wiped his chin and dabbed at the coffee pooling at the base of his newspaper and soaking through. He laid it down on the table, shaking his head, his appetite deserting him completely. "What the devil was Miss Cherville thinking?"

"Not . . . Miss Cherville," Mr. Trickett gasped, wiping at his eyes and cheeks with the palm of his hand. "She has too much sense to have been the author of this. On the other hand, Mrs. Urchfont . . ."

"Stevens!" Braden shouted before his secretary could complete his thought. When his servant arrived, he began issuing a string of orders. Within twenty minutes, he was climbing aboard his curricle, with Trickett in tow, and giving the reins a hard slap.

Twelve

When Braden arrived with Trickett in Upper Brook Street, the relatively narrow lane was in a state of chaos. At least a dozen coaches, curricles, gigs, and landaus jammed the thoroughfare.

"Good God," he murmured.

"Just so," Trickett responded, shaking his head. The carriage rocked as Braden's footman jumped to the ground and went to the horses' heads. "Why did you feel such an urgency to involve yourself in this?"

Braden glanced at him, a little startled. "I haven't the faintest notion."

Trickett smiled. "Probably for the same inexplicable reason I felt compelled to come with you."

"Your presence here is not inexplicable in the least, Cupid having landed you a leveler and knocked you flat!"

"So he did," Trickett responded congenially. "You as well, perhaps?"

Braden snorted. "Could anything be more ridiculous?"

"Then give me another explanation," he countered, jumping to the pavement.

Braden descended the curricle, wondering just what he could tell his friend since his present conduct was as much a mystery to himself as it was to his secretary. "A sense of duty, I suppose."

"To what? To whom? Alice Cherville? You cannot be speaking of the guardianship."

"No. I do not know. Oh, the devil take it! I desired to be of assistance to her in this situation in order to avert what will otherwise become a terrible scandal. You know what the *beau monde* is." He cast a scathing glance at his friend. "You need not smirk in that ridiculous manner. Only tend to this, will you"—he waved an arm over the crowd of vehicles—"while I go within and see what is going forward?"

"Of course," Trickett said and immediately set about dispersing the large gathering of hopeful suitors and their attendant carriages and horses.

Once admitted into the house, Braden did not hesitate to send six finely dressed fortune hunters back onto the flagway. He asked the house maid quietly, "Where is Miss Cherville?"

"In the drawing room, m'lord, with a gentleman."

He hurried to the fine chamber on the first floor, mounting the stairs two at a time, and arrived on the threshold to find Miss Cherville hiding her laughter behind a kerchief. A man whom he knew by reputation as Mr. Smith, was presently kneeling before her, his arms wrapped about her knees. He was professing his love quite violently, so much so that he did not seem to notice Braden's arrival.

Braden met Miss Cherville's gaze and between the sparkle of laughter in her beautiful blue eyes and the silent plea for help which shaped itself on her lips, his irritation somehow vanished.

He crossed the room in three long strides, caught Mr. Smith by the collar, and dragged him away from what he had just pronounced was the *deepest, most spectacular love of his entire existence.*

Mr. Smith gained his feet awkwardly. "Eh! What the deuce!" he cried. "Who the devil do you think you are to interrupt a man in his proposals? Good God—Bradenstoke!" His face turned the precise shade of a beet.

Braden lifted a single brow. "Her guardian," he stated.

"Oh, I say, I had heard as much but thought it all a hum. Well, then, is it to you I am to apply for her hand in marriage?"

"Should you attempt to even cross the shadow of my front door, I shall have my butler discharge his blunderbuss at you from my library window. Your choice, of course!"

"I see, I see. Well, then"—he glanced at Miss Cherville—"I shall be going. Farewell, my love."

Braden watched as Miss Cherville bit her lip quite deeply and turned hastily away from her devoted swain.

"Let me help you find your hat," Braden said, giving Mr. Smith's shoulder a warning shove as he began guiding him down the stairs.

A few minutes later, after ascertaining that Mr. Trickett's efforts had prevailed and the street had begun to clear, he once more mounted the stairs. This time a different noise sounded from the drawing room.

"We are ruined! We are ruined! And it is all my fault!"

Arriving on the threshold, Braden found Miss Cherville attempting to comfort her shatter-brained aunt.

"There, there," she soothed. "You meant kindly, I am sure."

"Oh, I did, I did," Mrs. Urchfont turned to her niece, tears streaming down her face. "We were all in need of a husband for you, Hugh and Nicholas most of all, and I thought, well, you did say I should place an advertisement in *The Times* in order to put an end to our difficulties."

Miss Cherville seemed perplexed for a moment, then her brow cleared. "Oh, Aunt, I was speaking of Hugh and I meant, but only in the most facetious manner, that if you were worried about his whereabouts, you could advertise for him to come home or something. However, I was not in the least serious and I certainly would never tell you to advertise for a husband for me. Do you understand?"

"No," Mrs. Urchfont whimpered. "You so much as told me to place an advertisement though I remember thinking it was quite an odd notion. I recall it quite distinctly. But do you not see that had you married Sir Benedict, none of this would have happened!" She began sobbing anew, exclaiming over and over again that the entire family was doomed and what was to be done about poor Hugo!

Braden met Miss Cherville's gaze for a brief moment then moved to stand by the windows overlooking the street. Trickett was still working to clear the street, one unfortunate fellow having turned his curricle too widely and was now blocking the entire thoroughfare.

"Dear aunt," Miss Frederica called out, "do but look! I have brought your favorite—oil of roses."

Braden glanced in her direction and saw that she and Miss Louisa were just entering the chamber, each carrying some article or other for Mrs. Urchfont's benefit.

"Oh, how do you do, Lord Bradenstoke," Miss Frederica said, pausing briefly with her sister to bow politely to him. "I daresay you have learned of our debacle?"

He nodded, bowing in turn as they moved to attend to Mrs. Urchfont.

"Do not fret, Aunt," Miss Louisa said in her soft, musical voice. "It was a simple mistake, a misunderstanding, and all our friends, *our true friends,* will forgive us for it. I beg you will not be so distressed. We are not, are we, Alice? I have brought your vinaigrette."

Mrs. Urchfont took the small silver box and popped it open. She took a deep breath and looked pityingly upon Miss Cherville.

"Of course we are not distressed," Alice assured her. "Not in the least!" She leaned close to Mrs. Urchfont and embraced her fully. "Cook is preparing your favorite macaroons. Pray dry your eyes. This is nothing but a storm in a teacup!"

At that, Mrs. Urchfont began to smile. "Teacups are very small, are they not?"

Miss Frederica patted her shoulder and embraced her as well. "Small, indeed!"

Miss Louisa dropped before her aunt and tenderly laid her head on her lap. "Nothing to signify!"

"Oh, my dears. I am so very sorry."

"Nonsense," Miss Cherville responded. "You have nothing to apologize for. You were merely attempting, in your own way, to make everything better for our family. How could even one of us find fault with that?"

"Yes, I was!" she cried. "Indeed, I was. I had no other purpose in mind but to be of use when poor Hugo has fallen into a ditch or something of the like." She pressed the kerchief once more to her nose, her chest rising and falling in quick succession with another series of sobs. "I should like my pastilles."

Braden watched Miss Cherville and Miss Louisa exchange a glance after which the latter said, "I am sorry, Aunt, but I could not find the little ceramic house in which to burn them. Jane would know where it is, but she has taken Nicky to Hyde Park this morning."

"Never mind. I shall be content with my oil of roses and vinaigrette."

Braden watched the ladies ministering to their birdwitted aunt and felt that his own irritation over the matter had been ridiculous. The gentle vignette was playing itself out in a manner that would very soon put Mrs. Urchfont's distressed mind at ease.

He withdrew to the hall and began to pace rather slowly. What an odd circumstance had brought him today to Upper Brook Street and how strangely happy he was to be in the presence of so much love and forgiveness. The experience was wholly new to him.

After Lady Dassett's ball on Friday evening, he had returned to his town house with the certain knowledge he had never enjoyed a dance so much in his existence as the one he had shared with his Nemesis. She was an easy, graceful partner and in the midst of it he had found himself drawn to her as never before, powerfully so. Of course later he had succeeded in reminding himself quite carefully that Miss Cherville was not precisely deserving of such a marked attention and that he would be well served not to raise her hopes further.

Yet here he was proclaiming to Mr. Smith and therefore to the world that he was the Cherville guardian and, the devil take it, enjoying himself hugely.

He had found that throughout the weekend, his thoughts had turned to Miss Cherville again and again, not less so than after his mother had asked to be introduced to the family and subsequently had expressed her admiration for them all. Her letter to "Mr. Pinfrith" still rankled of course but he hoped his presence today in her home and in support of her aunt's scrape would soften yet a little more the harsh opinions she held of him. Just why it had become important that she think better if not well of him, he could not precisely say but he rather thought it had something to do with his desire to kiss her again and not as "Mr. Pinfrith."

Although, he mused as he continued to pace the hall, another letter from Mr. Pinfrith might provide the means by which he could bring about the shift he desired. Only this time he meant to be a great deal more careful in precisely what he said to her since his last effort, with a similar object in mind, had had a completely opposite effect.

From the landing, he heard Quinney arrive and a moment more the maid's voice as she explained to him what had happened. He descended the stairs and greeted his old friend.

"The ladies are in the process of comforting Mrs. Urchfont but I suggest we leave them alone for the present."

Now that Mrs. Urchfont was calmer, Alice asked Freddie to accompany her to her bedchamber, where she might rest for a time. Once she was gone and the sound of her footsteps ascending the stairs to the second floor had faded from their hearing, Alice released a very deep sigh, feeling utterly bewildered.

"Whatever are we to do?" Louisa asked quietly, appearing numbed by the experience.

"I do not know," Alice responded, shaking her head. "What a disaster! I still cannot credit my aunt would place an advertisement in *The Times—The Times!*—for a husband for me." She pressed her hands to her cheeks. "I am still beyond mortification at the very thought of it!"

Louisa shook her head. "You know, if it had happened to

any other family, I believe I should have laughed myself silly."

At that, Alice chuckled. "I do wish you could have seen Lord Bradenstoke drag Mr. Smith from the room. Mr. Smith's arms were actually locked about my knees. I feared toppling over at any moment from the sheer eagerness of his addresses."

"What a sapskull."

"Indeed."

Louisa moved to the window and gazed down at the street below. "I think it a great curiosity that Lord Bradenstoke should come at all," she said. "And Mr. Trickett with him." She glanced over her shoulder at Alice. "Come. You must see for yourself how neatly Mr. Trickett has managed the business. There are only one or two carriages still stopped near the house but, oh dear, you should see the mess the horses have left behind."

Alice could not help but laugh as she, too, moved to the windows. "Our neighbors will be so very grateful." She stood beside her sister and watched as Mr. Trickett helped some unfortunate whipster back up his curricle and pair. "I do so like Mr. Trickett," she said. "He is the sort of man one might rely upon in any situation."

"I believe you are right," Louisa agreed. She glanced up the street, craning her neck slightly. "Lord Tamerbeck is coming."

"Oh, Louisa, I am sorry. I daresay by now he has read the advertisement. Do you think he will be very angry?"

"Undoubtedly," she said, her voice sorrowful. "He is very protective of his consequence."

When his lordship drew near to Mr. Trickett, who had just sent the unfortunate curricle heading in the opposite direction, Tamerbeck tossed his reins to him with the words, "See to my horses, Trickett! There's a good fellow!"

Louisa gasped. "How very rude!" she cried. "He has just spoken to Mr. Trickett as if he were a servant!"

Alice kept her peace.

Mr. Trickett, however, was up to every rig and row and

simply tossed the reins back. "Tend to your own cattle, Tam!" he retorted sharply.

"Well," Louisa murmured appreciatively.

"Just so," Alice responded.

For the first time in weeks, Alice felt hopeful. In such ways she was certain her sister's *tendre* for Lord Tamerbeck would diminish. Louisa had not readily forgiven the viscount for having snubbed her at Lady Dassett's ball and had only finally relented toward him when no less than three bouquets had been delivered to Upper Brook Street along with a most sincere apology as well as a promise that he would be more attentive to her.

Freddie returned to the drawing room and joined her sisters. "Aunt is resting now."

"Poor Aunt Urchfont," Louisa said, shaking her head. "Whatever was she thinking?"

Freddie, who could be less than tactful on occasion, stated, "She was not thinking. She never does."

Alice might have remonstrated with her for the harshness of her expression, but a new diversion presented itself in the form of Mr. Dodds, who had just arrived by hackney. He emerged from the vehicle, sporting his heavily decorated crutch and wearing a scarlet silk coat, bulky pantaloons, and an odd pair of shoes that appeared to be made of purple velvet.

"Oh dear," Freddie murmured absently. "And Mr. Quintin is just arrived."

"Are those Petersham trousers?" Louisa asked.

"I suppose they are," she responded.

Alice glanced at her and saw that her color had receded ominously.

"But in green plaid?" Louisa queried.

Worse was to follow when he entered the drawing room along with the rest of the gentlemen and complained loudly, "Do but think how the advertisement will reflect on me? Was no one thinking of me? Of my consequence?"

Since the entire party stared at him in some astonishment, he was satisfied, apparently believing he had made his point.

We'd Like to Invite You to Subscribe to Zebra's Regency Romance Book Club and Give You a Gift of 4 Free Books as Your Introduction! (Worth $19.96!)

If you're a Regency lover, imagine the joy of getting **4 FREE Zebra Regency Romances** and then the chance to have the lovely stories delivered to your home each month at the lowest price available! Well, that's our offer to you and here how you benefit by becoming a Regency Romance subscriber:

- **4 FREE Introductory Regency Romances are delivered to your doorste**
- **4 BRAND NEW Regencies are then delivered each month (usually before they're available in bookstores)**
- **Subscribers save almost $4.00 every month**
- **You also receive a FREE monthly newsletter, which features author profiles, discounts, subscriber benefits, book previews and more**
- **No risks or obligations...in other words, you can cancel whenever you wish with no questions asked**

Join the thousands of readers who enjoy the savings and convenience offered to Regency Romance subscribers. After your initial introductory shipment, you receive 4 brand-new Zebra Regency Romances each month to examine for 10 days. Then, if you decide to keep the books, you'll pay the preferred subscriber's price.

It's a no-lose proposition, so return the FREE BOOK CERTIFICATE today!

Say Yes to 4 Free Books!
Complete and return the order card to receive this $19.96 value, ABSOLUTELY FREE!

If the certificate is missing below, write to:
Regency Romance Book Club
P.O. Box 5214, Clifton, New Jersey 07015-5214
or call TOLL-FREE 1-800-770-1963
Visit our website at www.kensingtonbooks.com.

FREE BOOK CERTIFICATE

YES! Please rush me 4 Zebra Regency Romances without cost or obligation. I understand that each month thereafter I will be able to preview 4 brand-new Regency Romances FREE for 10 days. Then, if I should decide to keep them, I will pay the money-saving preferred subscriber's price for all 4...that's a savings of 20% off the publisher's price. I may return any shipment within 10 days and owe nothing, and I may cancel this subscription at any time. My 4 FREE books will be mine to keep in any case.

Name _____

Address _____ Apt. _____

City _____ State _____ Zip _____

Telephone ( ) _____

Signature _____ RN062A
(If under 18, parent or guardian must sign.)

Terms and prices subject to change. Orders subject to acceptance by Regency Romance Book Club.
Offer valid in U.S. only.

treat yourself to 4 FREE Regency Romances!

A
$19.96
VALUE...
FREE!

*No
obligation
to buy
anything,
ever!*

PLACE
STAMP
HERE

REGENCY ROMANCE BOOK CLUB
Zebra Home Subscription Service, Inc.
P.O. Box 5214
Clifton NJ 07015-5214

He took up a chair by the fireplace, crossing his arms over his chest and scowling heavily on anyone who chanced to glance at him.

Alice watched as Freddie stared at her beau for a long moment. Her expression was as a child who is perplexed when the cloud passes across the sky and the sun no longer shines.

Louisa drew near to Alice and murmured, "Look how Mr. Quintin grins."

Alice chuckled softly. "Why should he not be content when he is winning a lady merely by remaining silent."

"What do you think of his interest in her?"

"Only that I am grateful for his influence—Freddie is wearing but one necklace, a turban, though bright red, of unexceptionable size, and only half her hair is dangling to her waist. Beyond that, I am enchanted by how sweetly attentive he is to her, whether at the museum, the opera, or here in our drawing room. Does a lady require more than that?"

Louisa sighed. "Of course not." Her gaze wandered to Lord Tamerbeck, who sat staring at the carpet at his feet and appeared rather bored.

Alice could only laugh. "Go to him," she said. "He will soon enough become enlivened when he has you to converse with."

Louisa crossed the room and engaged her swain in conversation. Within scarcely a minute his expression had grown quite animated. Alice wondered what had prompted her to encourage Louisa to show the viscount even the smallest compassion, for he was entirely unworthy of such a kindness. She was even less satisfied when Trickett entered the chamber and saw how completely his rival had gained an advantage over him.

Bradenstoke approached her and in a low voice said, "Am I mistaken in understanding that your aunt's impulse to place an advertisement in *The Times* had something to do with Hugh's absence in London?"

Alice explained her aunt's unhappy reasoning, to which

Lord Bradenstoke merely chuckled before growing serious. "Regardless of her conviction that had you been married your brother would even now be in London, she seems quite distraught believing your brother's absence is due to some form of mischief. Do you share her concern?"

"At times, a little, but Hugh is a young man, wishful of adventure as I believe most young men are, and in my more sensible moments I am persuaded he is merely off on a lark. However, Mrs. Urchfont has convinced herself that he has suffered from some mischance and I cannot persuade her otherwise."

"How long has he been gone?"

"Approaching six weeks now."

"And he has been expected all this time?"

"Yes. Daily. Hourly."

"Then might I suggest, for your aunt's sake, that a person of experience in such matters be hired to find Mr. Cherville? Perhaps then she might be at her ease and less likely to act impulsively."

Alice looked at him for a long moment, weighing what he had just said to her. Finally, she asked, "Do you think there might be reason for concern?"

He was silent apace. "I cannot say," he responded. "I tend to think it is just as you have said."

She released a sigh of something near to relief.

"I know of someone who could perform this task for you," he offered. "For years he conducted every manner of investigation for Bow Street and now has his own firm. His name is Hicklade and I trust implicitly in both his ability and his discretion for he has performed several services for me in the past. I could arrange it, if you like."

Alice looked up at him and smiled. "Thank you. I would not have known where to begin and yes, I think it an excellent notion if for no other reason than to give my aunt some relief."

"As to the other matter . . ." Here he paused, frowning slightly.

Alice shook her head, bemused. "What other matter?"

"If you will recall, in the heat of the moment, I told Mr. Smith I was your guardian. By now half of London will know that I confirmed the recent rumors."

"I see. What do you wish to do about it?"

"I could put a notice in *The Times*," he suggested dryly, "refuting my claim of today."

Alice chuckled. "Yes, I suppose you could. Oh dear. I cannot credit my aunt could have done anything so harebrained. I am utterly mortified, my lord, and I do hope you will forgive us all since we have been so nearly connected with you these past several days." She lowered her voice further. "Though I find Mr. Dodds's complaints to be ridiculous in the extreme, I cannot help but feel that today's hapless circumstance will reflect badly on your consequence as well as your mother's. For that, I do most sincerely apologize."

"Nonsense," he said, a soft smile on his face. "A storm in a teacup."

Alice chuckled again. His gaze held her for a long moment and for that space of time Alice felt stilled within her heart as though she were listening to words that could not be spoken.

Finally, he cleared his throat and said, "I had meant to bring you a letter today from my brother, but in my haste in coming here this morning, I left it on my desk."

"He has written?" she asked. Her heart fluttered in her breast.

"Indeed, he has," he said. "When I return home, I shall send it to you by one of my footmen."

"Thank you. You are most kind."

He smiled, if ruefully. "You did not always think so."

"No, I did not." Oddly, she could hardly breathe as he met her gaze once more and that quite forcefully. She did not know what to make of him in this moment or why she felt so breathless.

"I must take my leave," he said, after a moment. "I have numerous appointments today."

"Of course," Alice responded.

She watched him go and Mr. Trickett with him. She still

could not credit the odd circumstances of the morning that had actually brought a man she had considered an enemy to her aid.

She moved slowly to the windows and watched as the earl emerged from the house, climbed aboard his curricle, and took the reins in hand. Once Mr. Trickett and the footmen were settled, he flicked his whip neatly over the heads of a finely matched pair of black horses. The equipage moved forward in a smooth motion and disappeared up the street. Lord Wroughton's words returned to her again, a chiming of bells in her head, *Marry him if you can, my dear. There is no finer gentleman than Bradenstoke.*

Thirteen

That afternoon Alice received a packet from Lord Braden-stoke containing both Mr. Pinfrith's second missive as well as a letter confirming the hiring of Mr. Hicklade. The former Bow Street Runner, it would seem, was already on his way to the Old Bath Road in search of Hugh.

Having just finished nuncheon, Alice took Mr. Pinfrith's missive to her bedchamber and sitting upon the edge of her bed, read eagerly the long-awaited response. She could not credit that a sennight had passed since his departure for Portsmouth.

My dear Miss Cherville,

I was deeply gratified to receive your letter but at the outset I must warn you that my business in Portsmouth will not be so swiftly concluded as I had originally hoped. Forgive me for not coming to you sooner. Only the most difficult of circumstances is preventing me.

Having read your letter a dozen times, I have come to realize how wrong I was to trespass on your kindness at Vauxhall for I am deeply chagrined at the depths of your dislike of my brother. Your ill opinions of him are distressing me deeply. I can only emphasize that he truly is just and equitable in all things. I believe this with my entire being. The only true discord between us concerns the property about which I have already told you and

*which I am coming to believe will be settled very soon
between my brother and myself in a manner that is
wholly agreeable but of that I will write more at a later
hour.*

*For the present, I much prefer thinking about the fu-
ture and about meeting your family. You spoke so
warmly of them in your last correspondence that I confess I desire very much to make their acquaintance.
Hopefully by the time I return from Portsmouth, even
your brother Hugh will have taken up residence in Upper Brook Street.*

Alice paused for a moment, considering all that had happened since Mr. Pinfrith's last letter—Bradenstoke had conversed with her in the nicest manner, he had danced with
her, he had even introduced her to his mother, and after the
morning's debacle because of the advertisement in *The Times*
had actually taken on an informal guardianship of her family.
She felt the strongest pleasure in being able to agree with
Mr. Pinfrith this time about his brother. She knew that in her
next letter, she would be able to offer such praise as must
surely set his heart at ease.

She considered Lord Bradenstoke for a long moment as
the letter lay quietly on her lap. She glanced at her windows,
at the shifting patterns of sunlight and clouds which passed
over the city, and realized she no longer thought meanly of
him. How could she, she thought with a smile, when he had
grasped Mr. Smith's collar as he had and fairly dragged him
from her drawing room? No, the sensations she was experiencing even now as she thought of the earl were entirely
warm in nature. Whatever his reasons for having refused the
guardianship all these years, his present conduct was altering
her opinions of him entirely.

With the strongest effort, she reverted her attention back
to the letter.

*I wonder if you would be so good as to tell me a little
in your next letter of your brothers and sisters. I desire*

*above all things to know something of each of them
before I make their acquaintance for I am convinced
such advance information would enhance a first introduction.*

*I think of you often and trust most sincerely that I
shall be in London sometime within the next sennight.*
Yours, etcetera,
William Pinfrith

With a smile, Alice moved to a small table in her bedchamber, which held pen, paper, wax, and seal. Her heart
was wholly warmed toward Mr. Pinfrith as she sat down to
write, to tell an anecdote or two of each of her siblings, and
to happily inform him that her opinion of his brother was
indeed undergoing a happy change.

Later that day, Braden entered his bedchamber, having just
returned from Westminster, when he noticed a letter propped
up against the candlestick on his nightstand. He recognized
the handwriting immediately and smiled as he saw his
brother's name written in Miss Cherville's beautiful script.

He unwound his neckcloth from about his neck, unbuttoned his coat and waistcoat, and sat down on the edge of
his bed to read. The words contented him at the outset and
he could see that he had finally achieved his object—he was
now in Alice Cherville's good graces.

My dear Mr. Pinfrith,

*How happy I was to receive your letter though dis-
appointed to learn that I must wait another entire week
before furthering my acquaintance with you. Though I
am anxious to do so. I wish to assure you that a man's
business must always come first for it is in his occupa-
tions that he is able to insure his own place in the world
as well as the security of those who depend upon him.
With a firm so large as your own, I can well imagine*

the numerous clerks, sailors, and overseas enterprises who rely on your steadfast effort.

I also wish to address a matter which I know from the manner in which you wrote of it caused you much distress—your brother. On that score, I hasten to inform you that of late my opinions and sentiments where he is concerned have been undergoing a significant change for if you must know—and I believe you will be astounded to hear of it—your brother actually attended Lady Dassett's ball on Friday evening. Yes, I know. The entire beau monde *suffered a shock that night. However, I chanced to both converse with him as well as to enjoy a waltz with him. His general affability both surprised and pleased me and I believe it was from that hour that I began to see the finer qualities in him which you were so insistent upon in your most recent letter.*

You will also be happy to know that on Sunday he introduced me to your mother and may I say that I found her to be an extraordinary creature. She has a marvelously open disposition which quite set my entire family at ease. You and your brother must love her very much and I do look forward to knowing her better.

The next portion of the letter described in detail the events of the morning, in particular his handling of Mr. Smith and afterward his offer to hire Mr. Hicklade. Finally, she wrote:

I can even see in my mind's eye your amazement. In truth, I feel utterly chastened in my opinions of your brother. You were right to upbraid me as you did in your last letter and how happy I am to assure you even now that when you return you will find me well disposed to liking his lordship.

Yours, etcetera,
Alice Cherville

He refolded the letter and leaned it once more against the candlestick. He smiled happily. He had more than achieved his object and ironically, had done so, not by intention but by responding in a rather impulsive way to Mrs. Urchfont's advertisement in *The Times*. It had not been by design that he had hauled Mr. Smith from the drawing room or offered to hire an investigator to find Hugh or to take on an informal guardianship. He had responded spontaneously and was even in this moment enjoying the fruits of having done so—Alice Cherville was *disposed to like him*.

The very thought of it pleased him so much that for several minutes he actually pondered the notion of attending Mrs. Orcheston's ball tonight.

This of course he dismissed readily enough. He knew quite well that his recent attentions to Miss Cherville and her family would quickly give rise to every manner of speculation were he to suddenly dance attendance on her at another fete. He would not for the world provide food for fodder in that direction. Good God, the very thought of it made him shudder.

No, he may be exceedingly content that her sentiments were softening toward him, but he had no serious intentions where she was concerned. So much seemed to have changed over the past sennight that his original desire to punish her had become something entirely different, something of a wholly roguish and quite unworthy nature. His sole purpose of the moment was to take her in his arms and kiss her again. To that end he would patiently make himself of service to her as the occasion would arise and in doing so would wait for the proper time to once more assault her lips.

Still, a terrific sense of triumph clung to him as he dressed for dinner, which he intended to enjoy in the sanctity of White's. Before he left, however, he wrote a brief note to Mrs. Orcheston and sent it directly by way of his footman.

Much to Alice's relief, Lord Bradenstoke had managed the business of the advertisement to perfection and upon her arrival at Mrs. Orcheston's town house had been greeted with the news that the earl had sent word to her to the effect that the advertisement had been the careless mistake of a novice at *The Times* for which there was no explanation. The *beau monde,* though skeptical, chose to make light of the entire incident.

Mrs. Urchfont's quakings and prophecies of doom, therefore, were laid to rest the moment Mrs. Orcheston cried, "Oh, my dear Mrs. Urchfont, what a great good laugh we all had when reading our *Times* this morning. I thought the advertisement the greatest joke in the world."

For herself, Alice's contentment at the ball began well enough but soon began to fade. For some reason, she kept looking at doorways and imagining a tall, broad-shouldered gentleman who would smile at her, cross the chamber to her, and engage her for the waltz. Alas, her vision would clear, the doorway would be empty, and she would glance about, wondering why the magic of the Season had seemed to have dimmed for her.

Four days passed in which Alice gradually came to accept that Lord Bradenstoke's appearance in Upper Brook Street the day of the unfortunate advertisement was unlikely to be repeated. That she had wished for his presence caught her entirely unawares except that she had enjoyed in his company a shared sense of the absurd which she did not generally find in the gentlemen of her acquaintance.

Her schedule reverted to normalcy though cloaked in the growing suspense of waiting each day for word from Mr. Hicklade. Now that a search for Hugh had begun, her brother's absence in London became of increasing concern to the entire family.

On Thursday evening, Alice traveled with Louisa, Freddie, and her aunt to Mrs. Fonthill's party at her mansion on the River Thames. At long last, Freddie and Mr. Dodds were to perform their vignette. The setting was unique and perfectly suited to the Barbary Coast theme of Mr. Dodds's epic poem, for Mrs. Fonthill had arranged for a large tent to be erected on the lawn nearest the river.

As the wheels of the Cherville barouche rolled across London Bridge, Alice glanced along the length of the river, and in the darkness below she could see a scattering of lights, for there were small boats navigating the waters at all times of the day and night. Already a smoke-laden fog was rising from the banks and she felt the river in such a state reflected her heart in an exceedingly precise manner.

Until this very moment she had not realized how low her spirits had actually sunk. Yet what disturbed her even more was the knowledge of why she felt downcast. She felt rather faint as she admitted to herself that somehow not having either seen or conversed with Bradenstoke for the past several days had caused her to feel quite blue-deviled. When had the earl become of even the smallest necessity to her contentment?

"Alice, is something troubling you?" Louisa asked. "For you have been sighing ever since we left Park Lane."

"Have I?" she returned, noncommitally.

"Indeed, you have," Freddie agreed. "At least half a dozen times."

"I suppose I had hoped to hear from Mr. Hicklade today." When her response caused Mrs. Urchfont's expression to grow pinched with worry, she added hastily, "Although I am still certain Hugh is perfectly well."

"Of course he is," Freddie stated, also glancing at Mrs. Urchfont.

"I for one," Louisa announced, "intend to box his ears when I see him. He has been selfish beyond permission!"

Both Alice and Freddie laughed, which finally gave relief to poor Mrs. Urchfont's features. Alice glanced at her sisters and knew that however much they might offer a joke now and then for the sake of their aunt, both Freddie and Louisa were concerned about Hugh's absence. Not less so Jane, who had decided to remain home with Nicky. No, there was not a one of them who felt entirely certain that Hugh had escaped some misfortune or other.

The performance of Mr. Dodds's vignette in which Freddie played an integral part was entirely informal in nature.

Mrs. Fonthill gathered everyone around and made a short but elegant introduction, after which Mr. Dodds began reciting a portion of his epic poem, entitled "The Bey of Algiers." Freddie, playing the role of an Englishwoman held ransom by the Bey, moved about a small makeshift stage, portraying in her mannerisms the general nature of the story.

There was something in the tenor of Mr. Dodds's voice and in the gentle yet purposeful rhythm of the words which held Alice's attention quite firmly. Freddie had been right, she was amazed. It would seem for all the unhappy parts of Mr. Dodds's temperament, to which she had become exceedingly well acquainted these past several weeks, she finally understood Freddie's adoration of her beau. Mr. Dodds was one of the most talented, affecting poets she had heard in a long, long time. Nor was she the only one to hold a similar opinion since the moment the vignette drew to a close, the entire audience, after a brief stunned hesitation, burst into a round of applause that fairly shook the canvas walls of the tent.

Mr. Quintin drew near. "I do not wonder she loves him."

"Good evening, Mr. Quintin," Alice said. "Indeed, her attachment to him makes complete sense when he is reciting his poetry, however, I would not despair. A woman may admire a handsome face, even great talent, but in the end she will choose steadiness of character."

She glanced at Mr. Quintin and saw him staring at Mr. Dodds and shaking his head grimly. "I fear I am not so sanguine as you," he said. "I have known a great many ladies who have married their Adonis when a dozen other 'steadier' characters were scattered about their feet."

Alice took his arm and gave it a gentle squeeze. "But I have the advantage of you, Mr. Quintin, for I have known Freddie these many years and more. She is not such a one, mark my words."

He smiled at that, if a trifle sadly. "I hope you may be right."

"I will tell you a secret," she whispered. Mr. Quintin eyed her curiously. "Last night at Drury Lane, Mr. Dodds paraded before the stage wearing a gold sash over a brilliant purple coat and at the end of the sash dangled a watch nearly as large as the clock on the mantel in my office. Freddie kept her expression impassive throughout his incredibly ridiculous display, but I knew she was entirely mortified. Worse still, he ignored her completely."

"Indeed?" Mr. Quintin responded enthusiastically. "Is this so?"

Alice nodded.

"What a Nodcock," he whispered.

"I could not agree more."

"You are a balm to my soul, Miss Cherville." With that, he moved away from her in the direction of the throng crowding about her sister and Mr. Dodds. She smiled, knowing quite well that it would not be long before the aspiring poet once more exposed those defects which she felt certain would in the end drive Freddie's affection for him straight from her heart.

She might have followed after Mr. Quintin with the purpose of reassuring him further but at that moment she turned to witness an astonishing sight—Lord Bradenstoke had apparently just arrived.

Alice flipped open her fan and began wafting it over her face, which for some reason had grown instantly flushed. She had not expected to see him tonight and yet here he was, dressed as elegantly as always in blacks and whites, and listening attentively to his hostess, who apparently could not cease thanking him for the honor his presence bestowed on her poor party.

Somewhere in the deepest part of Alice's mind, she knew she should move, seek out another group of people to join, or to even begin walking and appearing to be distracted by anything other than Bradenstoke, but she could not. She could only stand and stare and wait and hope, but for what precisely?

When he glanced at her, he smiled briefly, indicating his intention, and finally interrupted Mrs. Fonthill's rapturous compliments. What he said to her was received with another blush and a curtsy as he finally left her, after which that good lady was surrounded instantly by a dozen of her friends demanding to know how she had managed to entice the Earl of Bradenstoke to her fete.

Had Bradenstoke not been making his way directly to her, Alice might have enjoyed watching the bouncing group of ladies as they clucked, sighed, and exclaimed over Mrs. Fonthill's triumph. As it was, she could do little more than watch this man move toward her who had begun to consume not only her dreams but her waking thoughts as well.

"How do you do?" she began politely. "You have surprised me again. I only hope—" She got no further, for his expression had grown creased with anxiety and a dart of fear pierced her heart. "What is it?"

"I must speak with you at once," he said urgently. "I have had word from Hicklade."

Fourteen

News from Hicklade!

Alice should have been ecstatic, but the expression in Bradenstoke's eyes of the deepest concern forced her to lower her gaze. "You must tell me at once," she whispered, panic flooding her heart. "Is Hugh . . . dead?"

"On no account," he responded earnestly. He glanced about the tent. "I will tell you everything, but not here. Come, let us walk awhile."

She nodded and when he offered his arm, she took it quickly, for she was fairly trembling from head to foot.

Once strolling down the path which led to the river, he continued, "There was a bad business in Berkshire at a tavern called the Stump and Pelican just outside of the village of Theale. Apparently, your brother was attacked but by whom or for what purpose is as yet unknown. It is believed he was very badly wounded and left for dead in a ditch."

"In a ditch!" she cried.

"So it would seem."

"Then my aunt was not too far off the mark."

"I have thought the very same thing several times."

Several brightly burning flambeaux, jostled slightly by an erratic evening breeze, lit the path in darting patterns of light. "Where is he now?" she asked.

"Herein is the mystery. It is not clear what transpired or where your brother has gone."

"I do not understand."

"Mr. Cherville—Hugh—had been engaged in a card game at the tavern, but left sometime after midnight, at which hour he was apparently assaulted and left for dead. Around two o'clock, the publican of the tavern overheard one of his less sober customers speak of having seen a young gentleman in a ditch not far from the tavern, crying out for help."

Alice looked up at Bradenstoke, unable to credit what he had just said. "What?" she queried, incredulous. "A passerby chances upon an injured man in a ditch and does nothing to help but merely speaks casually of the event while sitting comfortably in a tavern?"

The earl hesitated. "The persons who frequent the Stump and Pelican are a rum sort, not to be relied on to behave like normal creatures. He was probably in his altitudes when he saw your brother. In such a state, it would not have occurred to him to extend his assistance to Hugh.

"The publican, however, went with lantern in hand to the location described to him by his customer, but your brother was gone, save for carriage marks in damp earth and this." He withdrew what Alice saw immediately was Hugh's watch, for she had purchased it for him several years past and had it inscribed. "No one in the vicinity of Theale has seen him since."

Alice felt her heart grow very cold. "This is too horrible!" she cried, taking the watch and pressing it to her breast. "Who would do such a thing and yet leave his watch?" For some reason at that moment the horror of the situation descended on her. "My poor Hugh," she cried, coming to a stop as tears suddenly spilled from her eyes. She withdrew her arm from his in order to wipe her cheeks with her gloved fingers. He quickly offered her the use of his kerchief, which she accepted gratefully. "And I thought he was merely being selfish as he is wont to be."

"Miss Cherville—"

"Oh, pray, please call me Alice," she said, attempting but failing to restrain her tears. "Given the circumstances, I need to feel we are friends, at the very least."

"Alice, then," he said softly, "try not to distress yourself too much. From everything I have heard, your brother is a strong lad, and he will have survived the attack."

She nodded, her lips quivering.

"Alice," he murmured gently.

She wiped at a fresh fall of tears and at the same moment felt his arm slip about her shoulders. He drew her close, which was her undoing. She turned to bury her face into his coat and with the kerchief pressed to her lips, wept freely. He stroked her arms and her back gently and never once told her to stop, for which she was profoundly grateful.

After a long moment, he said, "I beg you will not despair. I am convinced he is perfectly well."

Alice began composing herself. She had numerous questions yet to ask, but beyond that at some point she would have to tell her family what had happened. She would be of little use to any of them if she could not control her own tears. "If he has since recovered from these injuries, why have I not heard from him?" She blew her nose and wiped her cheeks again.

"He may have reasons for not having written to you or sent for you. Regardless, Hicklade is presently making inquiries in an increasingly wide pattern of search for a physician who tended to your brother."

"A logical progression," she murmured. She drew in a deep breath and glanced up at him. "I did not mean to become a watering pot and for that I apologize. It is just that you have given me a shock and you must remember that for days now my entire family and I have been in a state of suspense though we try very hard to keep a brave face."

"Walk a little more, Alice. You will feel better in a moment." Once more she took his arm and allowed him to guide her toward the river. He continued. "Hicklade was most encouraging. From what he has gleaned in his investigation, scarcely an hour would have passed from the time your brother was wounded until he was taken up in a carriage."

"What if the person or persons desirous of hurting my brother came back to harm him further?"

"Unlikely. A description of the wheel marks indicate an

elegant conveyance, hardly the equipage of someone intent on such a crime."

"Robbery, you mean?" Mrs. Fonthill's property was edged by a tall stone wall and broken only by a pair of wrought-iron gates which led to a small dock. Bradenstoke opened one of the gates for her and began leading her down a path that marched along the riverbank.

Alice looked up at him and saw the hesitation again in his eyes and in his manner. "What is it?" she queried. The air was chilled and she drew close to him. "Tell me," she whispered. "I promise I shall do better. I wish to know everything."

"Hicklade seems to think it was not a robbery at all, if for no other reason than that his watch was left behind."

Alice shook her head. "Then what was it? You cannot mean, you cannot be saying that you believe someone desired to hurt my brother, perhaps even to take his life?"

"It is a possibility."

"I must disagree," she responded emphatically. "I wish you were acquainted with Hugh for then you would comprehend how impossible it is that anyone would desire his death. My brother is the sort of fellow who is always laughing and joking. He is not in possession of a temper. If anything, he is far too biddable at times."

"There could be another reason. Is he not a wealthy man?"

Alice shook her head. "I would not account him such. Tilsford Hall gives him a comfortable living, but you must know that most of the rent rolls return to the property to sustain it, in repairs, in supporting the staff and retainers, the home garden, orchards, and farm."

"Is there a great deal of attached land, wooded land, per chance?"

"Yes," she remarked. "However—"

Lord Bradenstoke lifted a hand. "You are thinking as a responsible owner might think," he said gently. "However, I have had a great deal of experience with the practical worth of an estate especially if there are woods to be cut down and sold for lumber, and if there is land to sell."

Alice sighed. A growing fog crept from the river over parts of the path. "I believe I can see the direction of your thoughts but who would be capable of stealing Hugh's estate? Even if he had not survived the attack, Nicky is next in line to inherit and after him a cousin in Wales. So you see, an assault for the purpose of gaining control of the land makes no sense."

"What do you know of your cousin in Wales?"

"He is an older gentleman afflicted with rheumatic complaints. Hugh has been on the friendliest of terms with him and had received word from his solicitor just before leaving Wiltshire. I cannot say what the nature of his correspondence might have been, however. My last argument with Hugh was over the necessity of him answering estate-related letters more promptly than he was wont to." She stopped once more, and looked up at him. His face was lit only by moonlight and for a moment he seemed familiar to her in a way she could not quite explain. "Lord Bradenstoke, I wish to thank you for—"

Here he stopped her. "Will you do me the honor of calling me, as my friends do, Braden? For some reason, it seems the height of absurdity to hear you address me as you just have."

Alice regarded him thoughtfully. "I believe you are very right. Braden, then. I wish to thank you so very much for having hired Mr. Hicklade. Indeed, for having suggested the hiring of him in the first place. I feel wretched in not having pursued the matter sooner."

He lifted a hand to her face and gently pushed an errant curl from off her cheek.

The fragrance of his skin drifted over her, a redolence of leather and very fine soap.

"What is it?" she asked, for he had grown very quiet.

He shook his head and smiled faintly. "Nothing to signify," he murmured, "except that I love looking at you. Why are you not married with babes of your own?"

In any other setting such a question might have seemed either impertinent or indelicate, but slipping from Braden's lips, to which her gaze was now attached, she could only smile. "I suppose I am overly particular," she returned on a whisper.

"I am glad of it."

He leaned the short space between them and gently placed his lips on hers. Alice closed her eyes, uncertain why he was kissing her or whether there was even the smallest amount of wisdom in allowing him to do so. Yet the moment seemed oddly perfect.

All her fears and tensions about her brother's fate disappeared in the soft drift of his lips over hers. Had she truly kissed him before? How many days ago was it she had fenced with him and he had taken her so boldly in his arms? So much had changed, wonderfully so, and how much she had been longing to kiss him again.

The touch of his tongue prompted her to part her lips. She felt his hand glide gently over her neck as he plumbed the depths of her mouth. The next moment, he was kissing her deeply in a manner that removed any desire she might have been feeling to protest the kiss.

"Braden," she whispered, between assaults.

He circled her waist with his arm and drew her close. "I have been wanting to kiss you forever," he breathed against her lips.

"And I you," she whispered.

He kissed her roughly, his tongue dipping deeply once more so that she felt connected to him in a manner that was as mysterious as it was profound. The river, the path, the mansion all seemed to disappear and in their stead was a cloud upon which she floated, the earth but a faint memory. There were no troubles in this heavenly bliss to which Braden had transported her with a mere touch of his lips and of his tongue. Whatever animosity had raged between them had vanished days ago and in its stead was an inexplicable bond as firm as an aged, hardened wood.

He kissed her again and again.

Braden did not know how it had come about that he had finally surrendered to the desire that had been building in him for days to take Alice Cherville in his arms anew and slay her with a hundred soft, possessive kisses. She had in no manner disappointed him with the dovelike coos and moans that issued from her throat and of which he believed she was entirely unaware. Her fingers plucked at the hair just above the nape of his neck and occasionally slid through his locks until he felt he would go mad with wanting more of her. His years had not been innocent and for many of them he had lived a rogue's life so that he knew merely by kissing a woman what it would be like to take her to bed. Never had he known such a delightful response in a lady. She had not even murmured the smallest protest.

"Braden," she murmured again with a sweet smile. She seemed to like saying his name. He smiled in response and once more lowered his lips to hers. She touched his face with the tips of her gloved fingers.

When he opened his eyes, he found her gaze had grown serious and strong. He disappeared into the thoughts that beckoned him forward. He embraced her more fully, an arm about her waist and the other about her shoulders. He drew her so tightly against him that he could feel her legs and hips locked against his. She in turn enveloped him in her arms. She stroked the back of his neck and moaned his name softly against his lips.

Again he kissed her deeply, once more possessing her mouth. The arms about his neck tightened in response. Was he truly kissing Alice Cherville? Had he indeed achieved the object of his desire for the past sennight? Where was the sense of triumph? Why, instead, was his mind flooded with visions of chasing her through his ancestral home, of hearing her laughter ring through his halls, of catching her and carrying her to his bed, where he would delight in making her his true wife.

She drew back, a tear trickling down her cheek. "We should return to the fete," she whispered, stroking his face gently with her hand. "Oh, Braden, I am so very grateful to you. Thank you so much for everything you have done."

Her gratitude began clawing at something inside his chest. He kissed her again. Why had he begun to hurt?

She pushed him away slightly. "What is it?" she asked. "I can feel that you are overset. Have I offended you somehow?"

He released her, catching her hands up in his.

"This was madness," he whispered.

"The very best sort of madness," she countered. "Braden, I hope you do not mean to begin apologizing to me."

"I should not have kissed you," he said, willing her to read his thoughts. "Indeed, you cannot know how much I regret having done so."

"I have no such regrets," she responded, laughing. "Why on earth would you?"

How beautiful she was with moonlight shining in her eyes. "Not even one?" he queried.

She shook her head and smiled. "I enjoyed kissing you and it may come as a shock, but I did not suppose next to receive an offer of marriage. Do but think, Braden. I had learned my brother was badly injured and even now might still be in some danger if he has not recovered sufficiently from his wounds. What better or more soothing balm than to have the comfort and even thrill of being kissed by a man I admire? Perhaps it is I who should be apologizing to you for having taken such grievous advantage of you."

Braden wished she had not spoken so forthrightly to him about her feelings, for he could only think one thing, just how long it would be before he could kiss her again. Good God, did she indeed *admire* him?

"I shall try to restrain myself in future." He straightened his shoulders and once more offered his arm to her.

"I am glad to hear it," she responded teasingly, accepting the support of his arm again.

"I am most serious," he said sternly, guiding her back up the path.

"I can see that you are."

He scowled at her. "And you refuse to acknowledge that what I did was reprehensible."

She chuckled. "It was quite reprehensible but no less so than my own conduct. Besides, I have something of far greater import to fret over than whether or not you should have kissed me."

At that he sighed. "I suppose you do."

He had never felt so at sea as he did when he was with Alice. He did not seem to know what he wanted from her. One moment he was cruel and provoking, in another offering his assistance to her, and in another taking her roughly into his arms. In all other aspects of his existence, in society, in Parliament, in his shipping firm, in the business attached to his estate, even with most of the ladies of his acquaintance, he was as surefooted as a cat walking atop a narrow wall. However, in his dealings with Alice Cherville, it was as though with each new encounter he found himself in uncharted waters.

The worst of it was that kissing her seemed to be the most natural occurrence in the world, which, he supposed, was why his comings and goings with her were so complicated. He was never around her, even when she was squabbling with him, that he was not desirous of kissing her perfect lips or dragging her so tightly against him that he could not tell where he ended and she began.

He breathed deeply. That was the rub, he supposed. He knew damned well his intentions toward her had nothing in the least to do with matrimony and yet every other thought about her was lascivious in the extreme. He must do better, he promised himself, to restrain these impulses which would only serve one day to cause Alice a great deal of pain.

Alice glanced at Braden and thought he had never before appeared so somber. His remorse at having kissed her was entirely unlooked-for. She did not believe he saw her as a naive schoolroom miss, so she could only suppose that his present distress reflected more nearly his fear as to what her expectations of him might be. That, however, she felt was his problem to solve and not her own.

Of course she had enjoyed kissing him, but not for a moment did she think anything of merit would come of it. After all, she understood quite clearly the disparity in rank which separated her from the Earl of Bradenstoke, even if she was a gentlewoman. His choice of bride would come from more exalted ranks than her own. Besides, she was not particularly interested in Braden as a future spouse. He was not, in her opinion, the most reliable of men, nor the most generous, although she had been agreeably pleased by his involvement in her affairs since the morning she had awakened to find that her aunt had advertised for a husband for her. Since that time, he had been a wonderful support, but to what purpose, unless—and here she laughed, for she thought it would be so very much like a man!—unless he had been doing so merely to catch her in a weak moment that he might kiss her!

She felt she understood him in that instant and turned toward him sharply just outside the gates of Mrs. Fonthill's mansion. "You have done all this just so you might kiss me!" she cried, laughing.

"What?" he responded, startled.

She laughed anew. "Do not protest, Braden, for I can see in your expression that I have hit the mark exactly."

He opened the gate for her once more. "I am not proud of it," he confessed. "And dash it all, Alice, must you be forthright about everything?"

She began to laugh and could not stop. "Oh, how you amuse me! And it is so like a man! And yet . . . and yet, you have been wonderful in your support of me where my brother is concerned." She laughed so hard that tears began to pour from her eyes and every time she would look at Braden and see his bewildered yet guilty expression, she could only laugh harder still.

When something of her amusement had passed, he asked, "You are not in the least offended?"

"No," she responded. "I am flattered, deeply so, for if you have not noticed, this was an extraordinary amount of trouble over a mere kiss."

"So it was," he responded, smiling.

She looked into warm brown eyes that had once more

grown serious and speculative. "Do all men pursue kisses in such a manner?" she asked.

"I was never used to," he replied, "but then, generally the ladies were more accessible, even more willing than yourself."

"I daresay none of them would have called you terrible things as I did and then dared to cross swords with you."

He shook his head. "No, they would not have. Only you, Alice Cherville. Only you. My next question, however, has little to do with kissing you—how do you mean to tell your family of Hugh?"

"Not here, that much is certain. After the fete, once we are at home." She then frowned.

"What is it?"

"I am filled suddenly with dread. Though I believe my sisters and even Nicky will manage the news with at least some fortitude—however, my aunt . . . !"

"Would you allow me, then, to stand with you while you inform them of Hicklade's discoveries? I should be happy to do what I can to allay a complete descent into hysteria."

There was something so absurd in the way he spoke of it that caused Alice to smile. "And my aunt is given to *descending* swiftly upon occasion, you can have no notion. I therefore do most humbly accept of your offer." She was silent apace and then added, "You continually amaze me, you know, or perhaps you are not aware that you could not have offered a greater kindness to me at this moment."

His smile grew crooked. "Someone must be there to catch Mrs. Urchfont when she drops into a faint."

Alice chuckled, taking up his arm yet again. She was perfectly composed when she reentered the tent, which was at the moment full of guests going down a lively reel.

She was soon parted from Braden, he to dance with Louisa and she with Mr. Trickett. From the makeshift stage, Mrs. Fonthill beamed at the sight of his lordship doing the pretty with another of the Cherville ladies.

Fifteen

When the party finally returned to Upper Brook Street, Louisa descended the coach first. Glancing up the street, she queried, "Why has Lord Bradenstoke followed us home?"

Alice took a deep breath. "He has word of Hugh," she said, as cheerfully as she could, leading the way into the entrance hall.

"Did he fall into a ditch as I thought he would?" Mrs. Urchfont asked.

Alice glanced at her but quickly looked away. At the same moment, both Louisa and Frederica exclaimed their desire to know immediately what Mr. Hicklade had learned, but Alice shook her head. "I will not say a word until Jane and Nicky are present. Will you fetch them? Yes, I know Nicky will be sound asleep and Jane as well, but I want them present when I share the news. Would you bring them to the drawing room, please?"

Freddie glanced at Braden, who had followed them into the house. "Of course." Her expression was wholly serious as she mounted the stairs.

Mrs. Urchfont cried. "He is dead! I can see by your face, Alice, Hugh is dead!"

Lord Bradenstoke took the elderly woman by the arm. "Would your niece have danced for hours on end were this true?"

"Oh! I see what you are about! Of course not!"

"Then, come, let me escort you upstairs."

A few minutes later, Jane was seated on the sofa beside Nicky, both sleepy-eyed and wearing their nightclothes. Louisa stood behind Mrs. Urchfont who in turn sat on the chaise longue along with Freddie. Alice related what she knew of Mr. Hicklade's investigation at Theale.

A terrible silence ensued. Not surprisingly, it was Mrs. Urchfont who shattered the stillness of the air. "I told you he would fall into a ditch!" she wailed, and then began to cry.

"He did not fall," Louisa said, staring down at her aunt with a shocked expression. "He was put there by . . . by murderers and thieves!" Her face crumpled and she, too, fell to weeping as did both Jane and Freddie.

"He is dead! He is dead!" Mrs. Urchfont cried. "I know he is dead."

"Hugh is dead?" Nicky whispered, wild-eyed.

Alice went to him at once. "No, darling," she said, attempting to reassure him. How could he believe her, though, when Mrs. Urchfont had taken to wailing so loudly that the entire chamber all but reverberated with the noise she was making and when so many handkerchiefs fluttered over tear-stained faces? She did not know what to do, for in truth she could barely restrain her own tears.

She tried again. "I promise you, Nicky, he is not dead. Merely . . . merely injured. It is believed he was taken up by very good people and transported to some unknown place to recover."

"Then why is everyone crying?" he asked, his own mouth turning down ominously.

Braden moved away from Alice and poured out a glass of sherry, which he took immediately to her aunt. "Cease your ridiculous wailing, Mrs. Urchfont, and drink this, on the instant! You sound like a calf bleating after its mother!"

His voice settled over the room like a thick counterpane, dampening even the younger ladies' sobs. Alice noted that everyone stared at him and that the kerchiefs were soon put to better use as Jane, Louisa, and Freddie each blew their noses in turn.

Mrs. Urchfont, not used to being addressed in such a manner, drew in a sharp breath and stared up at Braden as though he had just struck her across the cheek.

"Drink this now!" he commanded her again.

With a surprisingly steady hand, Mrs. Urchfont took the small glass of sherry and swallowed the whole of it without so much as a blink of her eye. She coughed afterward, but her tears had ceased and the only sound that emanated from her was a soft sigh.

"And now," he said, leaning over her, "let us have no more of your nonsense for you are frightening even me." Then he smiled.

Mrs. Urchfont nodded.

"Another?" he queried, taking the small glass from her.

"Yes, if you please," she said in a small voice.

He crossed the room once more, refilled the glass, and returned to her.

Alice knew her mouth was agape but she could not seem to close it. A smile teased at her lips. She glanced at her sisters in turn, each of whom appeared nearly as astonished as she felt. She could not help but chuckle softly.

Louisa approached her, wiping away the last of her tears. "I have never seen Mrs. Urchfont grow so quiet so quickly," she whispered. "I vow Lord Bradenstoke is capable of performing miracles. Is he a saint?"

Alice thought back to the manner in which he had kissed her at the riverbank and shook her head. "No, he is but a mere mortal, I assure you."

"Well, at this moment I find I am utterly grateful to him."

"As am I."

Even Nicky was watching him in some amazement.

Braden had taken hold of Mrs. Urchfont's hand and was speaking in a low voice to her. She was nodding her head in response, staring up at him, and sipping her sherry. When Braden finished, Mrs. Urchfont rose to her feet, supported by the earl.

"I apologize, children," she said, a smile wavering on her lips. "Lord Bradenstoke has made everything clear to me.

Mr. Hicklade is even now searching out the doctor who undoubtedly tended to our dear Hugh." She patted Braden's hand. "And our dear Bradenstoke is sending a courier to him on the morrow so we should have word of Hugh before Nicky's birthday. Until then, we must be strong, each of us. We must say our prayers and believe that very soon Hugh will be returned to us."

"Admirably spoken," Braden murmured, nodding firmly to the lady beside him.

She smiled up at him, if tremulously. "I think I should like another sherry. Would you be so kind?"

"Of course."

He assisted her in resuming the chaise longue upon which she had been reclining.

Alice watched her usually fainthearted aunt rest quietly and only once in a while dab at an occasional tear that escaped her eye. She could not help but marvel at Braden's skill and wisdom in managing so well a woman who took delight in her hysterics.

Nicky approached Braden shyly. "I was wondering, my lord," he began.

"Yes, Nicky?" he inquired gently.

"Well, would you like to come to my birthday party on Sunday?"

Alice was a little taken aback by the request and glanced at Braden. She could not imagine what his answer would be.

"It is your birthday then?"

"Yes. I am to be eleven and Hugh was supposed to give me my first fencing lesson."

"Fencing lesson?" Braden inquired, glancing at Alice.

She explained that from the time Nicky was young and had watched his siblings fence he had been begging to learn the art himself. Hugh had told him that he must wait until he was eleven and had further promised that the lessons could begin precisely on his birthday, which would be Sunday.

"I see," Braden responded, smiling sympathetically at Nicky. "So your brother fences?"

"He is almost as good as Alice," Nicky cried.

"I have actually seen your sister fence so I must say I am greatly impressed with your brother's abilities if he even approaches a particle of her skill."

"He does!" Nicky assured him fervently.

Braden nodded. "I should be happy to attend your party."

A half hour later, with a sensible, calm spirit established in the family, Alice accompanied Braden downstairs to the door. "Thank you so very much," she said sincerely. "You must know that you have spared us a great deal of misery not just tonight but for several days to follow in dealing with my aunt as you have."

"You are quite welcome," he said. He appeared as though he wished to say more but in his hesitation decided against it. "I shall send word to you the moment I hear from Hicklade."

"Thank you," she said.

When she closed the door, she hurried up the stairs and moved to the window by which Nicky was standing. Together, they watched his coach depart, a light rain tapping at the windows.

"He should live with us," her brother whispered, awestruck. "If he could make Aunt stop crying, he could do anything!"

Alice chuckled. "I believe you may be right."

Late Friday afternoon, Sir Benedict entered Alice's office, bearing a gift for Nicky.

"I am so sorry," he said, "but business demands that I be absent from London for the weekend. Make my apologies to Nicky?"

"Of course," Alice said, smiling at her dear friend.

"However, I shall be attending Mrs. Swainswick's ball on Monday night. I hope you will save a dance for me?"

"With pleasure," she responded happily. "Will you not sit with me for a few minutes? As it happens, there is something I feel you should know."

"This sounds quite serious," he said, taking up a seat near the fireplace.

"It is."

She carefully recounted all that Hicklade had learned of Hugh's disappearance as well as the investigator's present efforts.

"I must say, Alice, this is the strangest tale I have ever heard! So unexpected, so horrifying. You must be utterly devastated not less so than because we all believed he was merely being selfish in not coming to London in the first place."

"You have spoken my sentiments exactly."

"And there truly was no indication as to where he might have gone?"

"Not in the least." Alice thought Sir Benedict was more mystified than any of her siblings had been.

"I only wish there were something I could do," he murmured, looking away from her.

"Mr. Hicklade is doing all that can be done at present. Braden, that is, Lord Bradenstoke, has complete confidence in his abilities."

"Very well, then," he said quietly. "I can see that I leave you in excellent hands."

"Do not frown so, Sir Benedict. I feel in my heart that all will be well."

"Of course you are right," he said, smiling tenderly. He rose and after once more extending his heartfelt sympathy for the dreadful situation, took his leave.

Sixteen

On Sunday evening, with nearly all the guests arrived for Nicky's party, Alice watched Louisa leave her post by the doorway and join Freddie, who was conversing with both Mr. Quintin and Mr. Trickett.

Lord Tamerbeck still had not come.

He habitually kept Louisa on tenterhooks, flirting with her in a most attentive manner one day, then ignoring her the next. Tonight, however, Alice thought it entirely possible that the viscount was wholly unaware of the critical nature of his appearance at so important an occasion. In her opinion, knowing her sister as well as she did, the viscount risked losing Louisa forever.

Louisa, on the other hand, was not the only Cherville lady having troubles with her beau. Freddie's circumstances with Mr. Dodds were hardly less onerous. Earlier, he had sent her a brief missive indicating that he was absenting himself from the party because he did not approve of birthday celebrations in general. Freddie had subsequently shared the contents of the absurd missive with everyone assembled but afterward excused herself for several minutes for the purpose, Alice thought, of regaining her composure. When she returned, she wore a smile and devoted her attentions to Nicky and to the entertainment of their guests. At odd moments, however, Alice would catch her sister staring at nothing in particular, her expression inutterably woeful.

Alice knew what Mr. Dodds clearly did not—it would be

a very long time, if ever, that he would be forgiven for this ridiculous if inadvertent insult to Freddie and her family.

Alice drifted to the fireplace, where Jane and Nicky chatted about their recent excursion to the Thames docks. Braden's partner, Mr. Frisk, showed them their latest acquisition, a very fine East Indiaman which was presently being made ready for the open sea. Jane had taken her aside upon their return and said she thought it most odd that not once had Mr. Frisk mentioned Mr. Pinfrith's recent arrival in England. Alice thought it odder still that not once in the past several days had she thought of Mr. Pinfrith.

She had been shocked, retiring to her bedchamber where she took pen in hand and scribbled a letter quickly on a piece of fine vellum. She felt she had been remiss in not writing to him again even though she had as yet received a reply to her last letter. Undoubtedly, his affairs in Portsmouth were keeping him much occupied 'else she would certainly have heard from him by now. If there was something frantic in her actions, in her haste, she refused to dwell on it overly much. So she had kissed Braden. Certainly she would not be kissing him again and there was absolutely no need to inform Mr. Pinfrith of it.

She did however think it wise to tell him of his brother's kind involvement in having hired Mr. Hicklade and of the initial results of the investigation. She asked after his health, his business, and completed her letter with a hope that he would be returning to London very soon, for she was looking forward to finally meeting him, without his mask.

She felt greatly relieved while sanding and sealing her letter. She would give the missive to Braden this evening to include with his various correspondence, which she was assured was sent daily to Portsmouth.

Braden joined her by the fireplace. "Is Miss Louisa waiting for Tam?" he inquired softly, casting his gaze briefly at Louisa, who was looking a trifle pale as she conversed with Mr. Trickett.

"Yes, but it is hopeless, I fear," she responded quietly.

"Is she greatly smitten?"

"I do not know," she responded.

Braden frowned slightly. "I know this may sound odd, but I have just come to realize that your sister, Miss Louisa, is very young. She cannot be twenty."

"Scarcely eighteen."

He started. "Indeed? Is this possible for she behaves with a fine degree of poise rarely seen in a lady her age?"

"For that reason, I believe she ought to be allowed a little of youth's follies."

He smiled rather thoughtfully. "When did you ever have need of a guardian for this family? From all that I have observed, you manage everything and everyone with remarkable skill and care."

She could only laugh.

Of all the expressions that Braden had seen cross Alice's face, he thought her smile the most beautiful. She was so very lovely, no less so this evening with her hair caught up into a tumble of curls atop her head. Her locks were laced with small daisies reflected in the embroidery on her muslin gown. As always, there was an elegance in her style of dress and in her demeanor that pleased him so very much.

"But what of you?" he inquired. "You do not seem much inclined to folly or do you merely conduct your follies with inordinate discretion?"

She glanced meaningfully toward Jane and Nicky. "Would you care for a glass of champagne?"

He took up her hints readily. "I should be delighted."

She led him across the room to a table near the window where the champagne rested along with several glasses. Once out of Nicky's hearing, she gave him a gentle, discreet nudge. "How could you have asked me such a question with both my sister and my youngest brother so nearby?" She poured two glasses of the champagne and handed one to him.

Braden glanced back at them. "I was not thinking," he responded with a smile. "But now that we can discuss the matter in private, do you mean to tell me of your follies?"

"Well, one comes readily to mind," she responded archly.

"On Thursday evening, if you please, when I permitted you to kiss me, or have you forgotten?"

"Do you consider my having kissed you a folly?" he inquired, his lips twitching.

"Very much so, you ridiculous man." She had the pleasure of seeing him laugh outright.

"Any other follies?" he queried.

"Kissing your brother. I should never have done so and I must say—" She broke off. "Are you all right?"

He had choked on his champagne.

"Yes, yes," he said, clearing his throat and coughing several times. "It is just that—I had forgotten you had also kissed William." In truth it was his own absurd masquerade he had forgotten. Apparently, however, she had not. He looked away from her and for the oddest moment he felt jealous of the phantom he had created.

He took a deep breath and once more sipped his champagne.

"As it happens," she continued quietly, "I have a letter for Mr. Pinfrith. I was hoping you would give it to your courier."

"Of course." He took the missive and quickly slipped it into the pocket of his coat. "But enough of my brother, we were having the most delightful discussion of your follies until you brought forward his name. So, do you generally consider kissing a folly?"

"Only when it involves a pair of brothers," she responded teasingly.

He shook his head and laughed anew. "Other than kissing brothers, is there nothing more?"

She leaned close to him and whispered, "I will confess something to you that no one else knows—I nearly ran away with a Gypsy caravan when I was eight. They had come to summer in our northern pasture and I had made friends with a young Gypsy girl. I adored her and the kindnesses of her family. Do not stare at me in that manner! I was bewitched by the life they led, traveling everywhere."

"You almost became a Gypsy, eh? Is there anything else you would add?"

She narrowed her eyes. "Challenging you to a fencing match was a terrible folly, particularly when even a simpleton could see I had not the smallest chance of trouncing you."

"On no account will I allow you to consider our fencing match in such harsh terms."

"I invaded your house, insulted you, and then fairly challenged you to a duel. You do not consider these things to be full of folly?"

"The kiss I took from you eradicated any such unfortunate stigma on your part. My folly erased yours."

"You frightened me that day, you know," she said, a teasing smile on her lips. "You were very wrong to have stolen such a kiss from me."

He smiled wickedly. "I will let you take it back, if you like?"

She gasped playfully. "What a scandalous thing to say!"

At that moment Nicky called to her from across the chamber, requesting to open his presents. Alice glanced at Louisa, and lifting an inquiring brow at her, she watched as her sister shrugged in a rather hopeless manner. Clearly, Tamerbeck did not mean to attend this evening.

Alice gathered the family around Nicky and one by one his gifts were unwrapped. He received a fine leather riding quirt from Mr. Trickett, a pair of York tan gloves from Mr. Quintin, a set of handkerchiefs which Freddie had embroidered in her perfect stitches with his monogram, a slingshot from Mrs. Urchfont, a book of proverbs from Louisa, a watercolor of his favorite hunting dog from Jane, and from Alice, which was brought out by a footman at her command, a hobbyhorse.

Nicky fairly shouted with delight. "Just like Peter's!"

The recent invention was attracting all manner of notice. It was designed with handlebars, two wheels in line, and a seat slung in between so that with a little practice, a fellow, by using his feet, could speed along the streets. He was so excited he fairly ran in circles.

"I shall take it out now!" he cried. "Oh, thank you, Alice!" He bowed to her hastily then took the hobbyhorse by the handles.

Alice stopped him in the process of turning the machine around. "I know you are excited, but we have not had our cake yet nor have you opened Lord Bradenstoke's present."

He was immediately reproved and stood upright. "I beg your pardon," he said, bowing to Braden.

"Perfectly understandable. I only hope you will like my gift half as much as Alice's."

"I am certain I shall," he stated diplomatically.

He moved to a large package on the hearth, untied the ribbons, and pushed the paper aside. A long, beautiful wooden box came into view. Alice was astonished, for she knew at once what was within. She turned to stare at Braden, who was standing beside her. "Again, you have surprised me," she whispered.

Nicky opened the lid. "Fencing foils!" he exclaimed.

"Yes, do you like them?" Braden asked. "But perhaps more to the point, do you think Hugh would approve of them?"

Alice moved to stand next to Nicky. The case itself was of a beautiful mahogany and the swords were of the finest oriental quality with neatly turned hilts.

"You will find them light and nicely balanced," Braden added.

Nicky removed one of them, completely in awe. "If only Hugh were here," he said.

Braden clapped him on the shoulder. "I have another present for you. Perhaps I should not have saved this one until so late in the evening, but, here goes—I had further word from Hicklade."

Nicky lifted wide blue eyes to stare at him. "You did? You have news of Hugh?"

"Indeed, I do," he responded, smiling. "Hicklade found the doctor who treated your brother." A general squealing arose from the ladies. "It would seem that a family, by the name of Merrymeet, took Hugh up in their carriage and conveyed him to Four Mile Cross, where he was attended by a certain Dr. Deane who resides there. The doctor said that though the young man had obviously suffered greatly, his wounds were not severe enough to have threatened his life."

"So, he is all right?" Nicky asked.

"The doctor saw no reason why he would not be."

"This is famous news!" he exclaimed. "Thank you ever so much!"

"What happened to our dear Hugh afterward?" Mrs. Urchfont queried. "Is he yet residing with Dr. Deane?"

"No, the good doctor could not tend to him and so the family took him along with them, to Sussex, or so the doctor thinks. He foolishly did not ask for their direction and in the difficulties of the moment a need for such information was not at the forefront of his thinking. He was abject in his apologies but felt the young gentleman was in excellent hands."

Alice interjected. "Hugh did not ask after his family?"

Braden shook his head. "He had difficulty speaking and any mention of sending for his family seemed to cause him so much distress that it was the doctor's opinion that the subject should be let drop until the patient was calmer."

Alice did not pursue the matter further, but it disturbed her greatly that in the six weeks that had passed since the attack, Hugh still had not contacted his family.

"But he is well?" Louisa asked again, wringing her hands. "Does this Dr. Deane truly believe he will recover?"

"The good doctor spoke of Hugh as a strapping lad who would undoubtedly live a great many years to come." Alice glanced at Nicky, who had grown very solemn and even now was returning both swords to the box.

"Nicky," Braden said quietly, "I know that your brother was supposed to begin your fencing lessons today, but do you think he would be offended if I performed that office for him since he cannot be here himself?"

Alice was absolutely stunned by the exceeding kindness of both the suggestion as well as the manner in which Braden presented the idea to Nicky. Tears brimmed in her eyes and even Louisa came and slipped an arm about her waist.

Jane moved to stand beside Nicky. "What a kind offer," she said, meeting his gaze. "I think Hugh would approve vastly of such a notion, do you not think so?"

Nicholas appeared uncertain.

Louisa stepped forward. "Hugh would want this for you, my darling."

Freddie approached the wood box and promptly retrieved both swords, handing one to Braden and one to Nicky. "I know my brother!" she cried emphatically. "He would be the first to cry out a rousing yes! Have I the right of it, Nicky? Would not Hugh do so?"

Nicky smiled and nodded several times in quick succession. "Yes, he would," he said. "For Hugh hates put-offs more than anything."

Since this was an absolute truth about their brother, who was well known for his impatience, the sisters all laughed as one.

"He does, indeed," Alice said. "And now, Mr. Trickett, Mr. Quintin, will you not help us push some of the furniture out of the way? A good fencing lesson requires a proper amount of space!"

Alice stood to the side of the room along with the rest of the family and guests and watched as Braden made Nicky's birthday wish come true. Never in her entire existence would she have believed that the very man who had so steadfastly refused the guardianship of her family would be the very person to have touched Nicky's heart in precisely the right manner on his birthday. She felt as though her own heart were being pummeled into an entirely different shape as she marveled at Braden, at the man he truly was, in strong contrast to the selfish creature she had believed him to be. She had never been more proud of him, nor more admiring than at this moment.

Later, after a delicious lemon cake had been devoured by the assembled guests, and the hobbyhorse tested under Mr. Trickett's steady eye at the top of Upper Brook Street, Alice bid goodbye to their guests. She thanked Braden warmly. "I will never forget this kindness," she whispered at a moment when everyone else was engaged in congratulating Nicky on having reached the advanced age of eleven. She took the opportunity to place a kiss on his cheek. "You live as a man at a masquerade," she added with a smile.

He seemed disturbed by this comment. "Whatever do you mean?"

"Only that you pretend an indifference to the world in general which it seems obvious to me you do not feel."

Alice swiped at a tear which tumbled down her cheek.

His expression grew rather serious and he took her hands in his. "There is something I should like you to know," he began. "Something I should have told you before now."

"Braden," Trickett intruded, addressing him from the doorway, "I am to go to my sister's home and she lives in Park Lane. Can you take Quinney up in your coach?"

"Yes, of course," he returned. Mr. Trickett noted that Braden was holding her hands, which caused the earl to gently release them.

"Alice," Nicky called to her, "may I take the hobbyhorse one more time up the street?"

"On no account, dearest," she responded. "The hour is far too advanced." He pouted a trifle, but nothing to signify as Alice chuckled and then reverted her attention to the earl. "What were you saying?"

He shook his head. "Another time will do. There is too much of a crowd this evening."

Since Quinney approached them just then, his warm evening cloak slung about his shoulders, Alice could only agree. "Good night," she murmured in response.

When the gentlemen left, and her family had retired to their bedchambers save for Louisa, Alice queried, "Isn't it wonderful news about Hugh?"

"The very best," Louisa murmured, making her way slowly to the windows overlooking the street below. Alice could see that she was laboring under some strong emotion and for that reason followed her.

"What is it, dearest?" she asked gently, though suspecting the nature of her unhappiness.

"He did not even send word," Louisa said. "Even ridiculous Mr. Dodds was considerate enough to inform Freddie, however stupidly, as to why he would not attend Nicky's party. B-but Tamerbeck was not even willing to do that much."

"Oh, my dear," she said, slipping an arm about her. A moment more and Louisa had buried her face in her shoulder and was sobbing as though her heart would break.

Seventeen

On the following morning, when Braden arrived in Upper Brook Street, the serving maid led him to Alice's office on the ground floor. He had read her letter the evening before, breaking the seal anxiously, and had been relieved by the nature of the contents, which had been a simple recounting of Hicklade's investigation. His greatest concern had been that she would reveal a growing attachment to "Mr. Pinfrith," who was nothing more than a phantom of his own making. As it was, he released a sigh of relief, for there was nothing in the style or substance of her correspondence that indicated anything beyond a friendly demeanor. He had already decided that, however difficult, he must tell her about his ridiculous deception. His attempt last night had been poorly timed, but there should be nothing preventing him this morning from telling her the truth about "William Pinfrith."

For the present, he had come bearing good news.

"What a wonderful surprise," she said, greeting him warmly as he crossed the room to her. "I certainly did not expect to see you this morning. Only tell me what has brought you to Upper Brook Street?"

He held up a letter. "Hicklade—again!"

Alice let out a squeal. "Indeed! So soon, only do tell me his news!" She waved him to a pair of chairs near the fireplace and seated herself adjacent to him.

He said nothing but smiled as he handed the letter to her. She opened it, quickly scanning the contents. "He says he believes my brother is somewhere in Brighton. These are wondrous tidings and it would appear that there can be no doubt of his having survived the attack."

"None, particularly since there was word of Hugh all along the inns heading south, that though it was obvious he was seriously wounded and that his head was bandaged, he was still able to take sips of brandy and tea on more than one occasion."

"Oh, Braden, how happy you have made me today. I am utterly *aux anges.*" On impulse, she rose from her chair and slung her arms about his neck in a reckless embrace. He hugged her tightly.

Alice withdrew suddenly. "I do beg your pardon. I did not mean—"

"Never apologize to a man for embracing him," he countered with a laughing light in his eye. "Only tell me where the rest of your family is. Are they in the drawing room? I would not keep such excellent news from them for the world."

"I fear I am the only one at home at present," she said, taking up her seat once more. "Mr. Quintin took Freddie and Nicky to the tower to see the lions and Mrs. Urchfont, Jane, and Louisa have gone to Hookham's."

Braden glanced at her, a powerful feeling sliding through him at the knowledge that he was most certainly alone with Alice. He would not have come at this hour had he suspected her sisters, brother, and aunt had all gone out, for he knew he did not have complete command over his impulses where she was concerned. Every step he took in her direction, whether it was the hiring of Hicklade or giving Nicky his first fencing lesson or bringing her word of Hugh, all brought him too close within her orbit to make him entirely comfortable.

His heart began sounding heavily in his chest. He should tell her right now, that the Mr. Pinfrith of the letters did not exist, that he was the author of both letters by that name as well as the kiss at Vauxhall. The words, however, would simply not rise to his lips.

When he realized he had been silent far too long, he said, "Quinney has certainly grown attentive to Miss Frederica. I only hope he is not destined to be disappointed for it has not escaped my notice that her affections are engaged elsewhere."

Alice smiled. "I would have long since hinted him away had I thought he did not have a chance with Freddie. Of course, when he first met her there was no doubt that her heart was fully engaged by Mr. Dodds. However, Mr. Quintin's patience has had an effect, rather like gently catching a nestling that has tumbled from the branches above. The fall was inevitable and Mr. Quintin has caught his prize."

"You are so certain?" he asked.

"You must understand. Freddie will never forgive Mr. Dodds for his refusal to attend Nicky's party last night. For all her appearance of outrageousness, she believes in at least consideration if not propriety."

"I was never more amused, as I daresay none of us were, at the contents of his letter. I doubt there was a greater fool born than Dodds."

Alice laughed. "I only wonder how long it will take before he becomes aware of what he has lost."

"An eternity, perhaps. I have no great confidence in his perceptions of those around him. It is only a wonder that his poetry, the vignette he wrote Thursday last for instance, is full of so much genius."

"A mystery, indeed," she said.

He should tell her about Mr. Pinfrith. The moment was right. Instead, another silence grew between them.

She politely filled it. "Are you to attend Mrs. Swainswick's ball this evening?"

He was taken aback by the question even though it was perfectly cordial. "Yes . . . no. I am not certain. I will have to confer with Trickett." He stood up abruptly. "I must go. I wish I could have been here when the remainder of your siblings were present for to be the bearer of happy news is a most satisfying experience."

She rose as well and extended her hand to him. "Thank you again, Braden, ever so much."

He took her hand in his but not for the life of him would he ever comprehend why he caught up her hand in both of his and placed a lingering kiss upon her wrist. He felt a deep connection to her that spoke of every famous sonnet ever written on the subject of love. How was this possible, he wondered even as he released her hand.

He found her cheeks flooded with color. Her lips were parted and her large blue eyes filled with every dream he had ever had. He knew he should take his leave, that he was in some danger were he to stay much longer.

"Braden . . . ?" she queried softly, her voice and the expression in her eye the sweetest invitation he had ever beheld.

He wanted to take her in his arms. His breathing grew erratic. Thoughts of Mr. Pinfrith disappeared entirely as other more scandalous thoughts replaced them.

"Alice," he murmured. A single step and he could slip his arm about her waist and drag her against him. He knew she would not forbid it. He wanted to. He would . . .

Running steps and laughter were heard just beyond the front door. A moment more and the door burst open. Braden gave himself a shake as a moment later Nicky came running into Alice's office. "We saw the lions!" he cried. "They were not nearly so frightening as I thought they might be although one of them paced back and forth like—oh, good morning, Lord Bradenstoke." He offered his very best bow, which Braden could see pleased Alice immensely.

Miss Frederica entered the chamber with Quinney close on her heels. She greeted him politely and glanced from him to Alice several times until Alice exclaimed, "I had nearly forgot!" she cried, holding the letter aloft. "Braden received more news of Hugh. He is in Brighton!"

The letter was passed from one to the other and Nicky gave a loud "Huzza." Braden stayed only a few minutes longer and as soon as he was able to, made his escape.

Once in his curricle, he cracked his whip over the ears of the leader and taking a glance back at the house, saw Alice standing at the window of her office, her expression deeply perplexed as she lifted a hand once to him.

That evening, Alice stood at the far end of Mrs. Swain-swick's ballroom, her gaze fixed on the doorway at the opposite end, when a man's voice intruded. "Who are you expecting?"

Alice turned in some surprise to find Sir Benedict smiling benevolently. She felt a warmth suffuse her cheeks. "Why do you suppose I am awaiting anyone?"

"Because your gaze has shifted to the entrance at least a dozen times in the past few minutes and may I say whoever he might be, he will not be disappointed. I cannot express how beautifully this shade of green becomes you. I suppose it is the flame of your tresses in contrast to the emerald of your gown. Lovely, indeed."

Alice smiled and thanked him for the compliment. She unfurled her fan and began to cool her cheeks. Her gaze slipped back almost of its own volition to the entrance once more. Who was she awaiting, indeed?

Braden had indicated he might attend, though he was uncertain, and for nearly twelve hours past she had thought of little else other than the prospect of seeing him again, hoping in doing so she might discover just what had transpired between them earlier that day.

When he had taken her hand in his and instead of giving it a polite shake had actually kissed her wrist, she had felt dizzy and warm in the way the air sizzles just before the breaking of a storm. He had looked at her in such a way that had put her forcibly in mind of the kiss she had shared with him by the Thames. She had begun to wonder if per chance somewhere between fencing with him and his kindness at Nicky's party, she had begun tumbling in love with him.

Yet, how could this be since he was the man that he was, who had so completely refused to help her over the past ten years? How could such a man, so indifferent to her family, ever be a man she could truly love?

Yet, here she was, hoping Braden would arrive, having dressed with the greatest of care, having changed her gown no less than three times before finally settling on the emerald green silk, having taken an entire hour to see her red curls arranged just so.

"So tell me," he murmured, "has Freddie given up Dodds at long last for though he is present, to my knowledge she has not danced with him?"

"Poor Dodds," she murmured behind her fan. "He will stand at the edge of the floor glowering at her without the smallest comprehension of how deeply he has offended her." She then told him of the ridiculous note Mr. Dodds had sent to Upper Brook Street with his pronouncement that he did not believe in birthdays.

"Good God! What a complete gudgeon!" he cried.

"I could not agree more."

He lifted his quizzing glass which hung about his neck by a maroon silk riband and moved the eyepiece over the dancers. "I see that Freddie is going down a second set with Mr. Quintin. You know, he has never to my knowledge singled out a lady in such a fashion before."

"So I have been given to understand. Lady Wroughton told her only an hour past that he is grown quite serious in his courting."

"And what was Freddie's response to such news?" he inquired.

"She spoke very politely to Lady Wroughton, expressing her admiration of Mr. Quintin and saying that should her ladyship prove correct she would feel greatly flattered to find that she was the object of such a man's attentions. Lady Wroughton had lifted a brow and nodded in a manner which could not be construed as anything other than her approval. What is most interesting is that a fortnight past, because of Dodds's unfortunate influence over her for so long, Freddie probably would have said something quite impertinent to her ladyship. Tonight, however, I was never more proud of her polite, humble response."

"Freddie has changed a great deal of late. Do but look at

her. The turbans and silly caps are gone, she is gowned in a lovely pale yellow satin, and even her slippers are embroidered only with pearls."

"I believe it to be nothing less than Mr. Quintin's influence and you know what a stickler he is. Yet to my knowledge from the moment he met Freddie—and, I believe, tumbled in love with her—he never once criticized her costumes."

"This is most promising," he said with a smile. "You must be pleased."

"Of course. However, I beg you will not speak further on the subject. It can only be conjecture after all."

At that, Sir Benedict chuckled. "I must take issue with you, Alice. Now that the dance is concluded, do but look at how he smiles at her and how he has taken possession of her arm. If I do not much mistake the matter, he is leading her in to supper."

"So he is," Alice murmured. Since the happy couple was walking in the direction of the doorway, her gaze flitted past them, searching the crowd which was moving from the ballroom. She suppressed the deepest sigh. There was very little chance, at so late an hour, that Braden meant to attend the fete.

A scurrying nearby, however, drew her attention to her left, where she discovered that Lord Tamerbeck was hopping about Louisa in what he intended to be a teasing manner.

"I pray you will cease at once, my lord," she heard Louisa snap. "I am not in the least amused."

Sir Benedict whispered to Alice, "He looks like a puppy yipping at her heels. Whyever is he behaving in so ridiculous a manner?"

"Because Louisa is fallen out of love with him and he cannot credit it is true."

"What prompted her shift of heart?"

"I believe she grew weary of his inconstancies. He had promised to attend Nicky's party last night as well, but never arrived. Louisa cried herself to sleep."

"I begin to think him as great a fool as Dodds. Why, then, is he behaving so queerly?"

Alice once more glanced at Tamerbeck, who was still bouncing about Louisa in an absurd manner. "Because he cannot believe for a moment that he has truly lost her. He thinks that all he must do is charm her a little and she will relent. Come. Louisa means to go in to supper with me. Will you join us?"

"With pleasure."

She took his proffered arm and when she reached her sister, she asked, "Louisa, are you ready?"

"Yes. I told Lord Tamerbeck that I was previously engaged. You will excuse us, my lord?"

Tamerbeck hurriedly blocked Alice's path. "You must help me, Miss Cherville, for I cannot seem to persuade your sister to allow me to escort her."

Alice was never so happy as she was at this moment when she could say, "I believe she has refused you, has she not?"

"Well, yes, but . . ."

"I would offer my support to you if I could but unfortunately I have always trusted my sister to know her mind. Ah, I see that Miss Reed is waving to you, rather frantically." She then bowed to him and with Louisa on her left and Sir Benedict on her right, as a group they moved past him.

Alice felt Louisa's arm trembling beneath her own. "I danced with him earlier and I should not have done so for he believed himself to be forgiven. I gave him a hint at Hyde Park only this afternoon that his absence last night caused me great pain, but he did not think me in the least serious. Oh, Alice, was he always so unfeeling? Did you see the manner in which he was bounding about my heels just now? He is being utterly ridiculous!"

"I would have to say that until this moment, when he is perhaps suspecting he has lost you forever, he has generally behaved the gentleman."

"I truly thought I loved him," she whispered. "I begin to believe I was the one who was ridiculous."

Alice gave her sister's arm a squeeze and glancing at her saw an unhappy tear escape her eye. "Dearest," she murmured sympathetically.

Louisa would have none of it, however. "Never mind that," she cried, quickly brushing the tear aside. "Only tell me when is Mr. Pinfrith to return from Portsmouth?"

"I do not know. I have not heard from him in days."

Sir Benedict interjected, "Pinfrith is returned to England? I had not heard of it."

"Yes," Louisa responded. "A fortnight past but he had to leave London on business immediately. We are all longing to make his acquaintance."

Sir Benedict frowned. "Have you actually seen Mr. Pinfrith, here in the City, I mean?"

"Yes," Alice said. "I spoke with him at Vauxhall the evening of the masquerade. I met him after you had quit the gardens. Did I not tell you as much?"

"No, I am afraid you did not. But you say you met him at the masquerade?"

"Yes."

Louisa changed the course of the conversation. "Sir Benedict, have you heard our wonderful news?"

"What is that?" he asked.

"I had nearly forgot to tell you!" Alice exclaimed. "Hugh is in Brighton."

Sir Benedict started. "He has been found?" he asked, obviously dumbfounded.

"No, not precisely," Alice said. "But Mr. Hicklade sent us word by way of Braden's courier, that his investigation has led him to Brighton where there are reports of him. We have the greatest hope Mr. Hicklade will find him very soon."

"This is excellent news," he said, smiling.

"Indeed, it is," Alice agreed. With thoughts of Hugh brightening her mood, she was able to enjoy the supper with only the mildest regret that Braden had not attended the ball after all.

On the following morning, Alice was still abed when a scratching sounded at her door. She called out "Come" and watched as Freddie brought a huge bouquet of daffodils into the chamber.

Alice sat up, her heart fairly leaping in her chest. Were the flowers from Braden? she wondered.

"I had to come at once to show you," she cried. "These are from Mr. Quintin. Are they not the most beautiful flowers you have ever seen?" Her expression was aglow. There could be no mistaking the pleasure the bouquet had given her.

"Indeed, the most beautiful," Alice agreed, smiling warmly at her sister. If at the same time she felt an irrationally profound disappointment, she put away such feelings for Freddie's sake. It was obvious that her sister had come to her bedchamber to have a comfortable cose. "Why do you not put the flowers on my nightstand and sit with me for a time?"

"I should like that." Freddie quickly settled the vase on the small table by Alice's headboard and situated herself at the end of her bed, her knees tucked beneath her blue calico gown. "Lady Wroughton told me that I could expect a proposal of marriage from Mr. Quintin at any time. Do you think she may be right?"

Alice smiled. "Even a simpleton could see how much he is in love with you, Freddie."

"I had no notion," she said, her eyes wide with disbelief.

"Why did you think he came to Upper Brook Street so frequently and why would such a fashionable man who travels only in the first circles deign to notice an insignificant set of ladies fresh from the country?"

"You cannot mean you believe it is because of me?"

"Have you truly seen nothing in his conduct that would support my opinion? Freddie, he has been fairly dancing attendance on you from the moment he met you. Has there been even a day when he absented himself from either our home or your presence?"

"No—o," she drawled, "I suppose there has not. And he does have a tendency to stare at me—not rudely, mind!— even when he is speaking with others. Jane said only yesterday that she had to repeat a question twice before he could draw his attention back to her sufficiently to respond."

"A certain indication he is in love with you," Alice said, smiling.

"But why would he be when he might have a score of others more deserving?"

Alice was taken aback. "In what way more deserving?" she asked.

"Larger dowries, finer connections."

"I do not believe Mr. Quintin cares for such things. He is a very good man."

"Indeed," Freddie agreed. "The very best of men, forever attending to Nicky when Mr. Dodds has ignored him completely and he was never critical of Mr. Dodds, not even after I read his horrible missive aloud to our guests on Sunday evening."

Alice could only smile.

"Do you know, I am quite at my ease around him. When he took me to supper last night, we spoke of everything and nothing all at the same time. Which puts me in mind of something he told me. It was quite odd. He said that Lord Bradenstoke was quite torn about attending the ball last night."

"Indeed?" Alice queried, her heart beginning to pound unsteadily in her breast.

"I cannot imagine why, though," she continued. "Do you suppose he believes we have come to depend upon him?"

"I do not know," Alice said, although she felt there was a chance that an entirely different interpretation could be applied to his lordship's dilemma, particularly after her encounter with him in her office yesterday. Only what to make of it? she wondered. She thought it possible he desired to attend Mrs. Swainswick's ball for the purpose of seeing her. If that was true, then what precisely had prevented him from doing so?

Eighteen

"So Miss Louisa is finished at last with Tam," Trickett stated, smiling broadly. "What excellent good news!"

Braden regarded his friend thoughtfully. They were traveling together to Upper Brook Street to attend the Chervilles at home, and he had just informed his secretary of Miss Louisa's conduct at Mrs. Swainswick's ball on the evening before, critical information which had been passed to him by Quinney only this morning. Had he been in doubt about Trickett's attachment to Louisa, he would have been no longer. His dear friend was beaming with the news that to all appearances Miss Louisa Cherville was no longer sitting in Lord Tamerbeck's pocket.

"Quinney's words to the letter," Braden said, smiling as he turned to glance out the window of his coach at a passing tilbury. "He was there last night and saw how she did everything but give Tamerbeck the cut direct and still he pursued her. I daresay he could not credit that a mere country miss would reject his attentions no matter how horridly he behaved."

Trickett shifted slightly and met his friend's gaze. "Are you surprised?"

"By what?"

"By my interest in Miss Louisa. After all, I know your opinions of the Chervilles generally."

Braden shook his head. "You are mistaken. I do not hold an ill opinion of the younger siblings. I never have, merely an indifference to their plight. To Miss Cherville's letters, however, I took the greatest exception, but even this circumstance does not seem so wretched to me as it once used to."

"I am glad to hear of it. I should not like to think you despised the lady of my choice."

"I did not like that she had set her cap for Tam."

"Nor I, but I felt confident that one day she would comprehend his character. If Quinney is correct then that day has arrived. Good God, what a coxcomb Tam must be not to have had the decency to show for Nicky's party and then to actually believe Louisa would soon forget such a slight! I am only amazed by one thing."

When he did not speak of it, Braden queried, "And what is that?" He glanced at his friend and secretary and saw that Trickett was smiling broadly. "What the devil are you grinning about?"

Mr. Trickett laughed. "Only that you have completely astounded me by attending the Chervilles at home."

"But have you forgotten?" he queried, smiling ruefully, "I am their guardian."

Trickett laughed in response but to Braden's relief did not pursue the subject further.

He had spent the prior evening pacing his library and sipping his brandy. He had debated a hundred times whether to don his evening clothes and make haste to Mrs. Swainswick's ball in order to see if Alice might have a waltz left to give him. When Quinney had arrived at an early hour to see if he desired to accompany him, he had admitted the depth of his ambivalence but stated emphatically that he had decided not to attend lest he give rise in certain quarters to a great deal of speculation which he could not possibly fulfill. Quinney had called him a fool and left him to spend the evening wearing out the carpet of his library a little more.

He had dined at White's and afterward lost a hundred pounds gaming with Lord Wroughton and some of his set. When he finally returned to Grosvenor Square well past midnight, he met Quinney on his front steps. His *good friend* had come for the strict purpose of tormenting him further by actually giving him an account of the ball, or at least, of Alice at the ball. Alice, it would seem, had been gowned in emerald silk, and had attracted the notice of every male present.

"She wore a matched pearl necklace," Quinney had said, "which pulled into a beautiful diamond pendant. An heirloom, no doubt, but exquisite beyond words, like the lady herself."

"I should like to have seen her," he confessed with a sigh. "For she is absolutely lovely to behold."

"She danced every dance, including a set with Sir Benedict Locksbury."

Braden scowled. "Someone should warn her."

"Sir Benedict took her in to supper."

"Indeed?"

"Miss Frederica explained the connection to me for it seems Sir Benedict has been Miss Cherville's strongest support all these years. She quite depends upon him."

"Some say he is deeply in debt to the cent-percenters," Braden murmured.

"So I have heard and Miss Cherville is an heiress."

Braden understood the nature of his friend's hints but what came to mind of the moment was how formidably she had fenced with him not so long ago. "I daresay Miss Cherville is equal to the task of defending herself against fortune hunters however clever they might be. Only, tell me, old friend, do you intend to offer for Miss Frederica?"

"Of course."

How plainly he had stated his intentions, as simply and as boldly as if he had ordered a meal at an inn. Braden had been stunned, feeling as though a lightning bolt had been suddenly shot through his tidy world. Quinney to marry and a Cherville lady had won his heart.

"Are you in any manner certain of the lady's affections?" he had asked.

"Not in the least," Quinney returned, smiling in a devilishly stupid manner. "But I mean to offer for her anyway."

"She would be a fool to refuse you."

"And if she does I shall try again in another fortnight and another after that until she says yes. But what of you? Where is your soul, Robert, for I have never known a man to be so determined to keep love at bay?"

"Is this how you see me?" he had inquired, stunned.

Quinney had merely smiled and shortly afterward taken his leave. Braden had been left alone once more with his thoughts. The questions he could not seem to answer were what precisely his intentions toward Alice were, what he wanted of her, and why the deuce she had taken such complete possession of his mind?

Mr. Trickett pulled him from his reveries. "We have arrived, Braden," he said, giving him a little shove.

Braden glanced about and realized how deeply he had fallen into thought. "So we have," he responded, stepping down from the coach that was standing quite still before the Cherville address in Upper Brook Street.

As he led the way up the stairs, a flow of people descended, all of the first circle, paying their respects to Alice and her family. Mostly Quinney's doing, Braden thought with a smile.

The well-appointed chamber was still rather crowded. In addition to the family, Lady Wroughton, Mrs. Swainswick and her daughter, Lady Dassett, Lady Orcheston, Mrs. Fonthill, and a dozen others were present, all showering their attentions upon Alice, who sat presiding over the tea tray with some dignity near the fireplace.

Quinney had already taken Frederica to a quiet corner and engaged her in conversation. He was not certain whom to address first. When he caught Alice's eye and saw a welcoming smile rise to her lips, he knew he had but one object, to make his way to her side as quickly as possible.

He would have followed his impulse to approach her immediately had not Mrs. Urchfont, obviously ecstatic at his arrival, called out to him.

"How do you go on, my lord? Is this not a merry at home?" She hurried toward him, her own enameled snuffbox open and stretched out ominously in his direction, like the prow of a ship. She continued. "We were just discussing the various snuffs and I know you to enjoy your own blend and thought you might like to try—"

The lady tripped slightly, regaining her balance but not before the powdery snuff left the contents of its little box and formed a wide band over the front of his dark blue coat as well as a portion of his waistcoat and small falls.

A gasp flew up from the assemblage and at the same time Mrs. Urchfont was all abject apology. "I am so very sorry! Oh dear! Oh dear! I was always used to be the clumsiest creature. Will you ever forgive me?" She whisked a lace kerchief from the pocket of her gown and began swiping at his stomach. Silence fell over the chamber. "I fear I have completely ruined your clothes!"

Braden glanced at Alice, whose expression was one of the deepest concern for her aunt, whose complexion had taken on the precise shade of a ripe strawberry. He did not hesitate, but quickly took her hands in his. "Of course you did not! In fact, you have done me a great service, for Mullens, my valet, has been a little bored of late with nothing better to do than to supervise the amount of starch required for my neckcloths. So, I will thank you, or I should say, Mullens thanks you."

Mrs. Urchfont stared up at him as though he had gone mad.

He then wrapped her arm about his and paraded her the length of the drawing room, speaking to her of inanities until her color had receded and the guests in the drawing room had reverted to conversing in their tight little groups.

Alice was overcome as she watched him walk poor Mrs. Urchfont up and down the relatively small chamber. What an unlooked-for kindness since she was in little doubt that had he not done so the poor lady would have taken to her bedchamber for an entire sennight. She was never more proud of Braden than at this moment. He could have been deeply aggravated that the clumsy woman had ruined his suit of clothes, instead, he had treated the matter with just the lightness of hand which the situation required, given Mrs. Urchfont's heightened sensibilities.

When he joined her a moment later, she bade him sit beside her and presented him with a cup of tea and a small embroidered napkin. "Thank you, Braden," she murmured. "My aunt will retell the story a dozen times before the day is through of your kindness to her. As for myself, I vow I will be forever in your debt."

"There was a time I would not have been so kind. You have taught me differently, I think."

Alice met his gaze, which was, as always, forceful and commanding. "Have I?" she queried. "I do not see how."

He chuckled softly. "In everything you do you are a model of compassion or do you not know as much?" He chuckled again. "Now you are blushing. Are you not used to such compliments?"

Her heart was beating erratically. "Not from you," she countered, hoping to allay the strong feelings rising in her chest.

Once more he laughed.

"So tell me," she said playfully, "will your Mullens indeed be delighted at seeing your coat, your waistcoat, and your pantaloons so badly stained?"

He leaned his head close to her and whispered, "I admit I told your aunt a whisker to protect her feelings. Mullens will undoubtedly fall into a decline at the sight of all this snuff on what he considers to be the articles of his particular domain."

Alice could not help but laugh. "I thought as much." When a silence fell between them, Alice queried, "When do you expect to hear from Hicklade?"

"I am hoping later this afternoon but if not definitely tomorrow. You must be anxious."

Alice shook her head. "After your wonderful news of yesterday, how could I be? Besides, I try not to dwell on the situation overly much. Better to get over rough ground lightly."

He shook his head, smiling ruefully. "How do you find

the grace to manage your circumstances with such wisdom and patience? You astound me."

She smiled crookedly and leaned toward him slightly. "Has it escaped your notice, my lord, that for the past sennight it is you who have been managing the whole terrible business?"

He said nothing but held her gaze with the force of his own. Alice felt all her thoughts drift away so that she was left only with the desires of her heart. Even the chatter of the guests in the drawing room dimmed to barely a hum. Her gaze fell to his lips and she knew a longing so profound as to bring a prickling of tears to the back of her eyes.

Braden felt lost. The expression on her face and the way she looked at his lips then blinked away what he could only determine was a surprising spate of tears, worked strongly within him. The tension he had felt yesterday morning when he had called to give her news of Hugh returned to him. Now it was no longer enough to be in the same room with her and to converse with her. He desired more than life itself to touch her.

For that reason, he let the napkin on his knee slide to the floor between them. He did not attempt to retrieve it but let it rest where it lay.

She glanced down and after a moment, reached for it, just as he supposed she would. At the same time, he scandalously slid his hand down the length of hers, his fingers touching her wrist, her palm, and extending to the tips of her fingers. She glanced at him and he could see that she was fully aware of what he was doing, for a faint smile crossed her lips.

She let him retrieve the napkin then withdrew her hand first, but not without letting the back of her hand rake across his in what seemed, given the circumstances, an extremely scandalous manner.

He could not credit she had responded in kind. He understood then what it was about her that had so captivated him from the first—she met every aspect of him fully like a strong wind blowing the sails of a ship to deeper waters. No wonder he felt all at sea whenever he was around her.

"Are you attending the masquerade this evening?" she asked.

He nodded. He had not previously intended to. Indeed, he did not know to which fete she referred but it did not matter. Trickett would know and before the afternoon was through he would see that the proper letter was taken round, informing the hostess he meant to attend. The real invitation was in Alice's eyes, one he would not have refused even if his life had been in jeopardy in doing so. "You enjoy masquerades then?"

She smiled. "Very much so."

He lowered his voice. "What is your costume? How will I know you?"

"A veiled Turkish maiden," she said. "And yours?"

"A domino only."

Trickett was beside him at that moment. "I am sorry to disturb you, Braden, but you have an appointment at three at Westminster."

"I suppose we should be going," he said. He rose to take his leave, returning the teacup and saucer to her. She rose as well, offering her hand. He took it but given the public nature of their surroundings merely responded with a gentle squeeze.

Alice watched him go, feeling as though her world had just been turned topsy-turvy.

"What a fine man," Mrs. Urchfont said, drawing up beside her. "So very handsome, his manners more perfect than even the Regent's."

"He is all these things," Alice agreed.

"I did not think I would like him. I am happy to have been mistaken."

Alice glanced at her aunt and saw a mixture of distress and relief in her expression. She took her hand and patted it gently. "I as well."

Alice began her preparations for the masquerade well in advance of the hour. Though no one would actually see her hair, she had her abigail dress it in a meticulous fashion, streaming in ringlets nearly to her waist. Her costume was of a simple design intended to reflect the pictures she had seen of Turkish maidens covered in their unusual gowns and veils.

She had chosen a white silk shirt such as a gentleman would wear and had had balloonlike trousers made up which were gathered at the ankles and made of a broadly striped silk in turquoise red and a pale yellow. Around her waist she wore a purple silk sash, heavily fringed and dangling almost to the floor when properly tied. Such a costume would have been scandalous in the extreme had she not overlaid it with what she understood to be called a Ferigee entirely of gold silk. It was a covering resembling a loose-fitting robe that floated about her when she moved. On her feet she wore simple purple slippers that curled at the toes.

The final exotic look was created by the two muslin scarves every Turkish lady wore, a shorter one that concealed her face from her nose to well below her chin and a longer one that was wrapped carefully over the head and hung half-way down her back.

"Oh, Alice!" Jane cried, moving into her bedchamber just as the muslins were set in place with jeweled pins and the veil over the face secured by a loop over a glass bead. "No one shall ever know you—oh, I see!—except by your hair. How truly wonderful and so distinctive."

"It is not too scandalous, is it?"

"You are completely covered from head to foot more than most ladies will be tonight. How could you think it anything other than befitting a modest lady?"

She pulled apart the front opening of the Ferigee to reveal the striped trousers.

Jane clapped her hand over her mouth and giggled. "I would recommend you not allow a breeze to come anywhere near you."

"I shan't," Alice returned, then looked her sister up and down. "But how happy I am that you are to attend this evening."

"You know how very much I love a masquerade," Jane said.

"You appear as though you must have stepped from the court of King Arthur." Her gown of white muslin clung to her figure in a lovely flow and ended in a length of fabric nearly four feet long. "Mind your train, however."

Jane whisked it up in her right hand and demonstrated how the unusual length permitted her to sling most of the fabric over her arm in a manner as charming as it was utilitarian. Her light blond hair, as well, was let loose of its usual confines and rambled over her shoulders and down her back in a succession of beautiful waves. She pirouetted in a circle, then proclaimed that she had come to fetch her to dinner. "Though I do not know how you are to eat without disturbing your veil."

With one hand, Alice slid the loop over the small glass bead and the veil fell to one side.

"How very clever!" she cried.

The ladies then descended the stairs together and joined the family.

Two hours later, Alice, along with all three of her sisters as well as Mrs. Urchfont, crossed the portals of Mrs. Murton's mansion. The house was one of several truly palatial dwellings in Mayfair. As London expanded and the area nearest Hyde Park developed, plans for large, sprawling houses were frequently discarded in favor of what had become over the past century the typical town house, built with adjoining walls from home to home and sent spiraling three and four storeys toward the sky.

Mrs. Murton's home was not such a narrow confined dwelling but occupied the place of four large town homes and enjoyed many of the conveniences of a country house, including gardens to tease the eye of the visitor both in front and back. Alice felt she was entering another world when she crossed the threshold to the elegant entrance hall. Her gaze was drawn upward immediately to view the deep blue-domed ceiling, which was decorated with exquisitely rendered figures from mythology.

"A perfect place for a masquerade," Jane whispered over her shoulder.

The party greeted their hostess and afterward moved into the massive drawing room, where scores of guests, most in costume and some in domino and mask, chattered in a lively manner. In the distance, perhaps in an adjoining antechamber, the delicate sounds of a string quartet playing a lively sonata drifted into the room.

"The Chervilles," a whispered voice announced as Alice and her sisters moved by. "All that red and blond hair."

Alice could only smile as she searched the costumes and tried to guess who each character from history or mythology might possibly be. One by one, her sisters were drawn away, Freddie by Mr. Quintin, Louisa by Mr. Trickett, and Jane by a giggling young lady who turned out to be Miss Fonthill.

Alice was left to roam the rooms by herself, a circumstance which suited her to perfection since she had never been to Murton House and delighted in a chance to view the extraordinary collection of art and statuary that adorned the mansion. If her gaze was also frequently fixed on any tall, broad-shouldered gentleman who happened to appear in whatever antechamber she was inhabiting, who would be the wiser? In her Turkish costume she felt strangely invisible to everyone around her.

Regardless, she was occasionally recognized and that by the red curls draped over her gold silk Ferigee. She did not, however, lower her muslin veil, for it was too much fun to be in disguise. She was soon dancing and for the next hour or perhaps two, her curled purple slippers were never still.

When she had grown heated, she chose to sit for a few minutes and watch the dancers go down the next country dance. If her gaze one second out of three drifted to the doorway, she did not care. She was in a perpetual state of anticipation waiting for Braden to arrive. Unlike the night before, this evening she was in no doubt he would come. He had said he would and this she knew of him, he was as good as his word.

Her gaze found the figures of Freddie and Quintin going down the country dance. He was dressed in the ancient clerical robes of a monk and she in the guise of a fairy. She was a veritable cloud of pink silk, white tulle, and spangled gauze adorned by a pair of small silver silk wings. Her hair was gathered into a knot atop her head and decorated with a dozen tiny sparkling stars. Freddie smiled, her gaze rarely leaving Mr. Quintin's face. He in turn had never seemed happier.

Mr. Dodds approached her. "It would appear to be all but settled," he stated rancorously.

"Indeed, I believe so."

"You are not serious!" he cried. "I—I was being facetious. Is this indeed what you think or do you merely hope she will get his fortune?"

Alice turned and glared at his scowling face until he begged pardon. "I—I just never thought she would cease loving me and all because I do not believe in birthdays. Oh God, look at how she watches him, as though his face has become the air in her lungs. Whatever shall I do without my beloved? I shall tear my hair out!"

"Pray do not," Alice said sardonically, "for I daresay you would hardly appear to advantage reciting your poetry with patches of hair torn from your scalp."

He seemed much struck. "I say, Miss Cherville, I believe you have the right of it."

"Do you know, I always thought Miss Reed in possession of an abundance of theatrical ability. Perhaps she can take the place of Freddie as your muse. Besides, I understand her to be a great heiress and should inspiration turn to love, she could be of excellent use to a man in your circumstances."

"By Jove, Miss Cherville, I believe the gods ordained our meeting tonight." With that he bowed low to her and turned in pursuit of his new quarry. She glanced at his receding figure and thought it greatly ironic that a man who had for weeks dressed in every manner of outrageous costume as a matter of course, would attend a masquerade in a simple black coat and breeches with nary a hint of a mask to conceal his identity. Even the tails of his coat were of an unexceptionable length.

As he moved away, Alice could shake her head at his complete inability to conceal even the smallest of his flaws.

Even as he moved, however, her gaze was drawn yet again to the doorway as a tall man appeared in a scarlet cloak, but it was only the Duke of Wellington. How odd, Alice thought, that she had become so used to the presence of notable figures in society that in her desire to see Braden, she would think of the military figure across the room as *only the Duke of Wellington.*

Nineteen

Alice had just thanked a young Mr. Fonthill for a rousing Scottish reel when Louisa drew close.

"Is not this a marvelous ball!" she cried. "I cannot remember being so happy."

"Is that because in your domino and mask you have been able to go down three sets with Mr. Trickett with none the wiser?"

Louisa gasped. "How did you know?"

"Because you are my sister, goose, and because I wish for your happiness more than anything else in the world."

"I am happy," she stated softly. "Though I must confess I did not expect to be. Do you think I am exhibiting an unhappy inconstancy similar to, er, my former beau?"

Alice turned to her and slipped an arm about her sister's waist. "On no account. Such a circumstance would be impossible for you. I merely think you are coming to your senses after having been battered into a state of insensibility by a greatly handsome face attached to more charm than would be good for even a saint."

Louisa giggled. "I believe you are right."

At that moment Mr. Trickett arrived and offered to escort both ladies to the blue drawing room, where cups of iced champagne were being served.

Alice had just lowered her veil and taken a sip of champagne when Trickett leaned down and whispered to her, "Braden is just now arrived."

"Indeed?" she queried, her heart suddenly in her throat. She saw him framed in the doorway and felt as though every bit of breath deserted her quite suddenly. "So he is."

From the corner of her eye she could see that Trickett was looking at her and smiling, but for the life of her she could not tear her gaze from the fine figure striding in their direction.

Braden greeted each of them in turn, though it could not have been more than the space of a minute before Mr. Trickett drew Louisa away with some excuse or other. Alice watched him go, thinking that she would be forever in his debt since he had given her what she desired, to enjoy Braden's company without the smallest distraction.

When the waltz was announced, a general scurrying followed so that the room emptied rather quickly. Alice wondered if he meant to dance with her again. She might even have given him a hint in that direction, but he offered his arm to her and with a wink said, "Come."

She smiled up at him, wondering if this dance would be as delightful as the waltz they had shared at Lady Dassett's ball. She overlaid his arm with her own, but instead of directing her toward the ballroom, he turned her instead to a doorway that led in quite the opposite direction, into a smaller antechamber.

"Have you ever been to Mrs. Murton's house?" he inquired.

"No, I have not," she responded, wondering what he was about.

"One of the few excellent mansions left in Mayfair. Her collection of art is superb."

"I took the opportunity upon arriving to see much of it," she admitted. "I was quite astonished. The works of Raphael, Rembrandt, others of the Dutch school."

"Have you seen the Constable?" he queried.

"No, I must say I have not."

"Then I shall show it to you." He turned down a hall and a moment later guided her into the long gallery where a handful of costumed guests were milling about viewing the enormous portraits on the north wall.

After a short march, she found herself in a deserted ante-chamber in which the painting was displayed. Alice caught her breath. "I have heard of his work but until now I could not have imagined it. The whole of the landscape appears brilliant with light."

She could feel his gaze upon her. "I knew you would like it." He pushed the hood of his domino back, and untied the strings of his mask. The latter he secreted into the pocket of the cloak. "Come, there is something else I would show you, a very beautiful garden."

He took her down another hall, at the end of which were a pair of French doors leading outdoors. Alice smiled as she looked through the windows. "Roses!" she exclaimed. "How lovely!"

The garden was delightfully cool after the heat of the drawing room and the fragrance of hundreds of blooms permeated the air. The welcome mist of the May evening settled on her face instantly.

"Jane would love to see all these roses," she cried.

"Do you miss the country as much as your sister?"

"Not nearly so," she said, "although home will be a welcome sight after such a long absence. But quite unlike Jane, I am amazingly content in London."

He drew her down a graveled path, saying very little. Alice's thoughts reverted quite suddenly to the afternoon just a few hours earlier, when he had stolen a touch of her wrist, her hand, and her fingers. She remembered how the experience had left a sort of tingling sensation on her skin and that she had wished the experience repeated a dozen times afterward. Alas, he had been called away to Westminster. But here she was, alone with Braden, in a rose garden, his arm wrapped about hers and her thoughts entirely taken up with the notion that in such a secluded place, if he wished for it, surely there would be nothing preventing him from kissing her.

Once in the shadows, he released her arm, slid his hand

about her waist, and drew her against him. "Alice, I have been longing to kiss you again for days now. How you torment me."

With that, so simply said, he placed his lips upon hers. She tried to return his embrace, but the Ferigee was proving cumbersome. He drew back and with a quick movement, unbuttoned the clasp at the neck which kept the loose fabric from sliding off her shoulders. The Ferigee in turn slid to the ground and she was left leaning against him in her balloonlike trousers, her purple sash, and white silk shirt. His arm held her in a vicelike grip.

She sighed against his mouth. "Oh, Braden, I feel so dizzy." Her arm stole about his neck and without the smallest hesitation he took possession of her mouth as though he had always had the right to do so.

Passion swept over her in a sudden blaze of wonder. She realized she had been waiting for this moment from the time he had kissed her by the river's edge at Mrs. Fonthill's fete. His hands dove beneath her long curls, sliding up her back, his fingers becoming tangled purposefully in her hair. With a slight pressure he forced her head back that he might look at her.

"You are so beautiful," he murmured, his lips gliding down her neck. She felt utterly lost in the sensation of being kissed by him again. Her chest tightened in the most delightful way and odd tears played at the edge of her lashes. He released her hair, allowing her to right her head, but he tormented her further by encircling her waist with his hands.

"Alice," he murmured, once more kissing her.

After a time, she drew back and looked deeply into his eyes. "Braden," she whispered, "I feel as though I could remain here forever with you. Is that not the oddest thing?"

He stunned her by falling to his knees and embracing her with his head pressed against her stomach.

She looked down at him, her heart aching with sentiments she did not in the least recognize. Was this truly the man who had refused the guardianship? Was this the same man who had so sweetly given Nicky his first fencing lesson?

She slid her fingers into his thick brown hair as he held her tightly against him.

"You touched my hand," she heard him say, his voice muffled against her purple sash.

"Yes," she whispered.

"Why?" His hands caressed her hips and the entire length of her legs. Alice could not credit he was doing so, nor that she was permitting him such a liberty except that she was beginning to suspect that there already existed between herself and the man before her a bond of attachment so strong as to be inviolable.

"I wished you to know," she responded, "that your touch pleased me. I felt anything else would be hypocritical and unfair to you. I knew you were not just dallying with me for you are incapable of anything of the sort."

He embraced her legs tightly. "We have been enemies."

"But no longer, I hope," she returned. "Or do I much mistake the matter? Do you have misgivings about courting me?"

A trickling of her own doubt stole through her. What was she doing kissing and embracing Braden when in truth she knew so very little about him?

"Kiss me again," she whispered, "before someone else discovers the beauty of this garden and ends our time together."

He rose up swiftly and gathered her strongly in his arms.

Braden heard the familiar moans of delight which warbled in her throat and was transported from the rose garden to a place of tranquility and infinite pleasure. A joy indefinable surrounded him, bidding him to remember a time in his youth when all things felt possible to him, even a great and abiding love. As he kissed Alice's lips anew, as he plumbed the depths of her mouth, as he held her tightly about her sashed waist, he felt changed deeply within. The thought drifted through his mind like a delicate cool breeze on a warm day—he was in love with Alice Cherville.

He drew back slightly and searched her eyes, cupping her face with his hands. How comfortable she seemed to be with him. How easily she tumbled into his arms as though she, too, were transported by the embraces they shared. Did she believe herself to be in love with him? Was love what seemed to flow between them whenever they were alone? Was she worthy of his love? Was he worthy of hers?

He leaned toward her and once more plied her waiting lips with his own. The questions that had tumbled over him could not be answered in a moment but there was one thing he could do, something he had resisted for ten years—he could read her letters, the ones that had sent Trickett to Upper Brook Street every day for the past fortnight. He would know then the entire scope of her character, for it would be in the stream of her correspondence that he would see the truth.

In the meantime, he would kiss her and hold her tightly against him and recall the dreams of his youth.

When it seemed that perhaps a half-hour had passed since they had entered the garden, he drew back and with a smile said, "Did I not tell you this was a lovely garden?"

"I believe I have never seen so beautiful a place in my entire existence." Since she lifted a hand to tenderly caress his face, he understood her meaning.

"Nor I," he responded in kind.

Finally, after he had assaulted her at least twice more, she said, "We should return to the masquerade or the discovery of our absence will cause a great deal more gabblemongering than either of us could wish for."

He retrieved her Ferigee and slid it about her shoulders.

He was struck suddenly with a strong desire to tell her the truth about "Mr. Pinfrith." He knew then that the time had come. He guided her back up the path to the French doors leading into the house. Would she understand? Would she forgive him?

As he opened the door and a rush of warm air struck his face, the magic he had just shared with her in the rose garden began transforming into patterns of propriety and doubt. He knew he must confess his misdeed to her, but suddenly he did not want to. He felt strange, as though he needed to hurry her back into the garden, that to move into the house was robbing him of something precious.

There was nothing for it, however. He must speak.

When once more they were in the long gallery, and the portraits of Mrs. Murton's ancestors were watching him, he began. "Do you recall the evening you attended the masquerade at Vauxhall?"

"Of course," she said, a frown furrowing her brow. He could not know her thoughts precisely but he thought it likely she felt guilty that while she was corresponding with Mr. Pinfrith, she was busily kissing his half brother.

"Well, there is something I wish to tell you. I should have told you sooner, much sooner, but the moment never seemed quite propitious."

"Do you despise me," she queried, "for perhaps continuing to give your brother hope when it is you I cannot seem to keep from embracing?" A smile accompanied her words, but he saw the concern in her eyes.

"No, no," he assured her, giving her arm a squeeze. He stopped their progress beneath the portrait of a man wearing a long, curling black wig and a pointed beard. "As it happens, I—"

At that moment, Freddie burst through the doors at the end of the gallery. "Alice!" she cried. "I have found you at last! Jane is hurt! You must come quickly! She has been taken up for dead!"

"Good God!" Braden cried.

Alice stared at her sister for a long moment, then her slippered feet began moving swiftly down the hall. "What happened?" she cried. "How was she injured?"

Freddie held the door for her. "Aunt Urchfont stepped on her train while they were descending the stairs together because Jane had not properly gathered up all the fabric of her gown. Aunt, seeing that she had impeded Jane's progress, released her foot almost at once, but the force of the restraint coupled with the sudden release catapulted Jane forward. She was but a few feet from the bottom of the stairs, but in falling she struck her head on the banister. She has been insensible since." Freddie's voice caught.

Alice ran beside her. "But is she breathing?"

"I do not know."

By the time Alice arrived, Mr. Trickett was bending over Jane and gently stroking her cheeks. Louisa patted her hands and rubbed her arms. The silence among the masqueraders gathered about her was so intense that for some reason Alice felt they were all shouting at her.

She kneeled down beside dear Jane, whose complexion was the color of a white dove, and whispered urgently to her, "Dearest, tell me you are all right." She saw the lump forming at her hairline and the blood that was trickling from a tear in the skin into her blond hair. She withdrew a kerchief from the pocket of her trousers and dabbed at the wound. "Jane! Jane! You cannot leave me. What of your sisters and brothers? What of your gardens and your pets awaiting you in Wiltshire? Oh, my darling, I shall take you home at once, if only you will breathe!"

With that, Jane suddenly drew in a sharp gasp and her eyes fluttered ominously. "Louisa," Alice cried, "do you have your vinaigrette?"

"Yes, of course. What was I thinking?" She retrieved it from her own pocket and handed it to Alice, who then popped open the lid and held the small sponge beneath her sister's nose.

Jane began to moan, a circumstance that caused the assembled guests to cry out happily that the young lady had not expired as everyone had feared.

"I must get her home at once!" Alice cried.

Mr. Quintin moved forward. "I took the liberty of ordering your carriage. It awaits you even at this moment."

"How good you are, Mr. Quintin."

Mr. Trickett did not hesitate, but lifted Jane easily in his arms. Alice took up the hapless train and draped it over her sister's inert form. A series of pitiful moans continued to escape her lips.

"I shall send my physician to you," Braden said, following Alice from the house.

"I should be greatly indebted. You have no notion." Her sisters followed her into the coach as well as a quietly weeping Mrs. Urchfont.

The journey was spent comforting in turns Jane, who was beginning to gain her senses all the while complaining of a terrible headache, and poor Mrs. Urchfont, who cried out repeatedly, "It is all my fault! It is all my fault! I vow I am more clumsy than poor Hugo! Oh, poor Hugo! Poor Jane. It is all my fault!"

Braden was as good as his word, for his physician arrived shortly after Jane had been settled in her bed.

On the following afternoon, Alice stood before her chest of drawers sorting through her gloves, determining which pairs were no longer serviceable. She was fatigued from having sat at Jane's beside most of the night, but rather than attempt so tedious a task as balancing the household accounts she had opened the top drawer containing her numerous pairs of gloves and began examining them one by one. Failing to find five matches out of a dozen, she concluded that the Season was harder on gloves than even on ballgowns.

She drew in a deep breath, for she was tired to the bone. Jane had been restless in her sleep hour upon hour. Alice had watched her anxiously, now and then nodding into her own slumbers, only to awaken minutes later with some fresh outcry from her dear sister. She had relinquished her post by the bed only when the household servants began to stir.

Her excellent maid, Betsy, replaced her, promising to keep a watchful eye on Jane and to apprise her if there was the smallest change in her condition, for better or for worse. Alice had then dropped into a very heavy sleep from which Betsy had awakened her at ten with the excellent news that Jane was sitting up in bed and eating slow bites from a bowl of thin gruel. Except for a dull ache in the vicinity of the bump at her hairline, she professed herself to be perfectly well.

Alice had insisted on seeing Jane for herself and after being satisfied that her dear sister was indeed recovering with all due dispatch, she crawled back into bed to finally arise well past noon.

She had just set aside three pairs of gloves which were wholly beyond redemption when Freddie entered her bedchamber bearing an enormous bouquet of red roses.

Alice smiled at her sister, who in turn was beaming. "From Mr. Quintin?" she asked.

"Oh, on no account," Freddie cried. "These are from Braden."

"Braden?" she queried. "For me?"

"Of course," Freddie responded, her expression knowing. "He also sent a bouquet, though not of roses, to Jane." She moved forward to settle the flowers on a table between the tall windows overlooking the street. "Our sister's bedchamber has come to resemble a flower shop for if you must know both Quinney and Mr. Trickett sent flowers in hopes of her quick recovery as well."

Alice moved to the tall vase containing what must have been three dozen roses, touching one or two of the velvety petals and sniffing the heady fragrance. Freddie's reference to Mr. Quintin as Quinney had not been lost on her and she wondered just how long it would be before the couple was betrothed.

She drew the card from the vase and read the inscription which read quite simply, "Braden." She smiled. How very much like him to spare his words, she thought.

"Are you greatly fatigued from having sat with Jane all night?" Freddie asked.

"A little. I was able to sleep from time to time though I must say her slightest moan awakened me."

"Her complexion is greatly improved this morning and the swelling is not nearly so alarming as it was. Well, I will leave you for I promised Nicky that I would hear his Latin conjugations this morning. If for no other reason, I do hope

Jane leaves her sickbed very soon for I vow there is only one thing worse than having to listen to Nicky's ancient Roman recitations."

"And what would that be?" Alice asked, taking a single rose from the arrangement and holding it beneath her nose.

"Greek conjugations, of course," she cried.

Alice laughed and just after Freddie quit the room, she heard a carriage on the street. Moving close to the window and glancing down, she saw that Mr. Quintin had arrived. She could not help but smile. Nicky's Latin lesson would have to wait now.

She moved to her drawer and settled the red rose over a long pair of evening gloves. Her mind was drawn back just a few hours earlier when Braden had taken her into the rose garden, leading her deeply into the shadows and kissing her for what seemed an eternity. She had not wanted the moment to end, she had desired more than life itself to remain in the charmed state of feeling his lips devour her own. When he had knelt before her, embracing her legs, his head pressed against her purple sash, something within her had altered forever. A sensation that at the time had been utterly indefinable had flooded her. Now, however, as her finger lightly touched the velvet petal of the rose as it lay atop her glove, she understood that love had swept through her, love for a man she had thought never to cease despising.

She glanced at the large bouquet and wondered what Braden might be thinking about her today and even what his intentions might be. She could not mistake the truth that he was as charmed as she, 'else he would not have kept her in the garden as long as he had, nor sent the roses this afternoon. Braden was many things, but one thing for certain, he was direct in his conduct. The truth of his heart was always spoken not in what he said, but in what he did.

As such, a whisper of doubt played at the edges of her mind. In his steadfast refusal of the guardianship he had spoken his heart quite plainly. She knew that he had had a difficult time when his father died, for Quinney had mentioned more than once that the estate had been left in sham-

chuckling, she continued. "And now, on such a happy day as this, with so much to celebrate"—here she glanced at Freddie and Mr. Quintin—"we simply must have some champagne!"

Just as she rang for one of the lower maids to bring a bottle of the elegant sparkling wine and several glasses to the drawing room, a welcome visitor was announced.

"Sir Benedict!" she cried. "What a propitious moment for you to have come to us for we are in a wondrous state of merriment. Both Louisa and Freddie are engaged to be married."

"Is this so?" he cried, entering the room and congratulating each of the sisters in turn.

Alice's cheeks hurt from smiling so much, that is until she noticed that the gentlemen greeted Sir Benedict with but the smallest of bows and scarcely exchanged two words with him. For a moment she wondered at the reserve both Mr. Quintin and Mr. Trickett exhibited toward her dear friend. She would have to inquire at some point as to the reason for their coldness but for the present she would revel in his obvious delight at her sisters' good fortune.

The champagne arrived, glasses and toasts were passed round, the latter no less so on behalf of Jane who was well on her way to recovery and reclining on a chaise longue near the fireplace. Nicky was seated on the floor beside her, reworking the leather portion of one of his older slingshots.

Alice turned her attention to Mr. Trickett and Louisa, congratulating them again on what she knew would be all future happiness. They were discussing a date for the wedding, which was to be as near to the day after the posting of the banns as possible when Sir Benedict begged a word with her.

He led her gently to the windows, away from the happy couples. "My dear Alice," he murmured, catching her gaze, "All these weddings have given me such a notion."

Alice felt herself pale. She attempted a light note. "That you will have at least two wedding breakfasts to attend during the month of June?" She hoped he would take up her hint.

"I can see that you mean to spare my feelings," he said softly. "Only tell me, do I have even the smallest reason to hope?"

Alice would not wound her friend for the world but she felt she must speak. "I have spoken of this to no one, but it would seem my affections are engaged elsewhere—completely."

He started. "Indeed, is this so?"

She nodded. "I only recently discovered the state of my heart."

A kind of horror filled his eyes. "Do you refer," he whispered, "to Bradenstoke, for I know you have been seen in company with him of late?"

She nodded. "I love him, Sir Benedict, so very dearly. He is not at all what I thought he would be. You cannot imagine the kindnesses he has shown me and my family over the past fortnight."

"You do not know him," he murmured, appearing distressed.

"I misjudged him. We all did."

He sighed. "I should not speak but to fail to do so would be to abdicate my role as your friend. I beg you will not act hastily. My dearest Alice, he is not what he seems to be."

Sir Benedict had been such an excellent friend to her that she could not imagine he would speak maliciously of Braden without cause. "You must tell me what you know," she stated, her heart thumping in her chest.

"I think it entirely necessary that Lord Bradenstoke tell you himself, which he will certainly do once you ask him a very simple question."

"What would that be?" she inquired, puzzled.

"Ask him about Mr. Pinfrith. I have every confidence he will know precisely what I mean should you address the subject with him."

"Mr. Pinfrith?" Alice strongly suspected that somehow Sir Benedict had learned about the long-standing dispute over the property in Hampshire. She wanted to reassure him that the gentleman in question felt the disagreement would soon be settled, but she did not feel she had permission to discuss the matter with him.

Thoughts of Mr. Pinfrith, however, brought a wiggling of anxiety to her heart. Though she felt it was odd that she had not heard from him in some time, to a degree she was relieved for she knew her next letter must by necessity reveal her interest in his brother.

Sir Benedict lowered his voice. "You are of such a trusting disposition that I fear he has used you ill where Mr. Pinfrith is concerned. Again, I recommend you ask him, but of this I will say no more."

"I appreciate as always that you are tending to my interests," she responded, smiling. "And I will ask him."

He seemed intensely relieved. "And now I must away. I am riding with friends at Hyde Park but before I depart, tell me, is there news of Hugh?"

"Not yet, but I suspect I shall have word very soon, perhaps later this afternoon. Please call on me then, if you wish for it."

"I shall," he said, smiling.

Alice watched him leave, wondering just how he might have learned of the discord between the brothers. At that moment, Freddie asked Alice whether they should marry in London or in Wiltshire. The prospect of discussing wedding plans was a great deal more enjoyable than anything else under the sun, so it was that Sir Benedict's anxious hints about Braden's character were promptly forgotten.

A half-hour later, Braden stood on the threshold of Alice's drawing room. Every sense was heightened at the prospect of seeing again the woman he loved, but at the same time he was continually reminding himself of his most pressing need to tell her of his absurd deception.

Moving into the chamber, he found a party of sorts in progress, for there was an abundance of laughter as well as champagne present. Even Jane was apparently well enough to enjoy the festivities, reclining quietly as she was on a chaise longue with Nicky sitting on the floor beside her.

"Braden!" Alice cried, approaching him, wreathed in smiles. "You have arrived at just the right moment, for we are celebrating not one, but two betrothals."

Braden glanced from one visage to the next and could not help but smile. Love had found nearly all of them, he thought, as he noted how sweetly Louisa smiled up at Trickett and how closely Freddie sat beside dear, immaculate Quinney.

He moved forward and congratulated the happy couples, greeting as well a beaming Mrs. Urchfont, who winked at him and said, "Only one thing could possibly increase the happiness I feel at this moment, my lord, but of course you would already know what that would be." She giggled as a schoolgirl might.

He said nothing but turned to look directly at Alice in order to let her feel the precise state of his heart. She met his gaze fully, as was her way, and after a long, portentous moment, he crossed the room to her.

"I am so happy you have come," she said quietly, extending a glass of champagne to him.

"I must speak with you later," he murmured. "There is something of great import I would say to you."

"Of course," she responded softly. He could see that she was enchanted by the notion and for the barest moment he forgot entirely about Mr. Pinfrith and wondered if in speaking with her he might also be able to kiss her a little and hug her a little more.

With such thoughts trampling his mind in the happiest way, he gave himself a shake and turned instead to inquire after Jane's health. He moved to stand next to the chaise longue and asked how she was feeling. She assured him she was mending rapidly and would very soon be able to walk about as though nothing untoward had happened.

"I know I should still be resting in bed," she confessed, "but how could I remain confined in such a dull chamber when there is so much happiness here in the drawing room?"

He lowered his voice. "And I have it in my power to add to your joy," he whispered, "for I have had further word of Hugh."

She gasped. "What a day of miracles!" she cried.

Alice joined them. "What is going forward?" she asked.

Braden summoned the attention of everyone present. "At the risk of overshadowing two of the finest events in history, the betrothals of my dear friends to Miss Frederica and Miss Louisa, I have come with news for all of you." He withdrew Hicklade's letter from the pocket of his coat.

The Cherville ladies, one and all, exclaimed their delight.

"Tell us at once!" Louisa cried.

"Hicklade must have found him," Freddie added. "Has he seen him? Is he perfectly well? Why have we not heard from our brother himself all these weeks?"

Braden revealed the contents of the letter to the effect that Hugh was pronounced in steadily improving health by his physician, though still extremely weak as would be expected due to the severity of the injuries he had suffered.

"It is very curious that Hugh is being so secretive," Alice said.

He gave her the letter. "Hugh's direction can be found within. Mr. Hicklade did not feel it appropriate to go to him without either you or myself present."

"Mr. Hicklade is a man of great honor," Alice said. "But, oh, I must leave at once!"

When her siblings indicated their intention of traveling to Brighton with her, she quickly demurred. "As soon as I am able to determine if our brother is capable of receiving visitors, I will send for you, I promise." In the same breath, however, she turned to Braden. "You will attend me, will you not?"

The impulsive request brought an odd silence to the chamber as everyone turned to stare at her. Braden watched her cheeks darken and realized the simple truth that it would seem everyone present was aware of their growing attachment. Even Mrs. Urchfont was suppressing a smile.

"Alice," Nicky asked, "why are your cheeks red?"

She pressed her hands to her face. "I have not the faintest notion," she said, glancing down at him.

Braden cleared his throat. "As it happens, Hicklade is expecting me since I have been acting informally as your family's guardian," he returned promptly. "So, of course I shall be attending you to Brighton."

"Alice," Jane called to her, "will you ring for some tea for me? The champagne, I fear, does not agree with me just yet."

"Of course!" Alice cried. She cast a grateful glance at Jane for relieving her sudden embarrassment.

Soon afterward the entire house was thrown into a whirlwind of activity in preparation for Alice's departure. It was agreed that her coach would be used for the journey since a portion of the interior could be converted into a bed, by which she confessed she hoped to bring Hugh back to London. Louisa and Freddie argued about who would pack her portmanteaux and Nicholas scrambled to his feet, saying he must write a letter to Hugh to be taken to Brighton.

In the midst of the scurrying, Braden drew Alice aside. "I promise I will be ready for you the moment you arrive in Grosvenor Square, since I know you are anxious to be going, but I must leave now. If Mullens does not have sufficient time to prepare, he is of just such a temperament that he could easily fall into a decline from the despair of not having a proper number of neckcloths ready for travel."

Alice smiled and hooked his arm. "I shall accompany you downstairs then for there is something I must ask you about Hicklade's letter before you depart."

"Of course," he responded. He bid everyone good-bye, then accompanied Alice from the chamber.

"You blushed so prettily a few minutes ago. Only tell me why?"

She drew in a deep breath. "I could see that my request for you to accompany me to Brighton had been misunderstood."

"I think your family comprehended it completely, particularly Mrs. Urchfont. She had a great deal of difficulty hiding her smiles."

"So she did."

"You are blushing again," he cried.

Alice lifted her chin. "Most certainly I am not."

Braden chuckled. When they reached the bottom of the stairs, he said, "I know you had something you wished to discuss with me but would you mind doing so in your office?"

She glanced at the door, which was but a few feet away. "Of course not."

He could see she was entirely unaware of his intentions. However, he left her in little doubt because as soon as he crossed the threshold, he shut the door and dragged her quite abruptly into his arms.

"Braden, you should not—!" she protested, trying half-heartedly to push him away and giggling. "My family, Mr. Trickett, Mr. Quintin—they are upstairs! Oh!"

From the moment he settled his lips on hers, she quieted her movements. A moment more and she was leaning against him. "Oh, Braden," she murmured against his lips.

He demanded entrance, which she obliged without hesitating. His tongue sought the deepest recesses of her mouth and he had all the pleasure of feeling her hands drift up his arms until her fingers were gently touching his face and neck. He drew her closer still.

How different this kiss was for him after having come to understand the depths of his love for her. The marriage bed took shape in his mind and for the longest moment he had no other thought but laying her gently down and making her his wife.

"Alice, my darling," he murmured over her lips, her cheeks, her forehead, "I shall enjoy our journey to Brighton immensely." He drew back a little and looked into her eyes. The moment was right, he should tell her the truth about Mr. Pinfrith. He opened his mouth to speak, but before the words could pass his lips, she was kissing him in the most delightfully wanton fashion as she slipped her arms about his neck and held him fast.

He groaned, surrounding her fully with both arms and lifting her from her feet.

"I realize we do not as yet have an understanding," she whispered, dangling in the air, "but I wish you to know that you have become incredibly dear to me over the past few days."

"My darling," he murmured once more. Her lips silenced him yet again and he gently returned her feet to the carpet. He knew now that he could not possibly speak of William, not with her lips driving him to a place of wonderful madness over and over. He eased his conscience, however, by promising himself that once they were on the road to Brighton he would tell her the truth in the sincerest, humblest manner possible.

After a moment, he asked her what it was she wished to know about Hicklade's letter, but she merely stroked his cheek. "Nothing," she said with a laugh, "it was a but paltry excuse to be alone with you, I fear."

He laughed outright. "And I thought you entirely innocent when I suggested we speak in your office."

"Going into my office was an inspiration," she admitted, "particularly since in the whole of my scheme I could conceive of only a single kiss by the front door."

He laughed appreciatively and could not resist kissing her again. A few minutes later, she walked him to the front door. "I shall come to you as soon as my coach is made ready," she said.

He stole yet one last scandalous kiss before finally quitting her house.

Twenty-one

An hour later, Alice paced Braden's drawing room, waiting for him to descend the stairs. She wore a poke bonnet trimmed in apple green silk, a sturdy traveling gown, a matching pelisse, and half boots of a fine kid. She tugged at her gloves yet again, anxious to be going, for at the end of the journey she would finally see her dear brother. She wondered what it was Braden had forgotten that was of so urgent a nature that he must return to his chamber on the second floor to retrieve it!

As she walked the length of the chamber, she could not help but smile as she recalled her last visit to Braden's town house when she had actually challenged him to a fencing match. She had been incensed over his conduct toward his half brother, which of course Mr. Pinfrith himself had subsequently tempered in his letters to her. Briefly, she wondered yet again why it was she had not yet heard from Mr. Pinfrith, although she still was not relishing the task of somehow explaining to him that while he was in Portsmouth she had tumbled in love with his brother. Time enough she supposed to sort through this particular difficulty.

She heard Braden's booming voice upstairs, calling to Stevens, his butler, about a wicker basket that was used to hold all of Miss Cherville's letters. Had she heard him correctly? Had he asked about her letters? Was it possible he had read them? The very notion of it made her smile.

Alice moved to the doorway, from which vantage the stairs

were visible, and glanced up the stairwell. The town house was of magnificent proportions and a great number of masterful paintings were hung on the stairway walls. Where was Braden? She was exceedingly desirous to be going, which of course he knew.

As she turned back into the chamber, she was reminded suddenly of Sir Benedict's hints to her earlier that Braden was not what she believed him to be. She had pondered his concerns several times, wondering if he had indeed been referring to the dispute over the Hampshire property. It seemed wholly unlikely to her that he would have known anything about such a disagreement between Braden and his brother. On the other hand, she could not imagine what else he had been referring to. She smiled anew, for it occurred to her that on such a long journey as a trip to Brighton, which would require the entire night to complete, she would have ample opportunity to ask Braden if there was a basis for Sir Benedict's beliefs.

Hearing a coach outside Braden's town house, Alice wondered absently if someone might be calling on his lordship and moved to the window to look down into the street. A man sporting a caped greatcoat and a tall beaver hat descended from a fine coach, which she noted bore the Bradenstoke arms. A second conveyance, appearing to be a small wagon, drew up behind the traveling coach. Servants from both vehicles began to unload any number of trunks, portmanteaux, and wooden crates. The gentleman, whose face she still could not see, spoke jovially to the coachman, sliding what must have been a generous tip into his hands, for the servant grinned broadly as he doffed his hat.

The man turned around and glanced up at the house, at which time Alice had a clear view of his features. He seemed vaguely familiar to her yet quite sun-bronzed. His hair was black and his eyes, from that distance, appeared to be blue. Though he did not see her, he smiled in what Alice felt was some satisfaction before bounding up the steps and throwing the door wide.

"Braden!" the gentleman called out loudly. "Where the devil are you! Come greet your brother, at once!"

Alice pressed her gloved hand to her lips. Mr. Pinfrith had arrived, only why had he brought so much baggage from Portsmouth? She took several steps toward the doorway, which was situated but a few yards from the entrance hall.

"Hallo, Stevens," he called to the butler, who was not within her range of view. "How do you go on?"

"Very well, indeed, Mr. Pinfrith, thank you."

Alice felt a chill pass through her. Whatever was she to do? Mr. Pinfrith had returned but at such an awkward moment.

Alice could just hear the butler speaking with him, but she could not determine precisely what he was saying, although his purpose was evident a moment later when Mr. Pinfrith appeared on the threshold.

"Stevens has just informed me that Braden has a guest. How do you do, Miss Cherville? Forgive me if I seem greatly surprised to see you here and of course for the manner in which I entered the house as a barbarian would." His smile was friendly, but in no way particular.

"I feel I should explain immediately, Mr. Pinfrith. So very much has changed in the past fortnight that I hardly know where to begin. Braden has been of extraordinary service to me in discovering the whereabouts of my brother, though I must have mentioned something of it to you in one of my letters."

"Your letters?" he queried, pulling off his gloves. He seemed perplexed, his brow puckered in a serious frown.

"You are Mr. William Pinfrith, are you not?"

"The very one," he responded, a half smile on his lips.

Alice scrutinized his face carefully. So, this was the man who had kissed her at Vauxhall and written two letters to her. Why was he being so backward? She looked him up and down. It was the oddest thing; for somehow he seemed wholly unfamiliar to her, even shorter if that was possible. "The letters?" she queried in response. "Why, the ones I sent you recently in Portsmouth."

"Portsmouth," he cried. "I beg your pardon, but I have not been to Portsmouth in several years. I am just now returned from the East Indies. To what letters are you referring, for I have no knowledge of them?"

Ask Braden about Mr. Pinfrith.

The servants were now hauling Mr. Pinfrith's baggage into the entrance hall. She moved toward the stranger before her until she was but a few feet from him, a certain dizziness assailing her.

At the same moment, Braden bounded down the stairs, a large wicker basket held aloft in his arms. Because a servant bearing a trunk on his back was just mounting the stairs at that moment, Braden shifted the wicker basket away from him. He lost his grip and the contents, which proved to be several scores of letters, showered over the railing onto the pile of trunks and portmanteaux, forming a mountain in the entrance hall.

She might have been diverted by the sight but she was far too intent on discovering the truth about the man before her.

"Mr. Pinfrith," she said, wanting to be absolutely clear on one point in particular, "were you at Vauxhall some three weeks past?"

He shook his head, apparently mystified. "I'm 'fraid not, Miss Cherville. I would probably have been off the coast of Portugal at that time, I am not certain. I am but just arrived this morning at our docks on the Thames."

"William!" Braden cried, entering the chamber and clapping his brother on the back.

Alice saw at once that his complexion was heightened.

Mr. Pinfrith immediately embraced his brother, drew back, and laughed loudly. "I see what it is. Stealing my name again, Robert?" he asked.

Braden glared at him. "This is not the moment, Will. I have committed the gravest of errors."

"I see." He glanced at Alice then turned away from her. "I shall be in my chambers. Very nice to have met you, Miss Cherville."

"And you, *Mr. Pinfrith.*"

"Thank you, Will."

Alice stared at Braden, the horror of what she believed must have happened settling on her like a swarm of bees. "You must tell me at once what this means though I believe I have guessed at the truth."

"I had meant to tell you, a dozen times. I beg you will listen to me." He took her firmly by the arms but his touch was a painful fire on her arms. He continued. "So much has happened in the past several weeks, so very much, and every day for the past sennight I have been intending, even longing to tell you, only there always seemed some obstacle to my speaking. At the masquerade, if you will remember, before Jane's concussion, I told you there was something I felt you should know and each time I brought news of your brother I wanted to tell you, but each time I was prevented. Even an hour ago, while we were in the office together, but your kisses were too sweet." He paused. "I finally vowed to myself that once we were on our way to Brighton I would tell you the truth."

"And what is the truth, precisely, that all this time you were masquerading as your brother, that you lied to me at Vauxhall, told me such a Banbury Tale about a piece of property in Hampshire that I might be seduced into letting you kiss me? It is all too horrible to be believed. Only a rogue would do such a thing." She grimaced. "I wish you would release me."

"No," he responded sharply. "Not until I have had my say. All those absurd purposes seemed reasonable at the time because we were nothing less than enemies."

"Three weeks," she murmured, remembering so many details all at once. "You have been deceiving me . . . I wrote to you and you wrote to me . . . everything you said in your letters! Braden, where do the lies end and the truth begin for I swear I cannot make it out."

"Forget the letters, I beg you. What is true is how I feel when I hold you in my arms." He let his hands glide down her arms then he held her fast once more.

"What do I care for that when all I can think of is how

shocked Mr. Trickett was when I told him you had withheld the Hampshire property from Mr. Pinfrith. Yet, you did not, did you?"

He shook his head. "That was a whisker. I made certain William was put in possession of the property shortly after the reading of my father's will."

"That at least is to your credit," she said coldly. "Mr. Trickett, however, knew of your masquerade, did he not?"

Braden nodded. "Alice, please listen to me. I have wished this deed undone innumerable times. You must believe me."

"Am I to applaud you for possessing such a sentiment?" she asked.

"No, of course not."

"I must go," she said. "I beg you will release me."

With apparent reluctance, he let his hands fall away. "I will still attend you to Brighton," he said.

She shook her head and walked swiftly into the entrance hall, where a slow trail of servants were moving up the stairs. It occurred to her that they had been privy to the entire exchange and that before long every soul in Mayfair would know of Braden's deception. Her chest ached with the depth of her disappointment in him.

"But I love you!" he cried, for all the world to hear, following closely on her heels. "So deeply. Please do not go, do not allow our future together to be affected by a foolish impulse I now regret infinitely. I beg you will forgive me."

She turned to him, glancing once more at the stairs where the servants had ceased their march altogether and were presently staring at her. She noticed that Stevens was gathering up a great many letters and returning them to the wicker basket. "Are those my letters?" she asked, stunned. Braden was but a foot from her.

"Yes, I was bringing them downstairs. I wanted to take them on our journey, to read them with you. You see, I spent the entire morning finally doing as I should have done years ago—I read them."

She released a sigh and shook her head. "I begin to think this happened for the best today," she said sorrowfully. "It is not just that you deceived me, though I believe such an action must speak to your character more greatly than you think it does, but do you not see, Braden, you will always be the man who refused the guardianship, for whatever your reasons. This . . . this childish deception merely reminded me of what I already know to be true. How could I ever trust such a man with what I value most?"

"Because I am changed," he stated. "Knowing you has changed me."

She could not resist touching his face gently. "That is not possible and well you know it if you will but search your heart."

He caught her hand. "Alice, please . . ."

"I must go to Hugh," she stated, and then she was gone.

Braden stood staring at the inside of his front door. He had been entirely unable to think of anything to say that he might believe for a moment would cause her to stay. In truth, he could scarcely blame her for responding as she had, after all he was the one, in his prejudice against her, who had taken on William's identity in the first place. There was no fault to be found in Alice Cherville, only in his own arrogance and stupidity.

He turned and saw that his servants were still gaping at him. He rolled his eyes. "Is everyone sufficiently entertained?" To the last man, the caravan began moving once more.

He turned and saw that Stevens had gathered all the letters into the wicker basket. "Thank you," Braden said. "I can only suppose that my brother is upstairs?"

"Yes, my lord," he responded quietly but with a faint cluck of his tongue almost too soft to have been heard.

"You cannot possibly reproach me more than I have reproached myself in this moment."

"I should think not, my lord."

He shook his head as he mounted the stairs. His thoughts turned to his half brother and he realized that however agitated he was that Alice had spoken as she had, he could not help but be joyous that William had arrived home safely after an absence of more than two years. Neither the difficult climate of the East Indies, nor storm, nor illness had separated him from his only sibling, half blood or not.

Entering William's chamber, he saw arrayed on his chest of drawers several porcelain objects.

"Lovely, are they not?" William asked as he drew another from a wooden crate stuffed with straw.

"China?"

"Yes."

Braden handled them. "They will do well here I think and on the Continent."

"Frisk had a look at them. He was most enthusiastic."

"As he should be."

"So tell me, Robert, how the deuce did you fall in love with your old Nemesis?" His smile was teasing but there was a sympathetic light in his eye.

"You heard me then?"

William chuckled. "You have never understood that your voice carries louder and farther than a sea captain's in a storm. I daresay your neighbors heard your declaration as well."

Braden took up a chair by the door and balancing a booted foot on the edge of another wooden crate, told him the entire tale, beginning at the very point, Vauxhall, which presently had him fixed so badly.

William chuckled throughout the whole of it. "Did not I tell you that one day you would regret not having taken up the guardianship?"

"Indeed, you did, more than once."

"Just think. Had you done so earlier, you might have been wed by now with a dozen babes running about your halls."

"Do not torment me. I am desolate enough as it is."

"You should go after her, you know."

Braden sighed and stared up at the ceiling. "I might have done so had it just been a matter of having deceived her but she said something that is troubling me deeply."

"What was that?"

"Something to the effect that she could never trust me because I had refused the guardianship."

"I see. That is serious. It would seem the lady has doubts which your ridiculous masquerade has only served to encourage."

Braden looked at his brother and smiled. "Regardless, I am happy to have you home, Will. You were gone far too long this time."

"I could not have returned a day earlier and once you have seen all that I have brought home, you will declare my absence to have been worth every minute I was away, although the physician who attended me said I would be wise to remain at home for a time."

Braden sat up, sliding his boot to the floor. "You were ill?" he asked. The fevers in the Orient could be deadly.

"There was a point I did not expect to recover."

"Then the matter is settled. You shall not leave these shores again unless it is to travel to France on holiday. Besides, Frisk has two sons who are both anxious to begin taking on larger duties."

"Then it is all but settled. However, I should tell you I have no intention of doing the pretty in London."

"You might want to this Season," Braden said, "for I believe I have found a country wife for you."

William laughed. "If she is a country wife, then what the devil is she doing in London?"

"Longing for her poultry, her dogs and cats, her rose garden, her beehives, her horses, she may even have the care of the pigs, I am not certain."

"Oh dear," Will responded, his lips twitching. "Care of the pigs, eh? What an adorable picture you paint."

Braden chuckled. "Her name is Jane, she is quite beautiful, light blond hair, blue eyes, the sweetest of temperaments."

"Why is such a Nonpareil unattached?"

"As I said before, she has no interest in company and suffered through every ball she attended. She is no Antidote, mind, just wishful of being elsewhere."

"And her name?"

"Cherville."

William glanced at him. "You are serious then? Having discovered that one Cherville will do for you, I must have the next?"

"Not the next, Trickett is betrothed to Miss Louisa and Quinney to Miss Frederica. I thought you would do well to take up the slack."

"We shall see," he said, chuckling.

Alice returned to Upper Brook Street. Having lost Braden's company, she had little desire to travel to Brighton alone and hoped she might be able to persuade Louisa to attend her. She entered the house to the amazement of her siblings, but fobbed off their queries with the simple statement that at the very last moment Bradenstoke had become violently ill. Her explanation appeared to satisfy everyone and she was about to ask Louisa if she would be interested in joining her in lieu of the earl, but at that moment Sir Benedict was announced. She had completely forgotten that earlier she had suggested he call on her to find out if they had had word of Hugh.

"You appear ready to travel, my dear," he said, entering the room with a smile.

"She is," Nicky said. "Hugh has been found and Alice is going to Brighton to fetch him."

"Indeed!" he cried. "But this is the very best of news!"

"We learned of it shortly after you called," Alice said. "Bra—that is Lord Bradenstoke arrived with a letter from Mr. Hicklade. I have Hugh's direction in my reticule. Now that you are here, I wonder if I might ask a very great favor of you?"

"Anything that is within my power," he said.

She glanced at him. "Are you well, Sir Benedict? You look a trifle pale."

"Perfectly well," he responded quickly.

Alice, though a little concerned by his increased pallor,

proceeded to extend her request that he accompany her and after a slight hesitation as he reviewed his engagements for the next several days, he accepted quite happily. "You know I would do anything for you or your family," he said.

With that, Alice took him up in her coach and returned with him to his home, where he quickly had his valet pack for a short journey.

Once within the coach, Alice noticed he had brought with him a long, wooden box. "I see you have brought your fencing foils," she said, chuckling. "Are you planning on engaging in a duel while we are tending to Hugh?"

He laughed as well. "Of course not, but perhaps you and I can engage in a little swordplay."

She shook her head. "After so many weeks without my brother, I know that I will be spending every waking moment in his company."

He smiled at her. "Do you know, after all these years, you have never fenced with me. Always, you have avoided it. I wonder why."

"I know when I am outmatched," she responded. Her thoughts took a very sad turn as she recalled not so long ago that she had challenged another man, who far outmatched her, to a fencing duel. She would not allow herself to repine, however. Instead, she asked why he had brought his swords on their journey to Brighton.

"Did you not know?" he responded. "I never leave my house for an extended time without them. Several of my friends fence. I even have a distant relation in Wales who was used to be quite fond of the art, but that was many years past. He is since deceased, quite recently as it happens."

Twenty-two

Later that evening, Braden was just sitting down to dinner with his brother when his courier arrived from Brighton with yet another letter from Mr. Hicklade.

"You will excuse me, Will?"

"Do not stand upon ceremony with me, old chap," he said, settling his spoon into a beautiful bowl of turtle soup.

Braden broke the seal and scanned the contents quickly. "Good God," he murmured, and once more read the letter. "I had my suspicions, but they were only vague."

To the courier waiting in the shadows, he said, "I will not be needing you again, Jack. Please go to the kitchens." When the courier departed, he addressed his butler, "Stevens, see that he is cared for and have my valet repack my clothes. I will need my coach brought round as quickly as possible. It seems I will be going to Brighton after all."

"Very good, m'lord."

"Whatever is amiss, Robert?" Will asked.

Braden glanced behind him and dismissed the two remaining footmen from the chamber. When they were gone, he said, "This letter is concerning that business I told you about earlier."

"The attack on Hugh Cherville."

"Yes. Apparently, this morning he invited Hicklade to come and see him. Mr. Cherville it would seem had come to believe that Sir Benedict Locksbury was behind the attempt on his life."

"Locksbury? Good God!"

"It would seem Mr. Cherville finally read some correspondence from his cousin's solicitor, not only did he discover that his cousin, who was next in line to inherit after Nicky, had died but that following him in the succession was—"

"Sir Benedict!"

"Just so."

William whistled long and low.

"In addition, the solicitor included information the cousin had been seeking on behalf of the Chervilles and himself, to whit, the exact nature of the baronet's finances. It would seem he is some forty thousand pounds in debt."

"Good God. Forty thousand! An entire fortune." He paused and set his spoon down. "But do you think him capable of murder?"

"I cannot say," Braden murmured. "Mr. Cherville has asked that I come to Brighton, but without Alice or any of his family, in order to plan a strategy by which he might expose Sir Benedict."

"Has not Miss Cherville already departed?"

He glanced at the clock on the mantel. "She will have been gone these five hours and more and as much as I am fond of you, Will, and grateful you are home safely, I must away—immediately."

"Of course," his brother responded, smiling crookedly. "You love her very much, then?"

Braden rose to his feet. "More than you will ever know."

When Braden completed changing for the journey, he descended the stairs only to find his mother just arrived. She was embracing William and patting his face as though he were a child of ten instead of a man of more than thirty years. William was beaming.

She caught sight of him. "Robert," she called out, "I was hoping to persuade you and William to accompany me to Lady Wroughton's soiree but Will said that you were leaving town."

"Indeed I am," he responded, his senses growing more

heightened with each passing minute. He had a prescience of danger which he hoped would in no way be justified by what he found in Brighton. Regardless, he felt strongly the need to be going. "I have been summoned to Brighton by Miss Cherville's brother, Hugh."

"Then you have learned his whereabouts."

"He is being cared for by a family residing near the Steyne but had refrained from communicating with Alice because he lives in some fear of his life."

"Good God," she murmured, "you are frightening me. And who is it that he believes wishes to see him to an early grave?"

"Sir Benedict Locksbury," he said.

She shook her head in disbelief. "But are you certain? Sir Benedict has always been most affable in company."

"I do not know if it is true, but there seems to be ample reason to believe it a possibility."

William interjected. "I will let you speak with Robert while I fetch my cloak. Oh, and if you do not tell her of Miss Cherville, I shall!"

"What has happened? Does she not return your love?"

"How did you guess!" he exclaimed.

"Only because I have known you, my darling, since you were a babe."

As William disappeared into the hallway beyond the entrance hall, Braden led his mother into the drawing room in order to allow his valet and footmen to begin preparing his coach.

"Alice discovered that I had been deceiving her, having pretended to be William at Vauxhall some three weeks past. She found me out in the worst manner possible. She had originally requested that I accompany her to Brighton this afternoon and was awaiting me in my drawing room when the deeply sun-bronzed man who burst into my home proved to be none other than the real William Pinfrith."

She chuckled. "What a goosecap you are to be playing at such antics. How old are you, Robert? Sixteen?"

"You need not reproach me, Mama. I have not ceased

doing so myself from the moment I saw the stunned expression on her face as she greeted my brother. She will never forgive me."

"Never? Oh, I doubt that very much. In time, she will see it for what it was, a momentary lapse in your usually brilliant good judgment."

He shook his head. "What she actually said to me was that she did not think she could ever trust me because I had refused the guardianship. This deception only confirmed a much deeper distrust of me."

"I see," she murmured. "Then might I make a suggestion?"

"I would welcome any you might offer."

"You must prove your worth to her and I feel certain that if you search your mind and heart you will discover just how that might be accomplished."

He nodded just as Stevens appeared in the doorway and informed him that his coach was in readiness. "I must go," he said. He leaned down and placed a kiss on her cheek. "Enjoy your evening with William."

"Of course I shall and pray do not fret. Life has a wonderful trick of sorting itself out in the very best of ways."

Braden smiled, if doubtfully, and quit the house.

He climbed aboard his coach but on impulse directed the coachman to Upper Brook Street, hoping perhaps that something unforeseen might have detained Alice. Twenty minutes later, when he was led into the drawing room where the family was merry with a game of commerce, along with Quinney and Trickett, he was greeted with expressions of astonishment that he had recovered so quickly from the illness that had prevented him from attending Alice to Brighton in the first place. He might have argued the point, but as soon as he realized she was already gone, he decided there would be time enough at a later date to confess his misdeeds to the rest of the family.

"She decided to travel alone?" he inquired, wondering why one of her siblings, all of whom were present, had not accompanied her.

"No," Nicky said, "Sir Benedict went with her."

"Sir Benedict?" he queried, stunned.

"He is a good friend," Mrs. Urchfont explained. "He has been Alice's greatest support all these years."

The sensation that passed through Braden was as of a lightning bolt striking him hard in the chest. If Sir Benedict had truly acted as maliciously as Hugh believed him to have done, then the woman he loved was in the worst danger, having been lulled to a place of trust and complacency by a man of so little conscience as to be incredible by any standard.

"I see," he murmured. "I shall away then." He did not think it wise to alarm the young ladies or Nicholas and certainly not Mrs. Urchfont of his dark suspicions.

Trickett followed him downstairs to the front door. "Is something amiss?" he asked.

Braden took a deep breath and explained all that he knew of Sir Benedict's involvement with the Chervilles, of his debts and of being positioned so nearly to inherit Tilsbury Hall. "It would seem that all these years he was careful to keep the knowledge of his distant relationship to the Chervilles a secret."

"I never trusted him, but I thought him merely an unfortunate gamester. You did know that he has been in pursuit of Alice's hand in marriage these past several months?"

"I did not but I am not surprised," Braden responded. "He successfully chased away every fortune hunter who dared to approach her, apparently hoping to win the prize for himself."

"Shall I accompany you?"

"No," he said. "I do not think it necessary and I would not for the world give the family cause for alarm. It would seem that Hugh is a guest in the home of a good family near the Steyne. How could Sir Benedict, who still believes himself safe, be of any danger to Hugh now?"

"I am certain you are right," Trickett said.

Braden chuckled. "The devil you do. Regardless, I shall

send for the family when I have ascertained that all is safe
and whether or not Hugh is sufficiently recovered."

"Very well."

Trickett clapped him on the shoulder. A moment more,
and his coach was traveling at a brisk pace up the street and
in the direction of Brighton.

Because of the depths of his misgivings, however, the
horses could not move swiftly enough to suit him. As it was,
he would be traveling the night through and could only hope
that Sir Benedict had no immediate plans to do Hugh further
injury, if indeed he proved to be the author of the attack on
the lad near Theale.

He sat in a state of supreme misery for a long, long time,
as London Bridge was crossed, as the coach changed horses
at the outskirts of London, and finally left the metropolis
behind. His thoughts ran in an unforgiving circle, that had
he just told Alice earlier of his ridiculous deception he would
even now be with her in Brighton and able to protect her
and her brother should such a need arise. Instead, he was
here, lumbering along at a mere six or seven miles per hour
into the night. He might as well have been separated from
Alice by centuries as hours should Sir Benedict choose to
act while he was yet on the road.

He pounded one fist against the other. He understood in
this moment that he would do absolutely anything for Alice,
so great was his love for her—anything!

"Alice," a soft voice murmured next to her ear, "we will
be in Brighton soon, only a few miles more."

Alice awoke to the dark interior of the coach, her head
resting awkwardly on Sir Benedict's shoulder. She had slept
here and there, the fatigue of traveling so great a distance in
an afternoon and a night finally overcoming the bounces and
jolts of the road.

"What is the hour, do you suppose?" she asked, yawning.

Sir Benedict glanced out the windows. "There is no sign
of the dawn as yet."

"As much as I long to see my brother, I vow all I can think about now is my bed."

"I as well," he said gently. "I only wish we could have left London earlier. You would have been reunited with your brother by now."

Alice looked out the windows. A faint light from the carriage lamps illuminated some of the passing shrubbery. She stifled another yawn and shifted in her seat. How glad she would be when the journey was over.

The journey thus far had been rather pleasant. Sir Benedict's company was always soothing, for he was exceedingly polite and whenever they would stop at an inn to refresh themselves, his sole object was her comfort.

The only true difficulty, beyond the weariness of road travel, had been how frequently her thoughts had turned to Braden and how with each thought her heart felt as though it would constrict tightly for a very long moment before finally releasing to begin beating again. She was, essentially, sad beyond words, for regardless of her conviction that he was not truly trustworthy, she still loved him, so very much. She was old enough, however, to comprehend that love was not the only necessary component of marriage. A deep and abiding trust must be equally present. She had spoken her heart clearly when she had told him that she did not feel she could truly rely on him because he had refused the guardianship so many years ago. Even Sir Benedict had agreed that she was being wise in her refusal of the earl.

Nonetheless, she withheld a very deep sigh.

"Alice," Sir Benedict said, turning toward her slightly, "there is something I would discuss with you, that is if you are not overly tired."

Alice smiled. "I am tired, but please speak whatever is on your mind."

"Thank you," he said, smiling. "I know this might not be the most appropriate moment, but given your recent disappointment in Bradenstoke's character, I was hoping you would give my proposals another consideration. We have been friends for so long, and I have loved you so dearly, that it would be my greatest honor to have the care of you and your family."

He had taken hold of her hand and pressed it lightly. She glanced at his hand and shook her head. She was a little startled that even after having refused him earlier that afternoon that he would press his suit yet again, however tactfully.

"My dear friend," she began gently, "I hope I have not unwittingly given you reason to hope."

"This does not sound promising," he said.

"It is not," she stated firmly. "I beg you will forgive me if I ever misled you, but I must refuse your kind and most generous offer. I do not love you as a wife should love her husband. I greatly esteem you, I admire you in so many ways, and I trust that our friendship will always be of as much importance to you as it is to me, but I will never be your wife."

She could see Sir Benedict's expression even as dimly lit as the interior of the coach was. The line of his jaw seemed rather hardened as though he were grinding his teeth. She had not thought he would become angry upon receiving her fourth refusal.

"You do understand, do you not, Sir Benedict?"

"Of course," he answered abruptly. "I merely thought that in time . . . well, never mind that. I suppose this changes everything."

"What do you mean? I trust our friendship will always remain as steadfast."

He shook his head and turned to stare out the window. "Nothing to signify," he responded.

He was clearly distressed, more greatly than she had thought he would be, but why the sudden shift in his demeanor toward her and why had he said that everything must change? She felt alarmed in a manner she could not precisely comprehend.

She tried to take his hand in hers, to offer what comfort and reassurance she could, but he snatched it away. "I beg you will not," he said curtly.

"Of course," she responded, clasping her hands together on her lap.

The remainder of the journey was a quiet one. Sir Benedict barely exchanged two words with her, which rather astonished Alice. She felt his conduct was so different from what she had come to expect of him that she thought she was well out of such a marriage were Sir Benedict of a more quixotic nature than she had thought he might be.

When the coach reached the Crown Inn, and a sleepy-eyed stableboy tended to the horses, his demeanor grew a trifle more affable. Alice chuckled to herself as she realized that clearly Sir Benedict was merely as fatigued as she was and would soon recover his usual composure.

Within a few minutes after sliding between the sheets, Alice fell deeply into her slumbers.

Just past nuncheon, a lovely young lady by the name of Miss Merrymeet showed Alice into the bedchamber that had housed her brother for over six weeks.

"Alice," he called out, sitting up in bed, *The Times* spread out on his lap, "I had not thought you were to come, but, oh, what a happy sight you are!"

Alice ran to his side and embraced him. The tears she had promised herself she would not shed in his presence rolled down her cheeks and dropped onto the sleeve of his thick nightshirt. He was so very pale and much thinner than when she had last seen him in Wiltshire. "My dear Hugh!" she cried. "We thought—well, we thought we might never see you again."

"There was a time when my fears were no less profound," he murmured against her cheek. "But come, let me present you to Miss Merrymeet, who has had the care of me."

Alice released him but could not let go of his hand as she turned to receive a more formal introduction to the young lady Hugh credited with his recovery more than any other individual, including the physician. "For it was Miss Merrymeet who sat up night after night, and fed me broth or laudanum, pressed cold compresses to my fevered head, and eased my general suffering with an endless stream of the prettiest songs."

Alice took in a deep breath. "Miss Merrymeet, will you accept a sister's eternal gratitude for your devotion to my brother? I promise you, should you ever require anything of me, you have but to ask."

Miss Merrymeet blushed. "I . . . I was happy to be of service, Miss Cherville." She turned to gaze upon Hugh and the soft expression that entered her eyes bespoke an affection far greater than friendship.

Alice glanced at her brother and saw the same affection returned in the warmth of his eyes and the tender smile on his lips. A love-match, she thought, her heart expanding wondrously. Well, if her brother had found love, and that so unexpectedly, she thought that at least a portion of his sufferings were not without some value.

Hugh glanced toward the doorway and frowned slightly. "Did not Lord Bradenstoke attend you?" he asked.

"No," Alice responded softly, "I . . . I thought it best I travel without him."

"You came alone? All this distance?"

"Actually, a most excellent friend accompanied me," she responded, moving toward the door. "I shall just fetch him."

"Alice," he called out, leaning forward and wincing slightly, "who came with you? I beg you will tell me."

"Sir Benedict. He is most anxious to see you."

Alice's smile froze on her lips as she watched her brother's complexion pale to a deathlike shade of gray.

"No," he called out to her. He pushed the covers back from his lap and with every sign of weakness, shifted his legs over the side of the bed. "I must get up. Charlotte, I beg you will help me."

Miss Merrymeet was beside him instantly. "No, Hugh, you must not! Your leg cannot yet bear the weight."

Alice, greatly alarmed, ran to his bedside. "Hugh, whatever is the matter?" she cried. "Do get back into bed!"

"Alice, you do not understand. Sir Benedict—"

"Was he the one, Hugh?" Miss Merrymeet whispered, her expression horror-stricken.

Hugh nodded.

"Good God," Alice murmured. "What are you saying?"

"The attack near Theale."

"But I do not understand? How can you say such a thing? There has been no kinder friend to us than Sir Benedict."

"Alice, do you remember that letter I received from our cousin's solicitor in Wales, the one you reproached me for because I had not taken the time to either read or respond to it?"

"Yes?"

"Well, I did so, that night in Theale. In it was the strangest information which I could not for the longest time credit."

Alice felt ill, for she could sense what was next to come. "Pray continue," she said, easing herself down on the side of the bed.

"Not only is our cousin dead, the one who would have inherited Tilsford after Nicky, but next in line is Sir Benedict."

Alice was stunned. "Why did he never tell us? How could we not have known of his relation to our family?"

"In the absence of male heirs, the line can become twisted and difficult to follow. Clearly, he wished it kept a secret. But there is more. He is in debt to the cent-percenters for over forty thousand pounds."

Even Miss Merrymeet gasped.

"He asked me to marry him just a few hours ago. I can now understand why he pressed his suit as he did for the past several months. And to think he made a great point of chasing all the fortune hunters away from our door. He wanted my fortune for himself." She gave her head a shake. "But, Hugh, do you truly think he was the one who attacked you?"

"I believe he hired thugs to do the job in his stead."

"I cannot believe it of him." She felt like weeping. She had trusted Sir Benedict so completely.

Hugh took her hand. "Dearest, do you remember the accident I had so many years ago when Sir Benedict was first come into the neighborhood?"

"Yes."

"Well, who arrived in time to help me?"

"But he saved your life!" she cried.

"I am come to believe not only had he hired someone to cause the accident but that his arrival was no coincidence. Had not our vicar appeared round the bend at the same time, I am persuaded he would have—"

"Do not speak it!" Alice cried.

"But there is something more. The night I was attacked, I saw Sir Benedict at the Stump and Pelican."

"Oh, no," she murmured. Her heart began pounding in her chest. "What are we to do? He is belowstairs even now."

When Hugh attempted once more to leave the bed, she stayed him with a hand on his arm. "Wait. Let me think. I will find a way to manage the situation, never fear." After a moment she said, "He will not harm you here, I am convinced of that, for it would be madness."

"What else is he if not mad?" Hugh countered. "The devil! I am as weak as a kitten and a hundred times as useless."

Once more, he fell back against the pillows, his expression agonized.

"Miss Merrymeet," Alice said, "where is your family?"

"On the Steyne but a short walk from here. They should be returning within the hour."

"I beg you will fetch them."

"At once," she cried, fairly running to the door.

"Charlotte," Hugh called out, "use the servants' stairs."

"I will," she returned. "I was thinking the very same thing." With that she slipped from the chamber.

"I know what I must do," Alice said, glancing at her brother. "I shall go downstairs and tell Sir Benedict that you are not well enough to receive visitors and we shall return to the Crown Inn. After that, I shall find some way of stealing away from the inn and return to you. Mr. Merrymeet should be with you by then."

"Alice, I have the worst presentiment. I beg you will not go. Pray, remain with me until Mr. Merrymeet returns. He is an able gentleman and will know quite well how to deal with Sir Benedict."

At that moment, a scratching sounded on the door and Sir Benedict's voice intruded. "Might I see our invalid?" he called out.

Alice rose to her feet her hand against her throat. "One moment," she returned, attempting a cheerful note. To Hugh she whispered, "Remain here, dearest." She leaned down and kissed her brother's cheek.

"Alice," he whispered urgently, his face crumpling, "be careful."

"I will," she responded, a smile faltering on her lips. Her eyes had welled with tears and she quickly withdrew a kerchief. She moved to the door and before Sir Benedict could enter she pushed him back, pulled the door shut and pretended to cry. "Oh, Sir Benedict, you cannot imagine how poorly he feels. I fear he is not well enough to see you. Indeed, I felt I should leave in order to let him rest."

"How's this?" he inquired. "I spoke with the doctor not ten minutes ago and he gave a much more hopeful portrait."

"I suppose he would since he is not looking at Hugh through a sister's eyes."

"Of course not," Sir Benedict said. He seemed to be watching her carefully.

"Where is the doctor now?" she asked, glancing down the hall toward the stairs and wiping at her nose.

"As to that," he said, smiling faintly, "I sent him away, of course."

"Why?" Alice asked, alarmed all over again.

"I shall explain in a moment. I beg you will attend me in the ballroom, where we might converse privately."

"I . . . I have been thinking, Sir Benedict. I should like to return to the Crown Inn. I am of no use here and I believe I need a few hours to regain my composure."

"I can see that you do," he offered sympathetically, "but

what I need to say to you really cannot wait and we shall be left to our own devices in the ballroom."

"How do you know where it is?"

"All fine houses are similar—a hallway or two and there you are."

Alice was trembling as she walked down the stairs. She could not imagine what he must needs say to her of such urgency, but she felt certain her best path was to seem agreeable. Still, she could not help but press him a little. "I am certain once we are within my coach we shall have all the privacy required for a conversation." They had reached the bottom of the stairs and the front door was but a few paces away. "Come," she added with a smile as she slid her arm about his in what she hoped was an inviting manner. "We are near enough to walk back to the inn, if you should prefer."

He smiled and she almost thought he meant to acquiesce. "How beautiful you are," he murmured on a sigh. "However, I do not wish to walk nor to speak with you in a coach. I prefer the ballroom."

"Very well," she said, chuckling faintly. "Only, I must say I think it quite odd of you."

"I imagine you would."

The smile he offered her, so cold, so unlike the Sir Benedict she had known all these years, set her knees to trembling.

Twenty-three

Alice stared in horror at a pair of fencing foils Sir Benedict held in his hands. "I do not understand," she said, her heart pounding. "Whatever do you mean by bringing me into a ballroom and showing me a pair of swords? Are they Mr. Merrymeet's? Wherever did you find them?"

"No, my dear. They are mine, remember? I always travel with them. After all, what is the purpose of acquiring such a noble skill and yet never being prepared to make use of it?"

He stood next to a pianoforte that was situated in the middle of the ballroom. The sword case lay on top of the instrument.

There was an odd light in his eye that she had never seen before, or perhaps because at her own need of his friendship over the years she had just never before noticed.

"But this is absurd," she cried, laughing lightly. "I certainly do not mean to fence with you in the house of my brother's host."

"You do not feel sufficiently prepared," he stated. "However, if you are able to hoist your skirts a trifle, and remove your half boots, I believe you will acquit yourself quite well." He reclined the swords in the box and began removing his coat. "Certainly well enough to suit my purposes."

"I will not fence with you, Sir Benedict, and I most certainly do not understand why you are pressing me in this manner. At the very least I would consider it a great rudeness to the Merrymeets."

"Fencing is an elegant sport. They will forgive you, I am certain of it."

"I believe you have gone mad," she said at last.

"I suppose I have, but you will fence with me." He removed his shoes and tested the feel of the wood floor against his stockings. "It will serve. And now, Alice, shall we? Boscombe always praised your abilities in the highest most ridiculous fashion possible and today I intend to test your mettle."

She turned on her heel, hoping a bit of bravado would win the day, and headed swiftly for the door.

"Do you actually think," he called after her, "that I chanced by Hugh's door a moment ago?" Panic seized her and she froze in her tracks. She turned back to him and found that his expression had grown as hard as flint. "If you leave now, I promise you I shall mount the stairs swiftly and complete what I failed to do in Theale so many weeks past."

She turned horrified eyes upon him. So it was true that he had been the author of the attack on Hugh. Tears started to her eyes. "I accounted you my friend and now you will confess to so terrible a crime?"

"You should have married me when you had the chance. Although, by God, you are so pretty I vow all you must do is give a nod of assent and I will take you to Gretna on the instant."

"I had rather be devoured by snakes," she responded coldly.

He laughed outright. "That is a bit of plain speaking. The foils, then?"

Alice glanced at the open box. She felt as trapped as a hunted animal might. "Should I come to grief, Sir Benedict, how do you intend to explain whatever injuries I might suffer at your hands? Even if you succeed in dispatching the pair of us, how will you explain it to Mr. Merrymeet?"

Her words had given him pause, but only for a second or two. "I shall not be deterred, Miss Cherville. You know too much and as I have already proved to you, I can be quite convincing when necessary."

She straightened her shoulders. "Very well, then," she said, "I will fence with you." She could only hope that the Merrymeet family would return from the Steyne before much mischief could be done.

She slowly removed her pelisse and settled it on the pianoforte. She stripped off her gloves and her half boots, the latter of which she knew would fail to glide about the floor in the manner she would require.

As she began adjusting her skirts, she considered her opponent. She knew Sir Benedict to be skilled in the art of fencing, for Boscombe had praised his abilities. Yet she had no real knowledge of Sir Benedict's style, having never seen him fence before. What she did know was that if she hoped to be successful against him, for her brother's sake as well as her own, she would need to concentrate fully on his every maneuver.

She finished arranging her skirts by once more tucking the bulk of one side into the ribbon at the high waist of her gown. Fortunately, she was wearing silk which was light and tended to float. She picked up a sword, stepped away from Sir Benedict, and stilled her mind. When she was ready she turned to face her enemy. He was standing where he had begun, an unnerving smile on his lips.

When she assumed her position opposite her partner, with her left hand raised and arced for balance, she saw at once that Sir Benedict believed himself to be her superior. Even if he was, his sense of confidence could work to her advantage.

The first clang of steel brought a familiar vibration up her arm and an odd thrill accompanied the sensation even though the circumstances were too horrible to be pondered. She entered into the contest with each of her senses alert. She watched his eyes for purpose, the shift of his chest and abdomen to determine his movements, she listened to his grunts as he thrust his sword venomously and with intent.

He thrust and parried, she countered, matching his speed

and determination. She saw that his weakness was that he often lowered his arm and his balance would falter, if infinitesimally. She pressed him each time and for her reward grazed Sir Benedict's right shoulder. A red stain spread quickly over his shirt.

She had expected him to slow a little, perhaps even pause after having been injured, but he gave no evidence of even noticing the wound. She realized the nature of the adversary before her, that little would keep him from his object.

By now, she was truly finding her feet. Her arms and shoulders ached for the lack of practice yet every skill she had learned under Boscombe's firm instruction returned in full to her. When he pressed her backward, she maneuvered in a circle to keep him from gaining an advantage.

For the next several minutes, with her heart beating furiously in her chest, the only sound she heard was the cold rasp of the blades as they slid off one another again and again, death seeking the tip that struck solidly into flesh.

She pinked him again, but as before he took no notice of it. She began to tire and when the fabric of her skirts caught slightly between her legs, she felt a sudden burning just above her left elbow. A searing pain followed. He had cut her well and smiled with the pleasure of it. The blood flowed rather freely and began to splatter everywhere, on her gown, the floor, across Sir Benedict's white shirt.

He drew back several feet. "Bind your wound," he commanded.

Alice felt dizzy at the sudden cessation of movement but quickly removed her kerchief from the pocket of her pelisse and wrapped it tightly about her arm. When Sir Benedict approached, she backed away slightly.

"I meant only to offer assistance."

"Stay your ground, sir, or lift your sword. One or the other but I shall not permit you to approach me."

"Have it as you will," he said, shrugging.

He appeared to be barely winded and as she secured the knot by using her teeth, she began to be truly frightened. Hugh came to mind and the weakness of his body. He would be no match for Sir Benedict should the baronet prevail. Her eyes started to fill with tears which she quickly blinked away. She turned to face him once more, drawing in a deep breath and strengthening her resolve.

Once more, she engaged him and felt a surge of energy as steel met steel in what seemed a slow, endless punctuation of thrusts. She knew that blood was seeping from the gash on her arm but there was nothing she could do except press on.

A strange slowness entered the feel of her movements. She did not know what was happening, only that her ears were ringing oddly. Her steps seemed sluggish or was she imagining it? No matter what was happening, however, she would meet his blade with her own so long as she had life. Sweat stung her eyes and all the while Sir Benedict's cold smile towered over her.

Braden had traveled straight through the night. He was unshaven when he drew before the direction Hicklade had sent to him, but he did not care. The last few miles had filled him with a sense of dread he had never before known. The coach did not even stop moving before he threw open the door and leaped to the pavement below.

Without ceremony, he burst into the unknown house. Neither a servant nor a family member was present in the lower rooms that fronted the street. He called out for Alice and then he heard the sound as of a door squeaking yet in the great distance. His feet knew the precise nature of the rasping sound before his mind did and he was running down a long hall before the thought burst into his mind that a fencing match was in progress.

A moment more and he entered a ballroom in the center of which near a pianoforte he saw Alice, splattered with blood and white-faced, fending off Sir Benedict's brutal attack. As though shot through with the power of heaven at the horror of seeing the woman he loved wounded so badly and still pressed by her enemy, he called out to the vile baronet.

"Locksbury!" he shouted, his voice filling the chamber and drawing Alice's assailant away from her.

"You!" Sir Benedict cried, his face filled with sudden rage. Braden bore down on him with the ferocity of a tiger. He ignored the paltry sword the man held out to defend himself. In one swift motion, he diverted the side of the blade with his gloved hand and balling his free hand into a fist struck Sir Benedict with a leveler so powerful that he flew backward onto the polished wood floor, slid several yards on his back, and came to a stop, unconscious, his jaw bruised and displaced.

Braden turned to Alice, who supported herself for a moment against the pianoforte and then eased onto the floor, where she sat in a state of shock, blood seeping steadily from the gash on her arm. A kerchief, having become soaked, now hung at her wrist. There seemed to be blood everywhere.

Braden unwrapped the neckcloth from about his throat and quickly bound her wound.

"You came," Alice whispered. "How did you know?"

He sat down next to her and drew her tenderly onto his lap, cradling her in his arms. "Your brother wisely sent word through Hicklade of his suspicions. Nothing would have kept me from you, Alice, nothing."

She nodded and leaned her head against his shoulder. "He meant to kill us both," she said, weeping. "I believe he is gone utterly mad. Nicky would have been next. Sir Benedict was to inherit, you see. How could any man be so vile . . . and I trusted him!"

"I know, my darling. Do not think about it a moment more. It is a tribute to your nature that you think only the best of everyone."

She chuckled through her tears. "Except you and yet here you are."

He could only laugh as well. "You had reason to dislike me. I hid neither my sentiments nor my opinions from you."

"No, you did not, which I believe is to your credit for I

was never in any doubt as to what you were feeling at any given moment."

He was silent apace then in a softer voice said, "You know that I would do anything for you, Alice. Anything in the world." She drew back slightly, searching his eyes. The pallor of her face distressed him further. He touched her cheek. "I should fetch a surgeon."

"In a moment," she said, a crooked smile on her lips. "I am only a little weak but otherwise perfectly well, I assure you. I should just like to sit as we are until I am more composed. And Braden . . . thank you for coming."

He petted her cheek lightly. "I love you so very much."

"And I love you," she returned, her eyes misting over.

"Sufficiently to wed me?" he asked softly.

When he saw the doubt sweep across her face, he sighed. "There is something I would say to you, perhaps when you feel better."

"Now," she said. "I promise you my wound is but a scratch and I am only a little weak. Pray, speak to me."

"Of all the missteps I have taken in my life—and there have been legion—the only one I truly regret is not having taken up the guardianship. At the time I learned of my father's promise to your family, I was full of rage. He had left me with so great a responsibility upon his death having, as he had, run the estate into the ground. I was utterly drowning in the host of decisions that had to be made daily when I learned of the guardianship. The thought that he had also made such a reckless promise was beyond what I could at the time bear. My youth, my inexperience, my grief all combined to place me against the guardianship. I hope one day you will be able to forgive me for not doing what was right and honorable ten years ago. However, I fully intend, when I return to London, to legalize the guardianship, that is, if you still want me to."

Alice stared at him. "I do not know what to say. Are you certain you truly wish for it?"

"More than life itself."

"Oh, Braden," she murmured, tears starting to her eyes.

He withdrew a kerchief from his pocket and wiped gently at her cheeks, which were dotted with both the blood from her wound and her tears. The setting could hardly be construed as romantic, yet there was only one thing he desired as he looked into her lovely blue eyes.

He settled his lips gently on hers. There was an immediate answering response and had she not been so badly wounded he would have engulfed her in a tight embrace and never let her go. As it was, he drifted a series of tender kisses over her lips which brought forth a familiar cooing sound from her throat.

He pulled back with a smile. "I love the melodies you make when I kiss you."

"What do you mean?" she inquired.

He touched her throat with his fingertips. "Here." He watched a faint blush rise on her cheeks.

"Oh, that," she responded, obviously embarrassed.

"I should have kissed you the moment you slid to the floor," he said, chuckling, "for it is a wonderful thing of the moment to see some color return to your complexion."

"Am I so sickly in appearance?" she asked.

"No," he drawled. "Whyever would you be?"

She chuckled in response and he kissed her again releasing her only when running footsteps were heard in the hallway beyond. A tall, strongly built man appeared suddenly through doors thrown wide. "Good God! Higgins, send for Dr. Thomas at once!"

"What has happened?" an older woman cried, drawing up beside him. "Oh, dear God!" She then turned abruptly to a very pretty young lady. "Charlotte, do not let the children come in."

"Of course, Mama." To her credit the young woman, though obviously aghast at the sight before her, kept her head and turned back into the hallway, clucking quickly to the brood that had followed her.

The older woman, clearly her mother, called after her. "And tell Cook we will need the muslin I keep rolled in strips and a basin of clean water. Oh, and perhaps a little restorative brandy. Go quickly, child!"

Mr. Merrymeet had already crossed to Braden and now dropped to his knees. "You must be Miss Cherville," he said, meeting her gaze. "I am Mr. Merrymeet and this is my wife." The lady, now on her knees as well, began unwinding the neckcloth gently.

"How do you do?" Alice murmured.

"More to the point, how do you do?" Mr. Merrymeet queried.

"Well enough," she responded with a smile. "Though I fear I made the worst of mistakes and brought my brother's assailant into your home. I am so very sorry, Mr. Merrymeet, but I had been horribly deceived."

"Never mind that," he said firmly. He glanced at the wound, which was still seeping badly. "Why, this is little more than a scratch."

"That is what I thought," Alice responded.

"Good girl."

He then asked who the fellow was lying unconscious on the opposite side of the pianoforte. Braden explained everything while Mrs. Merrymeet wrapped up the bloodied bandage. A moment more and Cook arrived a trifle out of breath but bearing a basin, the required muslin, and the brandy. The chamber then became a bustle of activity as Mr. Merrymeet took charge, ordering his servants to take in hand the scurrilous Sir Benedict and afterward to clean all evidence of the battle from the ballroom.

Braden encouraged Alice to sip her brandy, which she did, and soon grew drowsy in his arms. Within an hour, she was tucked between the sheets in one of Mrs. Merrymeet's several bedchambers.

A sennight later, Alice was seated in Mrs. Merrymeet's quite comfortable morning room on a small sofa, viewing through a window several of the eight Merrymeet children at play with Jane and Mr. Pinfrith.

Once it was learned of Sir Benedict's horrific betrayal of Hugh and herself, the remainder of her family, along with Mr. Quintin, Mr. Pinfrith, and Mr. Trickett, descended upon the Merrymeet home. Fortunately, the Merrymeets were of such a disposition that the entire party was housed within their commodious home. The stairs were a constant stream of motion, whether galloping with children, guests, or servants so that Alice felt the very walls breathed with life.

She smiled as she watched Jane, whose complexion had blossomed under the gentle Brighton sunshine. In that moment Jane turned and smiled at Mr. Pinfrith in such a way that could not possibly leave anyone in doubt of her growing affection for him. How odd to think that though Braden had posed as Mr. Pinfrith, one of her sisters was actually tumbling in love with the real man.

Louisa came to sit beside her, having brought her a cup of tea. Alice took it gratefully in her right hand, for her left was held immobile in a sling to give relief to her arm, which still ached a trifle. The doctor had already pronounced that the wound was healing admirably without the smallest sign of infection.

Even Hugh was sitting in a comfortable chair across the room, attended as he was constantly by Miss Merrymeet with whom, only last night, he had become betrothed.

Louisa's gaze was fixed out the window. "Do you think it is a match?"

Her question was timed extremely well, for at that moment, the childish game of ring-around-the-rosie had grown rather wild with all the children falling down on one another, which sent Jane sprawling across Mr. Pinfrith. She sat up quickly but it did not escape Alice's notice that Mr. Pinfrith's hand lingered a little longer than necessary on Jane's.

"Indeed, I believe it is," Alice responded. The sisters laughed together.

Alice felt tears start to her eyes. "What a curious adventure we have all had," she murmured, sipping her tea.

"You most of all," Louisa said, "for you are to be a countess after having nearly got yourself killed by a madman."

Alice chuckled. "How happy I am to have you remind me of it," she said facetiously. She then glanced at Braden, who was conversing with Hugh across the chamber, his expression faintly concerned. He chanced to glance in her direction and meeting her gaze, he lifted his cup of coffee to her in a silent salute. She returned the gesture, raising her teacup to him and nodding.

"He watches me all the time as though fearing I will disappear," she murmured to Louisa.

Her sister only barely hid her smiles. "It is most amusing. Even Trickett has noticed how altered his conduct is when you but enter a chamber. A mother hen is not more solicitous of her young than he is of you. And to think we thought him a monster."

"Life can hold such mysteries."

Freddie joined them, also sipping her tea. Directing her gaze out the window, she whispered, "Jane could not stop speaking of Mr. Pinfrith last night. She fell asleep with his name on her lips."

The sisters sighed together.

Mrs. Urchfont joined them. "He is too old for Jane," she announced, scowling. "I intend to tell her as much as soon as I have a moment alone with her."

Alice saw the worried light in her eye and knew its source. Mrs. Urchfont feared having nowhere to go should all the older Cherville children take spouses. She took her hand and said, "Aunt, Braden and I would like to invite you to reside with us at his home in Hampshire, along with Nicky, of course—that is, if you wish for it."

Mrs. Urchfont's eyes opened very wide. "Oh, I do not know if I could impose."

"But you must, for I am depending on you. I always have, you know. And what will Nicky do without his Aunt Urchfont to scold him?"

Mrs. Urchfont blinked several times rapidly and her lips quivered. "Well, then, I suppose it would only be my duty, Nicky still being so young as he is."

"Precisely."

Mrs. Urchfont once more glanced at Jane, only this time she smiled. "She will make a lovely bride for she has my complexion and Mr. Pinfrith is such a fine man."

Both Freddie and Louisa turned away to keep from laughing outright.

At that moment, Nicky entered the chamber, his lips compressed into a line of indignation. Following him was the Merrymeet daughter nearest his age. He took up a seat in the midst of his sisters and folded his arms across his chest.

"Whatever is the matter?" Freddie asked. "You are as cross as crabs."

Miss Eliza Merrymeet's expression was wholly triumphant as she took up a chair next to her eldest sister Charlotte.

"Alice, I beg you will tell Miss Eliza not to kiss me again," he whispered. Nicky's expression became very dark as he scowled at the young lady in question.

Alice could not restrain a trill of laughter, to which both Louisa and Freddie added their own boisterous mirth.

"I do not see why you are laughing. She was being impertinent." His color deepened with every passing second.

Freddie, seeing that her brother would soon become apoplectic, suggested now was a good time to visit the various booksellers on the Steyne. He agreed readily, suggesting that Mr. Quintin come with them as well. Miss Eliza was notoriously in awe of Mr. Quintin.

Alice watched Nicky glare at his enemy as he departed the chamber.

"A certain sign, that love will soon follow," Louisa whispered, still chuckling and wiping at her eyes with her lace kerchief.

"No doubt," Alice murmured.

Braden, obviously curious about what was going forward, crossed the room and begged to know why Nicky had taken such a pet. Alice explained the terrible circumstances of Miss Eliza having taken sore advantage of him. "I fear we men are ridiculous creatures from a very young age."

Alice smiled up at him, her affection for him rising so

sharply within her that she nearly lost her breath. "Would you be so good as to support me for a turn about the gardens?" she asked.

The answering light in his eye was more than enough assurance that he was happy to oblige her. "Of course," he said, offering his arm.

Alice rose to her feet.

"I should like a turn as well," Mrs. Urchfont announced.

The disappointment Alice felt was profound. "Of course you would," she said quickly. "Do come with us."

Louisa stood up hastily. "But, Aunt," she intruded ever so kindly, "you promised to, er, show me your new bonnet. I beg you will do so now."

"But you saw it last night," she argued.

"Yes, but it was very dark and I should like now to see it in the daylight."

"Well, if you really wish for it."

"I do, indeed. I am thinking of procuring a similar bonnet myself. Would you object to my trying it on?"

"Not in the least." Mrs. Urchfont appeared utterly gratified by Louisa's interest.

Alice, for her part, cast Louisa a grateful glance and with her heart singing, left the chamber with her arm wrapped tightly about Braden's. He guided her not toward the sounds of Jane, Mr. Pinfrith, and the younger Merrymeet children, but in an easterly direction, where Mrs. Merrymeet kept her cutting and rose garden.

A stone wall and beautiful arch separated the flowers from the sounds of the children's laughter and squeals. The day was exquisite, with puffy clouds passing swiftly over a deep bank of blue. A slight breeze buffeted her red locks as Braden opened the gate to the garden.

"I have been wondering," Alice began.

"About what, my darling?" He guided her down the longest avenue of roses, the air fragrant with the rich smell of the velvety blossoms.

"Do you think it truly wise to have merely shipped Sir Benedict off to the Colonies? What if he returns?"

"He will not come back, Alice. As guardian of your family, and with the full weight of the Earldom of Bradenstoke behind this office, I am certain that Sir Benedict will not dare to allow even the toe of his boot to touch the shores of England again. Trust me when I say he comprehends quite perfectly."

Alice released one of what had been many sighs over the past several days. She understood quite well how close she had come to losing her life and was not yet entirely comfortable with the notion that the baronet, whom she had trusted with all her heart, still roamed free. "I wish he could have been tried in a court of law," she said.

"There was hardly sufficient proof, though plenty of motivation was evident. Such a trial would have required months, even years and then, should he have been found innocent, he would have been free to live as he pleased in England. You would never have been safe."

"I had not thought of that. Braden, I am so deeply indebted to you." The path turned toward the east and a delicate, comforting breeze swept over her face.

He forced her to stop and gently took her in his arms, careful not to put even the smallest pressure on her wound. "My darling, it is I who am indebted to you. How can I tell you how vastly you have changed my entire existence? I was happy, even content, in my former life of work and politics. But now, I know joy and a sense of fulfillment that ever eluded me. I promise you, that whatever protection my rank, even my involvement in your affairs, has created, these cannot begin to compare with the sweetness, the tenderness, the passion that I feel just looking at you."

Alice smiled and touched his face with the tips of her bare fingers. "My darling," she murmured.

He waited for no further invitation, and kissed her hard on the lips.

Alice's breath caught. He was a passionate man who aroused every desire within her, for love, for his bed, for the creation of a family with him. When his kiss deepened, the breeze and scattered sunshine, the squeals of the children, even the heady fragrance of the roses about her seemed to drift to a point on the horizon so far away that they were like the distant cry of gulls to her ears. All faded in the bright swell of her love for him.

She received his kiss for what it was, the promise of a life together, of years of happiness, and through what troubles may come, his tender support.